A SHADE OF EVIL

A DARK MAFIA ROMANCE

THE DARK LORDS

STELLA ANDREWS

Copyrighted Material
Copyright © Stella Andrews 2023
v110923

Stella Andrews has asserted her rights under the Copyright, Designs and Patents Act 1988 to be identified as the Author of this work.
This book is a work of fiction and except in the case of historical fact, any resemblance to actual persons, living or dead, is purely coincidental.
All rights reserved. No part of this book may be reproduced or transmitted in any form without written permission of the author, except by a reviewer who may quote brief passages for review purposes only.

18+ This book is for adults only. If you are easily shocked and not a fan of sexual content, then move away now.

18+

NEWSLETTER

Sign up to my newsletter and download a free eBook.

stellaandrews.com

A SHADE OF EVIL

THE DARK LORDS

Revenge is a dish best served cold.
Shade Vieri has no mercy.
No compassion and no empathy.
He is cruel, enigmatic, and deliciously dark.

His instructions are clear.
Find the Achilles heel of the enemy and destroy it.
The enemy is a woman who slides across his soul like spun silk.
A breath of fresh air in a dark, depressing world.
A free spirit with a heart of gold and a woman who ticks every box he has ever thought of.
A woman he must destroy.

This dish is anything but cold.
This dish is so hot it burns.

For fans of dark mafia romance and hard-fought happy endings. Mad chaotic scenes and devilish behavior. Steamy, intense, and shocking. You have been warned.

PROLOGUE

ALLEGRA

I shouldn't be here. I should be tucked up in bed with a good book and a glass of wine because that is my happy place. Not a dark, depressing alley on the dusty streets of New York, clutching a brown envelope to me as if it's a bullet-proof vest. It needs to be. Hell, it needs to resemble an armored vehicle, because my life is distinctly under threat right now.

The wind whips against my ear, whispering in gleeful tones that my soul belongs to the devil now. I have sunk lower than the homeless man who slurps from the bottle wrapped in brown paper, cowering by the dumpster, watching me with blurred vision.

For a second I stare at him in the hope he's an undercover cop and will spring to my rescue. To end this misery once and for all and lock up the evil that waits for my downfall.

Our eyes connect and the weariness in his matches my own, telling me I'm fucked, and we both know it.

He shifts and drags his slight body to a standing position and gathers his possessions around him as if I'm the threat in this alley. I only wish I were because the person undoubtedly coming for me is the biggest threat to my life, my brother's life and probably anybody else's life that has the misfortune to cross his path.

I watch the homeless man shuffle away, like a bird fleeing from an approaching predator. A gazelle taking flight from a wild cat reminding me I'm a fool and I probably always will be.

My breath is racing, and my mouth is dry, causing me to lick my lips with a show of nerves I hate right now. I shouldn't give a shit. I shouldn't be terrified, but my clammy hands and shaking knees tells me otherwise. I am up shit creek without a paddle and all because of family.

The tears almost blind me as I think of the reason I'm here at all. My brother Rafferty. The one man I love with my entire heart and would kill to protect. He is in trouble, and I will never forget the stricken look in his eye when he confessed just how much. It was unbearable, and I foolishly told him I would sort it. Not to worry and to leave it with me.

Now I'm regretting my foolish bravery because I am so out of my depth I'm drowning. That would almost be welcome because I may not make it out of this alley alive anyway, and at least it would be a peaceful ending of sorts.

Cursing the fact I'm a strong swimmer in every way, I move further into the alley and glance around me with fear. Is he here already? Lurking in the shadows, watching my stupidity with an evil smile on his face. Preparing to ruin my life along with my brother's just for kicks.

I jump at a sound further inside and a cat races past me after a rat causing me to jump and shriek, my heart thumping as they pass, not interested in the foolish woman who has stepped out of her safe secure world for a walk on the dark side.

I turn back to the alley and stare into the abyss and only the light on the end of a cigarette alerts me that I'm not alone.

"Um, hello." I call out sounding like a complete fool and I timidly venture a little further, coughing nervously as I stand my ground.

"This is as far as I'm going." I shout bravely, although to anyone listening, I sound anything but brave.

A shadow steps out from the gloom and my chest tightens as I struggle to breathe. The sound of tires screeching to a stop behind me causes me to turn and I note the huge black car blocking my exit, protected by a huge shape dressed in black attitude.

The person advances and my knees tremble as I face my ruin and as he steps forward, my knees almost give way, so I grasp the envelope tighter and say as steadily as I can.

"I have what you asked for. Every dollar."

He steps closer and I make out a figure dressed in black. His attitude is set to couldn't give a fuck and his gravelly voice growls, "Ten thousand dollars."

"Yes." I hate that my voice is the barest whisper and laced with nerves and he reaches out his hand, causing me to step back a little.

"I want your guarantee this is the end of this."

He moves closer and I recoil at the huge scar dragging down his cheek as it promises this man walks on the wild side and any demands I make are worth nothing.

His face is cruel, rough, and repelling and I involuntarily step back as his arm reaches out and his hand closes around my wrist.

"You are in no position to make demands." He hisses, grasping me roughly and shoving me hard against the alley wall.

It winds me slightly and then I yell as he tears the envelope from my shaking fingers and growls, "You think this is the end?" He leans closer and hisses, "It's just the beginning, stupid girl. Your brother owes me and you're the one paying."

"But…" The tears burn and reveal my weakness as he snarls, "Your fucking brother messed with the wrong guys. His debt will only be repaid in death. His."

He leans closer and presses his lips to mine and whispers against them, "Ten thousand dollars is nothing to what I will get for you."

His hand reaches for my jeans, and I attempt to scream as he cruelly undoes them, whispering, "First I fuck you against this alley wall. Then I allow my men their turn."

His small laugh curdles my blood as he inches the fabric away from my body.

"Then we take you to a whore house and drug you into acceptance. You will lie on your back and earn me good money until your body gives up on you and you slip into the afterlife. You belong to me now."

There is a moment in life when you realize you don't have choices anymore. When it's game over and you should accept your fate because a far stronger adversary than you has won. The trouble with me is I've always been *that* woman. The one who never accepts and fights for what she believes in, and if this cruel fucker thinks I'm going down without a fight, he's as stupid as he looks.

Bringing my knee sharply up, I relish the contact as his groan of pain tells me I've hit my mark, but before I can escape, a flash of steel at my throat reminds me why I really should have played dumb.

With a hiss of anger, he kicks my legs apart, the blade cutting into my skin, causing the pain to almost finish me off and just when I think it really is game over, a shot rings out, sounding like the biggest clap of thunder in the alley, causing my assailant to release his hold and shout, "What the fuck?"

I watch in terror as in slow motion, he turns, and another shot ends up directly between his eyes and I scream as he falls backward, his head exploding on the dusty concrete, his brains decorating the alley with a sick painting of death.

My panicked sobs are the only indication I'm still breathing, and I sink to the floor, covering my head with my hands, expecting the next bullet to send me along with him and the sound of footsteps heading my way cause me to cower in fright as they move in no hurry toward me.

I am shivering with shock and fear. The envelope now red due to the contents spilling into the blood at my feet. Blood money for sure and it almost makes me laugh, telling me I've lost my sanity as well as my mind.

Somebody crouches down before me and a husky voice whispers, "Yours, I believe."

I peer though my eyes at the outstretched hand holding out the envelope and I'm almost fearful to look, but I just can't help myself.

I stare into a face I will never forget, even if I manage to dodge death for a thousand years. Rugged, handsome, but broken. His eyes flash and they reflect a soul of danger, depravity, and secrets. So many secrets and I am mesmerized. His hair is as black as the suit he's wearing and his penetrating gaze strangely compelling.

A serpent of evil that is waiting to strike and my heart beats to critical levels as he whispers, "Come."

He reaches for my hand, and, against my better judgment, I allow him to pull me to my feet and I stumble as my foot brushes against the body of the man on the cold ground.

My legs are shaking, and my mind fucked as the man tightens his hold and says huskily, "You really should take better care of yourself."

I'm not sure if he's referring to me or the dead guy and there really is no answer to that and for some reason, I follow him as we walk back the way I came in, and toward the black car blocking our exit.

The door is open, another silent assassin standing beside it and the man holding my hand says in a voice that feels as if it's caressing my soul.

"Come. Allow us to help you."

"No, um…" I pull back because what the actual fuck? If he thinks I'm going with him, he's got another thing coming because even in my crazy fucked up state, I realize this man is an even bigger threat than the one lying dead on the ground.

"No?" He sounds almost amused, and I say quickly, "Look, it's been well, interesting, but I should, well, um, go. I have work in the morning, and I really should be getting home to bed. I mean, um, thank you and everything, but I can handle it from here."

My breath is racing and I'm hyperventilating, and it's not helped when he wraps his hand around the back of my neck and pulls me close, whispering against my ear, "I didn't say you had a choice."

Before I can react, he pushes my head down and forces me into the car and as I tumble inside, he is quick to join me. The car door slams, and the engine starts, even before I turn and the hand that slaps against my mouth cuts off any angry response I have as he whispers, "We have a lot to talk about, Allegra. You would be wise to listen before you speak."

I am stunned and just stare at him in shock as he reaches past me and snaps the seatbelt in place, smiling with a wicked grin. "Safety first, princess. We wouldn't want anything happening to you now, would we?"

He leans back in his seat and reaches for his phone and all I can do is open and close my mouth, desperate to say something but unsure what the fuck would work.

As the car speeds off into the wailing city, I have an awful feeling my life is not my own anymore. It's his.

CHAPTER 1

ALLEGRA

TWO WEEKS LATER

My best friend Cecilia is staring at me as if I'm from out of space and I shrug.

"What?"

"You."

"What about me?"

"You're seriously not coming." She says in disbelief, her eyes wide and her hands on her hips, telling me I had better come up with an excuse, and fast.

"I don't feel so good." I groan and hold my hand to my temple and say with a gasp. "It's my head. It won't stop banging."

"Cut the crap, Ally. You've been hiding out here for close on two weeks now and you've missed some seriously amazing night outs. I mean, the guys have been insane just lately and as for that new club in town, Gyration, well, it's out of this fucking world."

"I told you…"

She cuts me off. "And I'm telling you, grab a kick ass outfit and draw your battle face on. We are going to celebrate your birthday tonight, whether you like it or not."

Cecilia is a fierce woman most of the time and she will not make saying no easy and yet I must. I can't go out there. It's too dangerous. I can't go anywhere, not after what happened two weeks ago.

I am still having night terrors because of it. Fearful of going out and being arrested for murder. That man was killed in cold blood and yet there was nothing on the news. I should know, I've searched every news channel going, even foreign ones and there is no report of a shooting in Cross alley at all. It's as if it was a figment of my own twisted nightmares and yet it happened as plain as Cecilia is glaring at me now.

What surprised me even more was I was dropped here. My rescuer didn't say one more word to me and just pulled up outside my apartment block and as soon as the door opened, I scrambled to my safety. It was the strangest experience of my life, and I couldn't get out of there quickly enough.

It's why I can't go out. Why I've ordered take out ever since and postponed my internship at The Social Queen. The PR consultants on fifth avenue.

Luckily, they were fine about it. They had two openings and one started later than mine, which was a good thing because I'm unsure how I would explain to my parents about my sudden change of heart.

Sighing inside, I realize my life is a fucking mess and all because of Rafferty, who hasn't even bothered to check on me outside of a quick phone call asking if everything went well.

If you count murder going peachy fine, then yes, it was a successful night. The trouble is, I have a feeling that night was the beginning of something, which is why I'm hiding away like Count Dracula, fearful of daylight.

"I'm waiting." She taps her foot angrily on the wooden floor and, realizing I am beaten, I huff, "Fine, but don't blame me if I leave after one hour. I've got my new job starting on Monday and I need my beauty sleep."

"You may as well be dead from the amount of sleep you've had lately." She grumbles as she reaches for the open bottle of wine and fills her glass for the third time.

"You have twenty minutes."

I say nothing and head into my room, realizing I have no choice. Cecilia Murray is a formidable adversary. My best friend since high school and my partner in crime. We were inseparable until she took up a position in a law firm as an intern. She wants to be an attorney and is learning from the bottom up. I set my sights on marketing and promotion and finally landed the position of my dreams here in New York. What happened that night almost derailed it, but the fighter in me stood her ground. Now I must push aside what happened and move forward with the rest of my life before anyone starts asking awkward questions.

I drag on a dress that really doesn't deserve its name. It's figure hugging and sparkles as it catches the light. The green in the fabric matches my eyes, and I'm not even sure it's a good choice. I should wear pants and a top that covers me entirely because I never want a man to look at me again — ever. The thought of what could have happened in that alley is still torturing me and yet the man who rescued me has me thinking different thoughts entirely.

He has since starred in every fantasy I have ever had. I wake in the knowledge I let him do despicable things to my body in my dreams, and then I scrub the image from my mind in the shower.

He has infiltrated my mind because I have never met a

man like him. So dangerous, sexy as hell, and a bad boy of the most devastating kind. Those rugged looks and his husky voice make me shiver with desire, telling me why I'm best locked up away from the world before I lose my sanity entirely.

I tell myself I'm pulling on this dress because it's my birthday and I want to look nice. I'm fooling myself if I think it's for any other reason than with him in mind. Part of me hopes I'll meet him again and the better half of me wishes the opposite. If I never see him again, it would be an extremely good thing, but the despair I have at that tells me I'm fucked.

As I brush my hair, it falls down my back, a brown curtain that shines as the light catches it. I was always proud of my chestnut hair. My brother said it reminded him of a conker, which is why he calls me that.

I hate it.

Who wants to resemble a nut anyway, and it's hardly cute? I told him that angrily once, and he shrugged and said that if I preferred, he could call me Beaver. I swear to God, I nearly murdered him myself and Beaver was dropped but conker remained, which is why I try not to go out in public with him. The fact he's just signed as the newest quarterback with the Jets makes for an evening spent watching him hit on by every female in the vicinity, which doesn't really rock my world. He may be drop dead gorgeous, but he's still my yucky brother and yet I would do anything for him. I *have* done everything for him and look where that got me.

"Time's up."

Cecilia stands in the doorway and whistles. "Man, you are hot tonight. That's my girl."

I turn and smile bravely. "I've got to try to keep up with you."

I smile because Cecilia is probably the most attractive girl I have ever met. Her beautiful brown skin glows with health and her deep brown eyes are framed by the longest lashes. She is going through her Beyonce era right now and her hair is golden and styled in waves, like the queen herself. Her figure is the envy of every model out there and she is so wasted hidden behind a desk in Washington when she should be gracing the catwalk and earning zillions as a super model.

"That's more like it."

She grins, revealing the most enviable set of white teeth that would make any dentist proud. "Let's go and celebrate your birthday and introduce that new club to the queens of clubs."

As we head outside, I fight back a moments panic as the night air reaches out and pulls me in, reminding me of the last time I ventured out.

The doorman nods, his eyes dragging appreciatively over us and as Cecilia drops him a wink, I try to hide behind her, desperate not to draw attention to myself.

My friend hails a passing yellow cab and as it screeches to a stop, I am grateful to jump inside, away from the curious gaze of the doorman and anyone else who may be watching.

I realize I'm being irrational, but it's as if I am being watched. It's probably just my guilty conscience, but it's surrounding me.

"Where to?" The driver says with a sigh and Cecilia yells, "Gyration, baby."

He rolls his eyes as we giggle on the back seat like two kids from high school and as we speed off into the night, I try to get my mind back on track.

I am a strong woman. I can do this.

Cecilia chats for the entire journey and only a few well-placed responses convince her I'm part of the conversation. I'm not. I couldn't tell you what we spoke of because I'm conscious of the interested gaze of the cab driver in the rear-view mirror.

He must be fifty years old, give or take a year, which makes me wonder if he's been sent to spy on me. It's making me nervous because there is an expression in his eye that's unsettling.

I'm happy when we pull up outside the club and Cecilia hands him the fare with a generous tip.

However, when I leave, his eyes follow me, almost as if he knows a secret concerning me. His expression is of interest filled with remorse and I don't know what the hell that could mean.

As we turn our back on the cab, I stare with dismay at the line snaking around the corner of the building and say with a sigh, "Are you kidding me? This is a disaster."

I shiver in my thin dress as I contemplate hours of lining up for a club I'm not even bothered about, and Cecilia nods. "I know, mad, isn't it? This place is super cool and sexy, and everyone wants to be seen here."

"Why don't we go somewhere else? Wait for it to be less cool and attractive."

"Girl, are you kidding me?" She rolls her eyes.

"This is your birthday, and you deserve the best. Leave it with me."

I stand awkwardly as she wiggles her way to the front and whispers something in the ear of the doorman, who immediately gives me a dose of post-traumatic stress when I note the black suit he is wearing and the dark shade covering his eyes.

A man walks past and whistles, causing me to jump, and he leers, "How much do you charge?"

I turn to tell him exactly what I think of that remark when Cecilia shouts, "Over here, babe."

I turn and note the disgruntled faces of the waiting line as the doorman parts the rope and beckons us inside. Feeling the hostility directed our way, I dive past the angry line and as I fall into step beside my friend, I whisper, "How did you manage that?"

She shrugs. "I don't know. At first, he was 'no can do under any circumstances' and then he stopped and adjusted his earpiece. The next thing I knew he said gruffly, Okay, grab your friend, you're in."

"Really!" I'm shocked and stare around me nervously, doubting it's because of anything other than my guilty conscience.

"Who cares? We're in, so what's the problem?"

She links her arm with mine and we head down a mirrored corridor to a booth at the side and as we reach the window, the cashier smiles. "Welcome to Gyration."

Cecilia reaches into her purse and the cashier shakes her head.

"Complimentary, ladies. Enjoy your evening."

My skin prickles as if a thousand razors are dragging across it as I sense we're about to walk into a situation I really should be running from but Cecilia whoops with delight and grabs my arm, "Wow, they must have heard it's your birthday."

The cashier smiles with interest and pushes two lanyards our way.

"Here. You have exclusive access to the VIP area. Go through the double doors and head up the staircase. You will need these to swipe for access."

She laughs at the shock on our faces and winks. "It's all complimentary up there. Prepare for the night of your lives."

Before I can react, Cecilia grabs my hand and almost runs to the double doors and I attempt to pull on the brakes, causing her to say with surprise, "What?"

"This doesn't feel right."

"The hell it doesn't. This feels so right I can't believe they haven't got our portraits up on the wall. I told you we are the queens and they bow down before us."

She giggles, and it's impossible not to react to that and rolling my eyes, I say with a grin, "Of course. Silly me. We are the queens, and they know it."

I follow her through the doors with a heart beating out of control. Why does it feel as if I'm walking into a whole heap of trouble with my name written on it in neon lights?

CHAPTER 2

SHADE

I lean back in my chair and fix a satisfied grin on my face, causing Kyle to roll his eyes and hand me a hundred-dollar bill.

As I drop it into a jar on my desk, he growls, "Every fucking time."

I nod toward the tray in the corner where a decanter of bourbon lives. "We should celebrate."

"Or drown my sorrows." He says moodily.

As he pours us both a glass of the finest, I stare at the growing pile of dollars and laugh softly.

"You're easy game, Kyle."

"Fuck you, Shade." He growls and drains his glass in one swift movement.

It makes me grin, and I turn my attention to the monitor and observe the two women striding through the doors to their damnation.

He hands me the glass and raises it in a salute of sorts.

"It's just a winning streak. My time will come."

I shrug as I empty the contents down my throat and slam the glass on my desk with a satisfied grunt of pleasure.

"Keep telling yourself that." I lean back, and he says with interest, "Will you make your move tonight?"

"Of course." I stare at her image on the monitor and like what I see—a lot. I have studied endless photographs of Allegra Powell, but none of them have done her justice. She is different from what I imagined. I expected a pampered princess whose idea of a wild night was to get trashed in one of my clubs and allow a frat boy's hand to creep to second base. Not the wild beauty I rescued from the alley. Not the woman who was struggling to hold her shit together in terrifying circumstances. Not the angel who stared at me through eyes of terror with a yearning I could almost reach out and grasp.

No, I have never met anyone like her, and it intrigues me. She intrigues me, which is why this may be a more pleasurable revenge than I first had in mind.

I watch them swipe their passes to gain access to the VIP area, the wild excitement in their eyes obvious even from where I'm sitting.

They spill through the doors with excited squeals and Kyle chuckles softly. "Fuck me, this is too easy."

I say nothing and just stare at my prize. The woman who will bring me delicious revenge against my latest enemy. Lucas Stevenson. Judge Stevenson to give him his proper title is about to have the rug firmly pulled out from beneath his pampered feet.

I stare at the woman he calls his niece, knowing full well she's his daughter. Only two people know the truth, him and her mother. Until a few weeks ago, when my grandfather casually mentioned it when we met to discuss our next battle. Knowing she is our enemy's most treasured possession is too good an opportunity to pass up on.

I will ruin her to slay him, and he will never recover. His guilty secret will be out, and he will lose everything. There is nothing he won't do to protect his saintly image and by the time I have finished with her, he will be begging to swear allegiance to the Vieri family.

To my grandfather, the supreme ruler of the Dark Lords. An organization Judge Stevenson is striving to take from us. They want us out and they are doing their darnedest to make it happen. However, my grandfather founded the secret society and fights dirty. He has three willing soldiers by his side to fight his battle, and this is mine. My brother Killian, who will succeed him as the Don, will bring about the destruction of the Judge's son Jefferson. I get the delights of his daughter.

As I stare at her, gazing around the VIP area in awe, I feel the stirrings of anticipation telling me I'll enjoy the kill. This is the part I love the most. The calm before the storm and what a storm is coming for the prim-looking princess who shines in my club like the brightest jewel. Well, I am a thief and I steal souls, so she had better guard hers well because my inner demon is slowly unlocking the door of his cage and preparing to step outside.

I turn to business and say with a sigh. First, we must wrap up the unfortunate business at hand before we can play.

"River?" Kyle raises his eyes.

I nod. "Show the fucker in."

I watch as Kyle heads to the door and set my mind to the business I must get out of the way before the pleasurable side of it can be enjoyed.

As the door opens, River strolls through it as if he hasn't a care in the world, although inside he must be pissing his pants.

"Mr. Vieri."

He nods respectfully, and I point to the chair before my desk.

He sits on the edge, the sweat on his brow the only indication he's shit scared.

"Rafferty Powell." I study his reaction and he nods.

"The new quarterback for the Jets."

"What do you know of him?"

He shrugs. "He's vulnerable."

"No." I fix him with a dark glare. "What. Do. You. Know. Of. Him?"

My words tell him everything and he pales significantly and stutters, "I don't understand."

"I think you do, River."

Kyle moves behind him and removes his gun, holding it to River's head, causing him to stutter, "I was paid to threaten him."

"Who paid?"

"He didn't give a name."

Kyle presses the gun in harder and River begins to shake.

"I swear I didn't get a name. He used Michelle as an intermediary. She told me there was ten thousand with my name on it if I arranged heat on Rafferty."

"Ten thousand." I think back on the money Allegra held in her hand, knowing exactly where it was heading now.

"What was the threat?"

My tone is conversational, but my expression isn't and River says quickly, "Blackmail. Frame him for murder and threaten to ruin his career before it began. I don't know why; he's obviously pissed off someone with more money than sense."

"So, you sent Diego."

I think back on the man I executed just for laying one finger on the woman waiting for me and to this day, I'm still not sure why it incensed me so much. Seeing him preparing to rape her and use her for his own gain unleashed the beast inside me. He was meant to collect, not twist it to his advantage, and his fate was sealed the moment he tried.

River says quickly, "I promised him a cut if he collected. I had business on the other side of town and it seemed the best option."

River is one of many men who slides under my radar. Low life criminals who scratch for a living doing shit just like this. I learned of it through my network of spies, and this time our paths have crossed. The trouble is, she is *my* soul to ruin, not his and whoever this fucker is who paid him had better watch his back because I'm coming for him too.

I lean back in my seat and my eyes flick to the screen, searching for the woman who is the star of the moment.

She is on a couch beside her friend with a bucket of iced champagne before her and I notice two men in suits sitting opposite them. It momentarily distracts me as I watch the guys apparently hitting on them, and my anger boils. I know those men. Two city dudes with platinum credit cards and no sense. They are regulars and leave with a different woman every fucking time. Their money is good and who the fuck cares how they get their kicks, but not tonight. She is mine and the only one who gets to ruin her is me.

With a frown, I dash out a text to security and watch as they move in on the group and whisper in the men's ears, their words designed to cut short any hope of hitting on the two women who will wait for me to do it instead. They nod and then smile apologetically and leave, moving to the other end of the bar, away from my revenge and away from her.

I switch my mind back to business and stare at River, who may be just about to shit himself.

"Murder. Whose?"

I remind him of his words, and he shrugs. "Some woman called Taylor Sutherland. She was found in a secluded area with her heart ripped out. Whoever wants Rafferty, framed him for it because he was dating her. Then again, maybe the fucker did it, which is why he's paying up."

"But he didn't pay up, River." I lean forward.

"He sent his sister. Why would he do that?"

He shrugs. "Doesn't want the spotlight on him to fall away. He's a big assed star now and can't afford to be seen in the underworld, so he got his sister to bail him out. Why the fuck do I care as long as I get my money and his blackmailer has his fun?"

"I want a name."

I state the facts and River shakes his head. "I could ask Michelle. Increase the pressure on her and get the information."

He sounds almost hopeful and yet we both know there is no way he is leaving this office alive because I leave no loose ends and this fucker is looser than most.

Once again, my gaze flicks to the screen and I notice the two girls move to the dance floor. Allegra is laughing at something her friend says, and the lights dance in the highlights of her hair. Her dress is short and heading up her thighs, offering me a glimpse of tantalizing flesh that would look good wrapped around my body.

I am wasting time, so I nod to Kyle who empties a bullet into River's head before he even sees it coming and as he falls to the floor, I congratulate myself on my choice of flooring as any trace of him will be gone before I return.

I stand and say to Kyle, "Call the guys and have him removed — every single fucking trace."

He makes the call as I reach for my jacket, shrugging into it while staring at the screen.

Yes, I'm coming for you, Allegra Powell. Prepare to be destroyed.

CHAPTER 3

ALLEGRA

This place is insane. Cessy is insane and I'm really beginning to believe I am insane to venture out at all. Despite an extreme show of bravado, I am quaking inside. Every person who glances in my direction is probably hiding an ulterior motive. I'm jumpy, anxious and wishing I wasn't here. However, there is no derailing Cessy from having a good time and as we take our seats in the VIP room, she stares at me with excited anticipation and giggles. "This is called living the dream."

"If you say so." I'm dismissive because this is currently my worst nightmare, and she stares at me long and hard and says with determination, "Okay. Spill."

"What?" I feign ignorance and she leans closer and whispers, "Something happened. You've been avoiding my calls for the past two weeks and now, when I hunt you down, you're scared of your own shadow."

I shrug. "Nerves I guess."

"What have you got to be nervous about?" She says incredulously and I sigh heavily. "If you must know, I'm worried about the internship. I will probably suck and my career will be over before it's begun."

"Really." She stares at me with a hint of anger. "Are you seriously telling me you're nervous?" She shakes her head. "For God's sake, Ally, you are the most 'I've got this shit' girl I know. It's why we're friends, because I'm one too." She grins. "We are the queens, remember, and queens don't have nerves. They create them in others."

As always, she lifts my mood and then she stops and stares in disbelief as a waiter hovers nearby with a bucket containing a bottle of champagne and two glasses.

"What's this?" Cessy says, her eyes wide and the waiter smiles. "Compliments of Gyration."

"Are you frigging kidding me?" Cessy's cool explodes in one excited sentence, and I roll my eyes as the waiter grins. "Enjoy, ladies."

We stare at one another in shock as the waiter moves away and Cessy dives on the bottle and I almost believe she will forego the glass.

I watch as she fills two glasses and hands one to me with a grin of pure pleasure.

"Happy birthday, Ally. May all your dreams come true."

"They already have, ladies."

I look up and note two men hovering nearby and before we can speak, they drop down onto the couch opposite and raise their own glasses of champagne.

"Happy birthday." They say and I catch Cessy's expression and try not to laugh.

"Brad and Julian at your service." One of them says, leaning forward and staring blatantly into my eyes. "I haven't seen you here before."

Cessy smirks as I smile politely. "It's our first time."

The other guy turns to Cessy and his eyes positively smolder. "We would have remembered you for sure. So…"

She almost purrs. "Cessy and Ally."

He stares into her eyes and his intentions are clear. Cessy is his target, and he is attempting a bullseye.

"I'm Julian. I hope you will allow us to join in your celebrations."

Cessy nods. "Of course. The more the merrier."

Brad turns to me. "So, Ally, do you live in New York or are you just passing through?"

"I live here now." I decide to be polite even though I'm not really interested.

"Now? Where was home?"

"Washington."

"So, you came here for…"

"Work." I smile as I lift the glass to my lips and he nods, his gaze sliding appreciatively the length of me, making no secret of his intentions.

I note that Cessy is chatting with enthusiasm to Julian and know she will be all over him like a rash, given half the chance. He is exactly her type. Smooth, slick and full of bullshit. Not that it will last. Her boredom threshold is almost immediate, and he will only last until something better comes along.

Brad says smoothly, "So, Ally. It's your birthday and while I would never ask a lady her age, I will ask what your plans are to celebrate."

I shrug. "We're doing it."

"Only the two of you?" He raises his eyes. "No boyfriend, family, or friends."

Thinking back on my mom's insistence I return home to celebrate with them, I push down the guilt and say firmly, "No. Just me and my best friend."

He smirks. "Then allow us to be your party. I can show you a good time."

Before I can even reply to that, a shadow appears and as I

glance up, my heart plummets at the stern-looking man dressed in a black suit and menace. There is another one beside Julian and Brad says with surprise, "May I help you?"

The guy leans down and whispers something in Brad's ear and whatever he says causes the blood to drain from his face and almost immediately he stands and nods to his friend. "I'm sorry, we must leave. Um, enjoy your evening, ladies."

Julian appears as confused as we are and yet the expression in Brad's eye leaves no room for argument and as they head off, closely followed by the two men, Cessy says in disbelief, "Wow, what just happened?"

I shake my head. "I don't know."

I really can't answer that and then, in true Cessy style, she bounces straight back and says with a slight shrug, "Whatever. Let's go and dance. It's time to get this party started."

Laughing, she drags me from my chair and onto the dance floor and, as the song fills my head, I almost forget. For once I am happy with no cares or worries and as we fool around on the dance floor, to anybody watching I haven't got a care in the world.

* * *

Three songs later and the champagne is calling and as we stumble back to our seats, my euphoria is quickly replaced with fear when I see the two men waiting.

It's as if Lucifer himself has entered the building and I should know, because that face will be forever imprinted on my memory.

It's him.

Cessy nudges me and whispers, "Fucking hell. What the actual fucking shit bullshit is happening?"

I'm not surprised she's gained a sudden bout of Tourette's

because I have never seen anything like this before outside of the movies.

There are four men dressed in black standing behind the couches, surrounding the seats with a ring of black menace. Sitting down are two men who wear their darkness like a badge of honor as they watch our approach with a predatory gaze. They are dressed in black suits, black shirts and ties, a uniform of sorts and the casual way they are sitting tells me they are arrogant, self-assured and probably assholes.

I stop and grab Cessy's arm. "Fuck this. I want to leave."

She whispers frantically, "Are you freaking kidding me? Have you seen those guys? They are so hot I'm already on fire and I am not going to pass this one up. We are so doing this."

"No! I mean it." I can feel his eyes on me the entire time, his expression almost amused, but those eyes tell another story. He is watching me closely, almost challenging me and my mouth dries and my skin pricks as I stare into the eyes of the devil.

A man moves behind us, and I didn't see him coming and says roughly, "Don't keep the boss waiting."

"The boss!" Cessy's eyes are wide. "You mean he owns this place? Fuck me."

"Um, there's been a mistake. We need to leave." I say foolishly and merely get a rough, "Non-negotiable."

Cessy grips my hand and says with determination.

"Come on Ally. I'll deal with this, um, situation. Leave it with me."

I have no choice and am dragged unwillingly into the black hole and as we drop down into the seat opposite them, I hate the way my body is burning up right now. Despite being the scariest man I have ever met, he is also the most attractive one and could be a movie star. From his velvet brown eyes to his strong jaw, incredibly smooth skin and delicious lips, he is extremely desirable.

He is also hiding an insane body under that shirt. I can already tell just from the fabric straining against it and he wears his arrogance with ease, knowing he can probably do whatever and whoever the fuck he wants.

As we sit, they stare at us with wicked eyes loaded with lust and Cessy shifts in her seat and is almost hyperventilating as his companion offers her a glass of champagne and says huskily, "You look as if you could use this."

I'm mortified when she downs it in one and says with an impish grin, "The bottle may be easier."

His eyes flash with amusement and as he undresses her with his eyes, even I feel the smolder of lust between them and yet I can't dwell on it because the man I am trying so hard not to look at, leans forward and whispers, "Dance with me."

He stands before waiting for a reply and holds out his hand and Cessy nudges me, whispering, "Go on."

Realizing I have no choice, I ignore his hand and head back the way I came, my heart racing so fast I may not make it there at all.

He moves behind me and as soon as we reach the dance floor, he grips my wrist and spins me against him, wrapping his arm around my waist and leaving me in no doubt I am not escaping anytime soon. He dips his face to my ear and whispers huskily, "Be a good girl. We have unfinished business."

Inside, I am crying buckets of fearful tears. I knew this was a bad idea. I should never have left my apartment. This is a nightmare.

As we begin to move in time to the music, I hate the fact I can only focus on his hard body sliding against mine. His hips are pressed against me, and I doubt there is any air at all between us. His hand splayed out on my ass as he presses me against him.

His face dips to my cheek and he whispers in his rough husky voice, "Some say when you save a life, you own it."

"Says the man who also took a life." I whisper back, a little of the fire returning to me as I struggle to fight back against the situation.

His soft chuckle makes me wonder if he's mentally stable and he almost makes me jump as his lips brush against my cheek and he whispers, "Just another day at the office. You get used to it."

I swear every part of me freezes because what the actual hell is going on?

I am frozen and unable to move and it's a good job he is almost carrying me around the dance floor.

"Allegra Powell." He whispers, causing my heart to beat a little faster.

"Now what will I do with you, I wonder?"

I can't even speak. My mind is racing so fast and it's not helping that his freaking gun is pressing against my left breast as he holds me close to his chest. This man wears danger like an aftershave and it's addictive.

Why am I a hot mess around a fucking criminal? He is dark, dangerous and focused entirely on me and I don't know whether to thank God for the opportunity or pray for my soul.

CHAPTER 4

SHADE

I like my women on edge, and she is about to fall over it. I can almost touch her nerves that she is trying so hard to conceal with indifference.

I feel her heart beating against my silk covered chest. She trembles in my arms and the sweat is forming on her brow. Her eyes are startled, and she is struggling to deal with the situation. She is perfect.

I never dance, but for some strange reason I needed her in my arms. When I watched her approach, I could read every thought in her head. She was trying to escape me. I loved it. I almost cheered her on, hoping she would run because for a man who loves the chase, it would have made my week.

Her friend was like every other woman I've met. Up for it. She was not and her fear is the tastiest dish that I feed from with delight. The terror in her eyes is mixed with lust, and that is my most preferred combination.

Her body slides against mine like spun silk. We fit together like the most absurd puzzle. It's an intoxicating situation that I intend to enjoy for as long as possible.

She is mine now. Mine to play with. Mine to corrupt and mine to ruin. My beautiful revenge.

The second song merges into the first and she relaxes a little. No longer as tense as she was when I first pulled her into my arms.

I rub slow circles on her back and then splay my hand on her ass, loving how it moves against my fingers, begging to be fucked.

She smells of expensive scent and corruption and I brush my lips against her hair, inhaling the sweet scent of forbidden fruit.

It amuses me to picture Judge Stevenson's face if he could see his beloved daughter now. In my arms, preparing to be ruined forever.

She is silent; her nerves standing in full view. She doesn't know what to expect, which is probably a very good thing.

I bend my head and whisper, "You know, birthdays should count for something."

She says nothing and I say huskily, "They are a first. The beginning of your life when you are born. Every year thereafter you should do a first on your birthday. What will your first be tonight?"

"I came to this club. That is my first for this year." She says quickly, causing me to smile and pulling back a little, I lift her chin to face me and stare into her eyes, loving how her pupils dilate and her breathing intensifies.

"You can do better than that, princess."

She holds my gaze and, with a wry smile, says huskily, "I know I can do better, so if you'll excuse me."

She attempts to pull away, which amuses me when I see the fire burning in her eyes as she hisses, "Let me go."

It makes me smile. "Now, why would I do that when we have so much to discuss? So much to enjoy—together."

I press in harder, and the desire lit in her eyes is a considerable turn on. If this was an ordinary night, I would be bending her over my office desk and delighting in an evening of debauchery, but I have a more extended stay in mind for my wild cat. She isn't leaving anytime soon, and she's a fool if she thinks she has that option.

Instead, I grip her hand and say pleasantly, "I have the perfect first in mind for you tonight."

Without even considering her response, I make for the exit, loving how she attempts to pull back and, as my bodyguard moves behind us, she has no option but to follow me.

We head through the exit and then move to another one at the end of the corridor.

"Stop, I..."

I ignore her pleas and as we push through the door at the end, my guard positions himself against it.

I pull her at speed up the metal staircase and through the heavy door at the top, spilling out into the night sky on the roof of my club.

The wind whips around us and the cold air chills as I guide her over to the edge and push her hard against it, facing the city below.

"Oh my god." She attempts to pull back as I press against her from behind and wrap my hand around her face, forcing her to look at the busy streets below.

"Look at the city, princess. Isn't she beautiful? Like a repeatedly fucked woman begging for more."

"You're insane." She says through gritted teeth, and I laugh softly. "Are you just figuring that one out?"

I whisper in her ear, "So, baby girl, why don't we make this a first to remember?"

"No!" She pushes back, attempting to get away, and I tighten my hold and press in harder. "Why don't you give in to what your body wants and fuck what your head is telling you?"

"Asshole." She hisses and I chuckle softy as the approaching rumble tells me this is just about to get interesting.

As the noise increases, she says quickly, "What's that?"

I don't need to answer her as my helicopter appears before us, rising majestically against the steel building.

I pull her back and grip her wrist hard and we watch as the bird lands on the helipad as arranged.

"Come."

I pull her after me and she squeals, "No. What the fuck are you are doing? I'm not getting in that thing."

She has no choice as I pull her after me, ducking under the rotor blades and pushing her through the open door.

Before she can run, I fasten her seatbelt and slam the headphones on her head and swing the door shut, loving how the bird immediately rises above the sparkling city.

My passenger may be shit scared, but her eyes are shining as we cut through the night sky like avenging demons.

"Where are we going?" She says through the headset, and I smile. "To your first."

I reach for her hand and squeeze it gently and smile my reassurance as she stares at me with confusion. The fact she leaves her hand in mine tells me everything I need to know. My ice queen is thawing and after what I have planned tonight, she will do everything I ask, and it will be the sweetest revenge.

CHAPTER 5

ALLEGRA

My mind is scrambled. It's as if I don't even know myself anymore. How has this happened and why am I enjoying it in a twisted, fucked up victim kind of way?

Every minute I am around this man, I am on high alert. There is not one of my senses that isn't affected by him, and it's exhausting. He scares the shit out of me, but I am ridiculously attracted to him. There is something so intoxicating about this man that draws me to him against my will.

Now I am holding his hand. What the hell?

It brings me to my senses, and I slide my hand away from his and point out at the skyline.

"Where are we heading?"

"To your first." He grabs my hand again and this time I let it settle there. It feels kind of nice and so I turn a blind eye to all the red flags waving around me and try to enjoy the experience.

This may be my first and my last birthday because I'm not a fool. I know he is a bad man. I watched him freaking murder a man in cold blood as if it's the kind of thing he does for kicks.

I shouldn't be attracted to that. I am fucked in the head, but right now, in this moment of time, I am living a life that is strangely turning me on.

The sky is as dark as this man's heart and as I steal a glimpse at him, I swear my whole body comes alive. He is so gorgeous, like a dark, decadent treat that is extremely bad for your health. A drug that is forbidden and yet you ignore the warnings and go there anyway. Maybe this will be a first because I tread carefully through life. I am the good girl. The valedictorian and sorority princess. He got that title right. I have never placed a foot wrong until I stepped into that alley and now look where I am. In trouble, that's for sure.

"We're here." He turns and points to a light in the ocean and I gasp, "You are freaking kidding me. I must parachute onto a frigging boat now."

He laughs and I love the way his eyes shine with excitement. It's contagious, and I even allow myself a small smile in return.

"Sadly, no. Not this time. It has a helipad."

"The boat has a helipad." I shake my head. "What is it, a US destroyer or something?"

"No" He grins and raises my hand to his lips.

"Just my boat."

As we dip lower, I brace myself for a watery grave and yet the pilot has obviously done this before because he touches down lightly, causing me to groan with relief. Thank God. Then again, perhaps it may have been better to drown because, from the expression in this man's eye, I'm about to face something even more dangerous.

The door opens and I note a man standing there dressed in a black polo shirt and chinos and he nods with respect.

"Mr. Vieri. Ma'am."

Committing his name to my memory to be revisited with google later on, if I make it back that is, I step out of the helicopter onto the deck of an enormous boat. It almost dwarfs the helicopter and I stare around me in awe as I follow Mr. Vieri to the front of the boat.

Despite the night sky, this boat is lit up like a firework. Fairy lights and discreet lighting illuminate a palace on the ocean.

When we turn the corner, I'm shocked when I see the table at the front, set against the rail. It's covered in a white cloth with beautiful flowers mixed with candles. Crystal glasses catch the light and sparkle in the night sky. The chairs have a fur throw resting on the back of them and the silver cutlery is set beside a starter that makes my mouth water.

"Happy birthday, princess."

My kidnapper pulls out one of the chairs and I drop into it in a state of shock.

As he sits opposite, a waiter dressed in white steps forward and pours a glass of champagne for each of us and then retreats into the shadows.

Before I can speak, soft music plays and my eye travels to a deck above and there's a string quartet serenading us, and I blink in disbelief as I struggle to wrap my head around what is happening.

"I don't understand." I stare at the man before me, and he takes a sip of his drink before setting it down on the table and saying huskily.

"I want your first with me to count."

"With you?" I am melting inside because this is the most romantic yet frightening experience of my life and I'm shocked when he reaches out and grasps my hand and lifts it to his lips.

"I have been waiting for you, Allegra. I am not letting you go until you fall in love with me."

"Excuse me?" I'm stunned and he whispers, "I saved you. I told you. You belong to me now."

Now I'm considering he has escaped from a mental institution and gulp, "Listen. Mr–"

"Shade."

"What?"

"My name is Shade."

"Of course it is." I shake my head as he chuckles softly and I say quickly, "Well, um, Shade. This is all rather amazing and completely over the top, but I'm struggling here. Yes, you saved me, and I thank you for that, but well, you don't really own me, you know. I'm a free woman. I always have been and aside from the, um, extremely bad experience of the other night, I can look after myself."

He leans back in his seat and regards me with a hooded expression, causing me to wonder if I've offended him. Then he nods toward the food. "Eat. I have employed the services of the finest chef in Manhattan. It would be rude not to enjoy his creation."

Thankful for the distraction, I set my mind to sampling this stunning cuisine.

It appears to be lobster dressed in a mouth-watering sauce, with intricate salad leaves that taste divine.

I decide to play this to my advantage and say with interest. "Tell me about yourself. What business are you in?"

He shrugs. "I'm in the mafia, Allegra. I think you can guess what that involves."

The fork hovers halfway to my mouth and I stare at the food as if it speaks in riddles and then I set it down and say weakly, "The um, mafia, as in The Sopranos type of thing?"

"If you like." He carries on eating, his eyes glinting with amusement, but I fail to see the humor in this situation at all.

He points to the food on my plate.

"Eat."

I jump as if his words burn and start shoveling the food more as a distraction than anything else because where I hoped he was just a hot billionaire who had fallen inexplicably in love with me like the romances I read, it appears that I lifted the wrong book off the shelf.

CHAPTER 6

SHADE

I love how nervous she is. She should be. In fact, if she saw inside my mind right now, she would be jumping overboard, a fight with the fishes more attractive than the one she has coming with me.

I love this. The anticipation of the attack. The moment when my prey realizes its game over—for them, anyway.

Allegra Powell is my revenge on her real father. The man who dared to think he could push our family out of the very organization they created. He's a fool who will suffer the consequences.

I smirk. "Hand me your phone."

"Why would I do that?"

I grin. "No big deal. The occasion calls for a memento. Raise your glass and smile for the camera, Allegra."

She slides it nervously toward me and her hand reaches for the glass on autopilot.

I do the same and take the selfie and waste no time in posting it on her social. If Judge Stevenson doesn't follow her, he will soon be told because this photograph will be the first of many.

She stares at me in confusion. "Why are you doing this?"

"I told you." I shrug. "I own you. A life for a life. Isn't that how it goes?"

"No, it doesn't." She slams her glass down and says with fire in her eyes. "I'm not some dimwit who thinks the sun shines out of your ass, you know. Newsflash, I didn't ask for this. I was perfectly happy enjoying a night out with my friend who will probably be calling the cops on you. Kidnap carries a jail term, so you should be pissing your pants right now."

I can't help it and burst out laughing and she stands and faces me with pure anger shining from her eyes.

"Take me back. Now!"

"And ruin the party I arranged. You were brought up better than that, princess."

"You know nothing about me." She snarls and I shake my head and lean back, switching my mood from hero to bastard in a nanosecond.

"Sit down."

My voice offers no disagreement, and she pales and drops into the seat she vacated with a worried frown.

"Firstly, you are my guest, and nobody has kidnapped anyone."

I lean forward, loving, watching the blood drain from her face as I scowl. "Secondly, you are in a shitload of trouble, and I am the only man who can help you and your brother."

"Rafferty!" She gasps and I nod.

"Your brother is in deep shit, and you had better tell me everything you know if you want to save him from spending his life behind bars."

"He's innocent." Her voice cracks and I smirk.

"That's what they all say."

"He is." She says louder, the tears gathering behind her eyes.

"He may be innocent, but if somebody wants to prove otherwise, he has no chance."

"Who?" she says with urgency.

"That's what I'm going to find out, with your help."

"But why would you help us?" she says with suspicion.

"I have my reasons."

I sit back and drag the glass to my lips and say, "Now, shall we continue?"

She nods miserably as the waiter appears to clear the starter and refill our glasses and the musicians play on as if nothing happened.

She gazes around her and says wistfully, "It's beautiful out here."

"It is."

"You are very lucky."

"You make your own luck, princess, and I make a lot of it."

I drum my fingers on the table and say wickedly, "If I help you, I want something from you in return."

"What?" Her attention shifts back to me, and I salivate over the alarm on her face.

"Seven days and seven nights."

"I don't understand."

I lean forward and stare into her eyes, loving how terrified she is as she gazes back at me.

"You will be mine for seven days and seven nights. On the seventh night, I will return you to your life. Debt paid, never to be repeated."

"I'm sorry." She shakes her head and stutters. "You will really have to spell it out for me because I haven't got a clue what you are talking about."

"I think you know exactly what I'm talking about, Allegra. You just don't believe I'm asking."

The blood drains from her face and she whispers, "I'm not a whore."

"I disagree."

I laugh softly at the furious expression on her face.

"You already proved you were when you attempted to pay your brother's debt. You may not have offered sex, but you offered money."

"I was being blackmailed, you fucking bastard." She says through gritted teeth.

"Then why didn't you go to the cops if you are so certain your brother is innocent?"

"Because…"

She falters and slumps in her seat. "Because he begged me not to. He told me his career would be over if there was a whiff of scandal attached to his name, let alone murder."

"And he used you to save his own skin." I hiss, wishing I had one hour with her fucking brother.

"He didn't know. Not at first."

"I thought he was being blackmailed."

I'm surprised at the tears that spill as she says with a sob. "It's not just Rafferty. I've been getting calls, notes and I'm sure I'm being followed."

This is news to me, and I growl, "Perhaps you should start at the beginning princess because you are in deeper than I thought."

She glances up and I detect a faint spark of hope in her eyes before she shakes it away and takes a deep breath.

"I'm probably being silly. I can deal with it. It's not so bad."

She lifts her glass and attempts to smile. "What's taking that main course so long?"

I click my fingers without tearing my eyes from her for a second and as the waiter serves two plates of filet mignon, I allow her the distraction to get her shit together. If anything, her confession has only made her more attractive to me. I love shit like this, and she will soon learn that I always get my man and woman. It's only a matter of time.

CHAPTER 7

ALLEGRA

I'm not sure why I blurted out my darkest secret like that. I'm such an idiot. Now what? He will make it so much worse, whatever this is.

I think back to when it started. A note through my door one morning that I passed off as a prank. It said.

I know your secret.

I shrugged it off, but then the calls started. A rasping husky voice whispering filthy things in my ear. I blocked the number, but they rang with a different one every single time.

The threats became obscener, deranged even, and I set all my calls to voicemail. Then the emails came, and I reported them. They kept coming. There was a note on my car promising I would die in a horrific crash. There was the letter sent to my parent's home telling me I would be kidnapped and sacrificed to the devil.

Then I got the letter saying that unless I paid ten thousand dollars, my brother would be framed for murder.

Rafferty knew about the other stuff, but I didn't want to burden him with that as well because the woman who was murdered had spent the night before in bed with him. He was so freaked out about it anyway, I didn't want to increase the pressure, so I raided my savings and that's where this began.

I stare at the man opposite and wonder if I can trust him with this. The trouble is, he's hardly a superhero, more like an anti-hero and I should be more terrified about the imminent danger I'm in rather than what's waiting for me back in New York.

However, despite everything turning to shit in my life, one sentence has me more worried than anything else. Seven days and seven nights. What the hell does that mean?

We finish our main course in silence. I wish I could be happy about that, but he spent the entire time staring into my eyes while he ate, and it was kind of unnerving.

As soon as the dishes are cleared and the wine once again topped up, he leans forward and says huskily, "What is your answer?"

"No." I shrug. "It will always be no."

He nods and for one foolish second, I think he's accepted defeat and I jump when he stands and moves to my side of the table, reaching for my hand.

He pulls me to my feet and for one terrifying moment, I believe he's going to toss me to a watery grave. I jump as he pulls me into his arms, hard and tight, and whispers, "Wrong answer."

I struggle to move, but he has me in some kind of super hold, and I hate that he must feel my terrified heart beating against his black one.

He dips his lips to my ear and whispers, "Seven days and seven nights is a small price to pay for my help."

"Only you think that." I hiss back and he chuckles softly

against my ear and says in a low voice, "I will treat you like a queen. You will want for nothing, and I will show you a world you will never believe."

"My answer is still no."

I am fading fast because he is overpowering my senses. There is something so desirable about a dangerous man. I never appreciated that before, but I am falling hard for his charm. I want to sample the forbidden fruit so badly, but I am terrified of him and the fact I may fall so hard I'll crack.

He whispers huskily, "There is something I forgot to mention."

I still as his hand wraps around my hair and tightens his grip, and the tears spring to my eyes.

He pulls my head back to face him, and the dark expression on his face sends shivers down my spine.

"You have no choice."

There he is. The man I guessed he was. No different to the man he murdered, reaching out and taking what he wants regardless, and it makes me so angry I can't even see him through the red mist of anger.

"You don't scare me." I lie in a futile attempt to gain the upper hand.

"Are you sure about that, princess?"

He smirks and tugs my head back and brushes his lips against mine.

"You should be scared." He whispers as that infernal string quartet keeps playing as if their lives depend on it and they probably do.

My eyes water with the pain, but there is something so compelling about those eyes that stare at me with a chaotic madness. They contain a broken beauty that hides a thousand secrets.

I am so caught up in them I forget what an asshole he is and reaching up, I shock him by stroking his face and whisper, "So many secrets Shade. Just like your name, they are hidden away from the light."

If it's possible, his eyes darken and the light reflects in them as he says huskily, "Then we are the same, Allegra. You are hiding secrets from me, and guess what?"

I lick my lips and whisper, "What?"

"I know a secret that you don't. One that concerns you and if you discovered it, your answer would change to yes."

My heart jumps because I knew it. This man has an agenda concerning me and it's vital I have all the facts if I'm going to survive this mess, so I seize the opportunity and whisper, "Then you should tell me to change my answer."

Once again, his lips brush against mine, and I taste the alcohol mixed with his intoxicating scent.

It appears that danger turns me on because I am dripping for him and that is a very inconvenient reaction right now because I want to hate him, not lust after him.

My head and heart are engaged in a fistfight right now because I am conflicted. I hate that I'm cheering my heart on because it would be so easy to agree to his demands. Seven days and nights of his attention is no hardship. The trouble is, I have a feeling it will cost me my soul.

CHAPTER 8

SHADE

She is stronger than most and I like it. I admire it and I applaud her, but it's also inconvenient. I'm not kidding, she doesn't have a choice, but forcing women isn't something I'm used to. They come willingly every fucking time, but she is holding out on me.

The fact she's so attractive is a bonus. It will be no hardship spending the next seven days with her. The way I will corrupt and break her is so delicious I am eager to get started. Her fight is getting in the way of that, so I revealed one of my cards.

Now I have her interest and I spin her around so she is facing the black ocean and I stand behind her, locking her between me and the rail. I grip her face in my hand and force her to stare out to sea and whisper darkly, "There are many bodies in that open grave. Never to be found which makes it the perfect place to stage a suicide."

She tries to get out of my grip, and I laugh in her ear. "I have no heart, no compassion, and no mercy. I am a man of secrets, that is true, but when that secret will tear your world apart, I really think you should pay attention and stop fighting the inevitable."

I feel her tears splash on my fingers and her body shakes against mine as I say darkly, "Seven days and seven nights, Allegra, and you will love every fucking minute of it."

I release her and, grabbing her wrist, I spin her around and stroke her face lovingly as she did mine, staring into her eyes and whispering, "I can tell you need further encouragement. I will tell you what you need to know and in return for helping you, I will demand your company in return. Then, we will head back to land, and you will carry on with your life knowing exactly who you are."

"Tell me." Her eyes are wide, and the fear has been replaced by a thirst for knowledge.

I smirk and nod toward the table.

"After we finish our meal, we will make our deal."

"Okay." She nods, her eyes bright but different from before. Fear has been replaced by a hunger for information and that will seal the deal far more effectively than threats and intimidation.

The third course arrives, a delicious trio of delights that make conversation easy as we discuss which one we prefer and, to anyone looking on, they would think this was any ordinary date. I decide to take the time to question her a little and refill her glass and say easily, "I understand you are here to work. What does that involve?"

"Please don't remind me."

"Why? Don't you like your position?"

She shakes her head. "It's not that, well…" She sighs heavily. "My mind just isn't there, which is inconvenient."

"Why not?"

"Listen, Shade." She rolls her eyes at my name, causing me to smile.

"This may be just another day at the office for you, but I have led a very sheltered life. Watching a man murdered in cold blood isn't something I can stop seeing. Then there's all of this. You."

"Me?" I'm amused at her obvious discomfort, and she nods vigorously. "Yes. I still don't understand why you are doing this, but to humor you, I will hear you out. There's the fact I've been dragged into a world I know nothing about. The endless calls, messages, and threats are really beginning to creep me out and for all I know, you are responsible."

Now I'm getting somewhere, and I lean forward, fixing her with a dark glare that causes the blood to drain from her face.

"What threats?"

She swallows hard before glancing at the musicians who are heroically still playing.

Then she leans forward and whispers above the music, "It started with a note left on my car he delivered to my home and some crank messages and calls on my phone."

"What did they say?"

She rolls her eyes. "Well, let's assume it's not you for a second. Mainly threats to kill me, telling me they knew my secret and to watch my back. The thing is, I don't have secrets, not really. Sure, I may have maxed out my credit card and got in the shit with my mother. Possibly there was the time I tried a cigarette at a party and the time I attended a strip club in town and may have got a little drunk and pretended I was better than them but well, it's hardly breaking news, is it?"

Her admissions make me laugh out loud because she is fucking Barbie, so innocent and so naive, it's ridiculous.

"I'm glad you find it funny." She says angrily, the embarrassment evident on her face.

"Anyway, then Rafferty's date wound up murdered and the threats notched up a thousand levels. He was home that weekend and when the news broke, he cornered me and told me he had spent the night before she died with the woman. He had just signed for the Jets and was shit scared that he would be involved in the investigation, but nobody came. The fact he learned of my own threats was inconvenient because he told me to move in with him and he would look out for me. I had already secured an internship at The Social Queen and so it made sense."

She drains the glass of champagne and glances around the boat before whispering, "Then I got the note telling me Rafferty was going to be framed for Taylor's murder."

She sighs. "He was so happy, Shade. If I told him, it could ruin his big chance, so I dealt with it behind his back. I thought…"

"That the money would stop the threats."

I shake my head, marveling at the naivety of these people.

"Yes."

She looks so broken I almost pity her, but I don't.

"I'll ask you again. Why didn't you go to the cops? It's obvious there's a hate campaign against you. They would deal with it."

"Because of Rafferty. He is riding high, and the scandal would never go away. I thought I'd pay the money and that would be the end of it."

"Where did you get the money?" I ask out of interest, wondering if she borrowed it from anyone else she may have told.

"My savings."

She pushes back her plate and says miserably. "The fact it's soaked with a man's blood means I've lost that as well. If that doesn't implicate me in his murder, I don't know what will. I have been so scared to go out ever since, waiting for the cops to hammer on my door and arrest me for murder. My prints must be all over that alley along with my DNA. It's only a matter of time before they come for me. Tonight is the first time I've been out since."

The fact I already know may be best kept to myself before I freak her out anymore. I've had eyes on Allegra Powell for several weeks now, and I know every inch of her routine. Did I send those threats? Fuck no, which means someone wants her scared. It's not only me who is using her for something, which is an inconvenience that needs to be dealt with.

Leaning forward, I lift her hand and this time she doesn't attempt to snatch it back and I smile a reassurance that only I can offer her.

"Seven days and nights, Allegra. The deal hasn't changed, however, in return I'll make it all go away. I will find the person responsible for blackmailing you and I will deal with it."

"Empty promises, Shade."

She cocks her head to one side and rolls her eyes. "For all I know, that person is you. I'm not that gullible."

She makes to snatch her hand back and I hold on to it tightly and growl, "I never lie. You will soon learn that about me. I tell it how it is and I'm telling you now. By the end of this evening, you will be begging to stay. You don't realize it now, but you need me far more than I need you, so you would be wise to smile prettily and say the words, thank you, Shade. My answer is obviously yes."

To my surprise, she throws her head back and laughs, much like she did at the club while I stalked her on the monitor. It completely transforms her, and I stare as if mesmerized. She is so beautiful, like a rare orchid blooming in the wilderness and it captures my attention in a way I never saw coming. Yes, Allegra Powell will make for an interesting seven days, and I am going to ruin her father in the process.

As I raise her hand to my lips and steal a kiss, this time she stares at me with a smile on her face and a spark of desire in her eyes that I knew she was hiding the entire fucking time.

CHAPTER 9

ALLEGRA

I'm not sure why, but the relief hit me hard. When he told me he wasn't my stalker, it drove the tension away that's been building for weeks now. Finally, I have offloaded my secret to someone who didn't bat an eyelid. A man who deals with shit like this every day and can sort things. I already know that about him.

Men like Shade Vieri don't play by the rules which is why he's the perfect man to help with my problem. The fact the payment he desires is almost certain to be my body doesn't seem as appalling as it did earlier. In fact, the more time I spend with him, the more interested I get and for a girl who has played it safe for her entire life, I am fast falling down the blackest hole, desperate to experience something I probably never will again.

We finish our food, and he stands, offering me his hand and saying firmly.

"Dance with me."

This time I don't protest. It's an impossible situation because I have never been treated like this before. My past dates have taken me for dinner and then expected my body in return. But not like this. Not in this romantic movie style way.

From the moment I met him, Shade Vieri has overtaken my world, my senses and my mind. He fills them and owns them and the romantic in me is swooning under his attention.

The practical side of me knows that seven days is probably all his attention span will allow him and if this is what he promises the next seven days will be like, I would be a fool to pass up the opportunity. He will expect me to have sex with him. I'm not naive. I know the score and for some reason that doesn't repel half as much as it should. To be honest, I should be begging him because I have never met a man quite like Shade Vieri and I like what I see.

This time, as he pulls me into his arms, I go there willingly. It's as if he has stepped inside and claimed my darkest secret and is holding it in his hand. It doesn't matter anymore because it's his to deal with now. He will remove me from my responsibilities for seven days and when I return, it will be with no shadows hanging over me. I can start again knowing there will be no threats. I have an avenging angel watching over me, and I will use his time wisely. I want to see how far I will go. How different it is when you walk on the wild side. Then I will return to my normal life and–

"Shade."

My voice is laden with disappointment as I stare up at him.

"What?"

"I can't stay."

He raises his eyes. "You don't have a choice. I thought you knew that."

"You don't understand." I say, the disappointment crashing through me.

"Then enlighten me."

"I'm due to start at The Social Queen on Monday. I've already delayed my starting date and I'll lose my internship if I don't show up. My family will also be informed because my mom is good friends with the owner."

He shrugs. "I'll sort it. It's an easy problem to solve."

"How?"

"I'll call your boss. Your mom isn't the only person who knows Evangeline Solomon and by the time I've finished with her, that internship will be a firm offer of employment with a generous salary. Leave it with me."

"Are you kidding me? You really have that much power. She's a rock star in this business."

"And I'm a rock star in mine."

He dips his head to my ear and whispers, "Trust me, princess. There is nothing I can't do."

His words send ripples of longing through my entire body. Power must be one hell of an aphrodisiac because there is not one part of my body that isn't turned on right now. He has the ability to crawl inside my soul and make it is. Any fear has been tossed over the side and I am drowning in desire—for him—this lifestyle and whatever else he has planned.

I almost blurt out a desperate yes to his question, but he told me he knows a secret about me. I'm keen to learn what that is, so I keep my words to myself and just enjoy swaying in his arms on the deck of a boat that really resembles a small ship. The wind caresses my body, and the stars shine brighter than the fairy lights that dress the boat in a warm, sultry light.

Out here I am free. I can be whoever I want to be, and I am in the arms of the sexiest man alive. The fact he's a killer is inconsequential now. Just for once, I am going to leave my perfect self back in that apartment. I am releasing my wild spirit and fuck the consequences because I have never felt more alive in my life.

I am disappointed when the music stops and Shade pulls away and grasps my hand, his mood switching in an instant.

"Come, we will discuss our business."

My heart hammers as I follow him up some stairs to the top deck, noticing the musicians are packing away their instruments.

"Are they staying on board?" I enquire, jerking my thumb in their direction, and he shakes his head. "No. They are about to take a short ride in my helicopter."

"Will it come back for us?" The fact it's there is a security I'm not keen to see fly away, and he nods his head. "Of course. In seven days."

His wicked grin somehow makes me laugh and if anything, he appears surprised at that but says nothing and guides me into a comfortable seat filled with cushions and drops down beside me.

He is so close, unlike when he was opposite, and I can almost touch the heat radiating between us. He turns me on. I can't deny it and now the fear has gone, it has only left interest. More interest than is good for me and so I cough nervously and say, "So, what's this big secret I'm supposed to be hiding?"

"All in good time, princess."

He slings his arm along the back of the chair, and his fingers brush against the skin on my neck, causing ripples of desire to pass through me.

Then he says in his husky drawl, "Tell me about your family."

"What have they got to do with this?"

I am curious but not annoyed, and he smiles softly. "Humor me."

I shrug. "Okay. It's pretty unexciting, though. We live in Washington where mom is a successful attorney, and my father runs a freight company. They met at university and have been together ever since. I was born and eighteen months later, they had Rafferty. We live a normal life, brunch on weekends and family dinners. Nothing wild, just well, as I said, normal."

"Tell me about your extended family."

His tone is conversational, but I detect the meaning behind his words and my heart starts beating a little faster.

"Mom has a sister, Aunt Rosie, who married an insurance broker in Maine. They live in Portland, and we visit with them once a month. Dad has a brother, Lucas Stevenson. He's married with a son, my only cousin, but we don't see him very much, or my aunt actually."

"Why not?"

"I don't know, really. Aunt Mary is heavily into charity work and is always busy. My uncle visits more, I guess because he's close to my father."

"Your uncle is Judge Stevenson."

He says it so casually I almost miss the warning flag and then reality hits me. Shade wants something on my uncle, the one man who could keep him from jail and he is using me to get something on him.

I turn and gaze at him with suspicion.

"So, that's your plan."

"Tell me. I'm aching to know." He seems almost amused, and I pull away and say angrily, "You want to use me to get something on my uncle so he will keep you out of jail. Is that it? I'm right, aren't I?"

"Good guess, but no, princess. I already have your father exactly where I want him."

"My father?" I'm surprised. "I thought we were talking about my uncle."

I don't like the sudden dark gleam of excitement that

sparks in his eye as he blows my world apart with one devastating sentence.

"No, Allegra. I'm talking about your real father, who also happens to be your father's brother, Judge Lucas Stevenson."

"You're lying." I can barely get the words out as his words strike a direct hit.

"I'm not." He says it so casually, as if we are just passing the time of day. Not ripping my world apart.

He carries on brutally destroying my safe and secure life.

"Your mother has been having an affair with Lucas Stevenson since she met your father. He doesn't know, by the way." He shakes his head in disgust.

"Both you and your brother are Lucas's because your father's medical records threw up an interesting fact that he has a low sperm count. There's also the fact both your blood type matches Lucas's, who has a rare one."

"But that's just hereditary. It runs in families and Lucas is family, my father's brother."

I really don't believe a word he is saying, and Shade sighs and reaches for a folder on the table.

"I can tell you don't believe me, so I apologize in advance for this, but you leave me no choice."

As he hands me the folder, I take it with trembling fingers. "What's this?"

"Open it and see."

I turn away from him and open it, and my vision blurs as I regard the first one. My mother is naked and sitting on top of a man. They are obviously having sex and as I turn it over, the next one reveals the man is my uncle Lucas. As I flip through them, there are more. Different rooms, different places and it's as if I'm seeing their lives flash before my disbelieving eyes as they age through the photographs. This tells me it wasn't one time only and is a snapshot through the ages. It's obvious they do this regularly and my hands shake as I stare in morbid fascination at the two people in the pictures who could be strangers.

"Does my father know?"

I whisper as I sift through the evidence and Shade replies, "No."

"But how did you get these pictures? It's disgusting. They must go back years." I'm appalled and Shade says gently.

"My grandfather." He shrugs. "He has been monitoring the situation ever since your father/uncle became a member of the society he runs."

"What society?"

"The Dark Lords."

I stare up at him. "What?"

"The Dark Lords. It's an organization where powerful men like to play. They protect one another and the rewards are great."

"Is my father one of these, um, lords?"

"Not Richard Powell, but Lucas Stevenson is."

"This is sick."

I stare in disgust at the photos, and Shade merely shrugs. "There is nothing my grandfather doesn't do to protect his organization. This is his guarantee, and he is cashing it in."

"But why?" I still don't believe him. My uncle is not my father. He can't be.

My hands are shaking so hard I'm surprised when Shade takes the photos from my hands and says gently, "It must be a shock."

"Why?"

"Why what?"

"Why are you doing this?"

"Because secrets have a habit of getting out and it's obvious that I'm not the only one who knows this. This is going to destroy your family, Allegra, and it appears that may not be down to me. We need to discover who else knows, and

I'm guessing that will reveal the identity of the person blackmailing you."

As I stare into two turbulent pools of malice, I see my own reflection staring back at me. Gone is the innocent sorority girl who lived life in a pink bubble. The woman staring back at me has had a rude awakening and, far from being upset, I am angry. So angry with the two people in those photographs.

My entire life has been built on a lie, and they have been carrying on a sordid affair behind my father's back the entire time. I hate them so much I feel the rage consuming me. Now I am no different from the man watching me with interest. I understand what drives him. I love the power it gives when you hold a secret this explosive, and I have the desire for revenge consuming my entire soul.

Yes, Shade Vieri has just pushed me over the edge, and I am holding his hand as I fall.

CHAPTER 10

SHADE

Another successful day at the office.

It was a harder battle than most, which makes the victory sweeter somehow. Now it's time to claim my reward.

Allegra is stunned as she holds the damning evidence in her hand and I reach out and carefully prise it from her fingers and whisper, huskily, "What is your answer now to my request?"

She lifts those gorgeous green eyes and stares at me with no fear.

"Yes."

Her breathing is erratic and her expression wild and right in this moment, she has never looked so beautiful.

This is the moment when her life has changed forever, and she is at a crossroads.

I lift my hand and touch her cheek, loving how she leans into my hand, not away from it.

Everything has changed between us because she is hurting. She is no longer thinking rationally and is allowing the pain to guide her decisions. She will do anything I ask as one big 'fuck you' to her mom and uncle, and I am the bastard who will exploit the situation to his advantage.

I lean in and steal a kiss. A soft kiss that causes her lips to part and welcome me in.

I wrap my tongue around hers and enjoy corrupted innocence. My favorite flavor in the world as I groan with longing. This is what I love. The kill and as she shivers before me, I know she is ready.

Gently, I ease her dress from her shoulders and pull it down to her waist and unhook her bra. Her breasts dance before me, full and magnificent, and I bend my lips to sample their delights.

It's as if she is frozen in place, probably not realizing what predator has her in his grasp and as I kiss a light trail up to her neck, I take great delight in sucking hard, with the intention of marking her skin for everyone to see.

Her eyes are closed as if she is refusing to acknowledge the situation. She is turning her back on her inhibitions and seeing where this takes her.

As I cup her chin, I bite down hard on her lower lip, the trail of blood that falls, delicious nectar on my tongue.

Then I run my hand around the back of her head and grip her hard, pulling her head back as I kiss her deeper, with more passion.

She is an unexploded firework in my arms, and I am interested in lighting the fuse. To watch it rapidly burn before the explosion of majesty at the end.

I pull her dress further down and push her back onto the couch, ridding her of her clothing, wasting no time with words.

She is now naked before me on the deck of my boat, exposed to the elements and the curious gazes of my crew. They know better than to hang around and are probably locked safely inside, but she doesn't know that. She is so far gone she isn't thinking straight and as I part her thighs, I gaze at the creamy skin hiding a center of wantonness.

I dip my fingers inside and her pussy clenches against them, the sticky heat telling me how much she wants this.

I insert three fingers inside, curling them against her G spot and she gasps, "Oh God!" before she comes hard, her entire body shaking as she gives into just the merest touch.

I don't wait for her to recover and, pulling her over my knee, I run my hands across her shapely ass, loving how it feels under my hand, desperate to watch it change color before my eyes. She purrs with satisfaction as I caress her body and I whisper, "Do you like that, princess?"

"Yes." Her voice shakes and I smirk. Perfect.

I lean down and whisper in her ear, "Then show me."

"How?" she says with a gasp, and I place her hand on my raging cock and say lustfully, "Fuck me with your mouth."

To her credit, she says nothing and just slides from my lap onto the floor and kneeling between my legs, she unbuckles my belt.

I love that she stares into my eyes the entire time and I am fascinated by the flashing eyes of a beauty I never really appreciated before.

Her dark hair shines in the light and her skin resembles the moon's beams. Her green eyes sparkle, and her perfect ruby lips are resting in a smile and as she frees my cock, I love how they widen as it dances suggestively before her face.

She runs smooth fingers around it and grips it hard and tentatively licks the crown.

Her soft gasp excites me further and as she slides it home, I groan with pleasure.

She carefully takes it all the way in and sucks gently. The sound of her slurps a strange turn on for a man who has experienced this a thousand times before. However, there is something special about this and I don't know why. Possibly

I had too much to drink. It could be because of the revenge swirling in my black heart, or it could just be her.

That thought disturbs me a little and so I shake my head back into business and grip her hair tightly as I fuck her mouth rough and hard. She gags as I hit the back of her throat again and again, loving her on her knees at my mercy. Loving the control I have over her.

I power on regardless of her feelings and use her mouth for my own pleasure, not hers. The whole time I picture her father watching us. Helpless to do anything about it and hating every second as I demean his flesh and blood. Ruining her, breaking her and stripping away her dignity, just because I can.

Just the thought of his anger causes me to explode violently into her mouth, holding her head in place as my cum streams down her throat. She frantically tries to swallow, and I don't release her until I'm certain she has downed every last drop and as she falls back on her heels, I feast my eyes on the wild beauty before me. Her face is flushed, and she has cum dripping down her chin that she tries desperately to clean up with her fingers.

Far from appearing angry, she is loving it. I can tell by her heightened color and erratic breathing. She is going to be a pleasure to corrupt because she won't even realize what this is.

"Come."

I reach for her hand and pull her to her feet, fucked and gorgeous as the moon bathes her in its ghostly light.

I pull her over to the edge, much like before, and position her with her back to the railings, kicking her legs apart.

"What is your answer now, princess?" I whisper against her lips, and she says breathlessly, "It's still yes."

"Do you trust me?"

"Fuck no," she says with a wicked smile, and I smirk, "Good answer."

The fact I am still dressed gives me more power because I am shielding her from view as she shivers in my arms.

Knowing the rail will be cold against her back offers her a certain kind of discomfort that I'm looking for.

As I begin to kiss every inch of her silky skin, she comes alive under my touch, her breathing fast and her moans of pleasure music to my ears.

The sound of the helicopter starting up causes her to shriek and I say roughly, "Stay with me, princess."

I flick her clit with my tongue, causing her to groan and as I suck and tease her the helicopter takes flight. Knowing she is naked and putting on a show, I'm certain of the photographs that will arrive on Judge Stevenson's desk in the morning. I almost wish I was there to watch, but strangely, I am having far too much pleasure to leave what I'm doing.

She comes hard on my tongue, and I roll the delight of her around my mouth, loving the sweet taste of revenge. Yes, everyone will soon discover that sweet little Allegra Powell is fucking a criminal and her perfect life will never be the same again.

CHAPTER 11

ALLEGRA

I am on sensory overload. It's almost too much as I throw decency overboard and allow myself to be corrupted in such a demeaning way. The pleasure this man is bringing to my body is heightened by the location, along with the fine wine running like a river of damnation through my veins and the pain of betrayal that is driving my actions. There is also the freedom being out here brings. The fact we are in the middle of the ocean with nobody around for miles, experiencing the salty spray on my body and the wicked heat of this man's mouth.

I am experiencing sensation overload and couldn't stop this if I tried. I don't even care that I'm naked for anyone to see. It's strangely liberating and I'm hungry for more of the euphoria I am experiencing now. He could ask anything of me because out here I'm no longer Allegra Powell. I am reinventing myself and grabbing the experience by the balls.

As I cum hard, I swear I see fireworks. He is that good and yet when I collapse against him, he won't let me fall and carries me to the couch and lies me flat on my back. As I peer up, he tears off his tie and shrugs out of his shirt, his hard ripped body a feast for my eyes. I watch with delicious anticipation as he tears his belt from his waist and then grips my wrists and uses it to fasten them together. The bite of leather and cool steel of the belt make me gasp and as he hooks them over the back of the chair, he drops his pants, kicking them away, standing before me naked and magnificent.

"I'm going to fuck you princess and there is nothing you can do about that."

His dirty words cause me to pant because why the fuck would I want to say no to this?

He drops down over me and stares into my eyes with the look of the devil and as he bites down on my lip it draws blood, causing me to squeal, "Ow."

He merely laughs and turns his attention to my breasts, biting the nipples so hard it makes me scream and then he grips my hips and says darkly, "Birth control?"

I nod, my voice not my own anymore as I stutter, "Condom?"

"Not a fucking chance." He grins and with one thrust spears me hard and deep, causing me to cry out as he pounds into my body as if it's under attack. He's merciless as he tears through me like an out-of-control beast, and I can do fuck all about it. He grips my neck in an iron hold and commands, "Look at me."

I open my eyes to stare into two dark pits of evil as he ravages my body. The fact it excites me is a very good thing because this is a frightening experience for a girl used to life inside a pink bubble. But its him. Shade Vieri. He is so damn attractive I can't think straight and I'm loving everything so far.

He pushes in deeper, causing me to moan, "Shade, Fuck me, that is so good."

He pounds relentlessly, owning my body and teaching me how good it is to be dominated because all my inhibitions, fears, and anxieties have left me. I am free. I am his now. He controls me and has taken my burden as his own. He has everything. He owns me just like he said he would and as I clench around his cock, I'm shocked when he pushes harder against my neck and growls, "Don't you dare fucking come."

It shocks me as he pushes in harder, faster, deeper and I can hardly breathe as he cuts off my air supply and just when I think it's all over, death by fucking, he releases his hold and yells, "Now you can come."

As he explodes inside me at the same time the air reaches my lungs, my orgasm crashes through my body in one violent attack. It overcomes me as violent waves shock my body. Causing it to convulse as if I'm having some kind of sex seizure.

I can't breathe. I am riding a wave so high it may drown me. I swear I even black out for a second as my soul leaves my body and suspends above it, watching the destruction of a woman who never knew sex could be this good. As my soul comes back to me and my body starts to behave, I am left with an overwhelming urge for more. Am I a sex addict now? Will I be seeking this high from any potential donor just for the euphoria I want to bottle and keep for my pleasure?

I don't even care that he has moved away and is dressing, as if I'm a whore he picked up off the streets. He has used me and got what he wanted. Then again, I never doubted his success, just my own ability to refuse him.

He could leave me here and I'd be happy. I am delirious and feel as if I kind of used him in a way. This wasn't making love. This was downright dirty sex and now I know what all the fuss is about I want more of the same. Yes, seven days and nights is not enough. He was right I would love every minute. But I'm here now and this is the beginning of the best week of my life.

* * *

I'm not sure how long I sleep for but when I wake the sun is caressing the burns on my body and I am sleeping under a fur throw that somebody apparently tossed over me in the early hours of this morning. Bleary-eyed, I sit up and rub my eyes, clutching the throw to my body as the events of last night remind me what happens when you let your guard down. Apparently, you become a wanton whore and I'm almost convinced I look like one.

I note my dress spread over a nearby chair, my panties strangely missing, along with my bra. My face burns with embarrassment as I reach for my dress and slip it on, hating the walk of shame waiting for me.

Before I can move, a man appears dressed in a white polo shirt and white shorts and he is carrying a tray with a glass of orange juice resting on it.

"Ma'am."

He hands it to me, and I feel my face flame as he says respectfully, "Allow me to escort you to breakfast."

I can't even speak I am so mortified and as I grasp the crystal glass, I allow the cool liquid to slide down my throat, loving the sweet taste of purity.

I follow him barefoot back down the stairs to the rear of the boat, where a table is set overlooking the most fantastic sunrise.

Another white tablecloth billows in the breeze and the silver cutlery sparkles against the fresh flowers and crystal jug of water.

It is beautiful and as I drop into the white cushioned chair, I stare at the sunrise with an empty heart. Today is the first day of the rest of my life. My eyes have been opened, and I have learned a valuable lesson. I never was Allegra Powell, not really. I always was Allegra Stevenson and the bastards have stolen my childhood. It ceases to exist. They have robbed me of my security and my history, but they will not rob me of my future. That is mine to mold into the perfect one for me and fuck the rest of them. I'm on my own now.

CHAPTER 12

SHADE

She is waiting for me, a vision in her dress from the night before, her hair messed up and the evidence of my brutality on her neck and body. She glances up as I head toward her, my own appearance flawless, courtesy of the good night's sleep in my bed, followed by a shower and a fresh change of clothes.

She, however, looks as fucked as I wanted her to look and so I pull her phone from my pocket and snap a memory, posting it to her Instagram before she even registers it.

"Is that my phone?" She reaches for it, and I place it back in my pocket with a shake of my head.

"It's my phone now for seven days and six nights. You will get it back at the end with a camera roll of memories to cherish in your old age."

"But…" She opens her mouth to make her demands and I say with a wicked grin. "I am the one controlling you, Allegra, as I demonstrated last night. This is your payment for my help and for keeping you out of jail. Remember."

She sighs heavily and gazes out on the sunrise that is particularly fine today.

"So, what now?" She says with a slight shrug of her shoulders and I'm loving that she has accepted the situation.

"We eat."

I state the obvious as the steward delivers two plates of scrambled eggs and smoked salmon, along with some warm crusty rolls.

I watch as he fills her glass with water and sets two mugs of coffee before us and then retreats, leaving us alone.

"You live like a king." She sighs, gazing around at the view.

"I do." I sip my coffee and stare at her long and hard. "This is your life for six more days. Enjoy it."

"That's up to you." She shakes her head and shrugs with resignation.

"I know." I chuckle softly because I am intending on having the time of my life this week and she may not survive it.

"Tell me about your life, Shade." She interrupts my depraved thoughts as she lifts a forkful of salmon to her mouth, and it momentarily distracts me. Knowing she is still sticky with my cum and unwashed is strangely satisfying.

I shrug. "My family runs the Vieri mafia. My grandfather is the don who will be succeeded by my brother Kill."

"Your parents must have really hated you." She laughs softly, causing me to grin.

"It appears they did. My mom ran away to Australia and my father ordered a hit on us."

She drops her fork and stares at me incredulously. "Are you fucking kidding me?"

"No. I'm not. My brother dealt with it and the threat was averted."

"And your father?"

Her eyes are wide and widen still further when I say with a shrug. "Dead."

"And I thought my family was fucked up."

I nod, raising my glass of water in a toast. "To two fucked up families."

She nods and raises her glass, clinking it against mine with a wicked smile.

"I'll second that."

As she sips the water, her face catches the light and despite the night she had, she has never looked so attractive to me. So beautiful, very natural with none of the make-up that wore off sometime in the night. Her eyes sparkle and her face is flushed and there is an acceptance in her that is begging to be tested.

I wonder what her limits are and what she will back away from. I intend on finding out and this week should be interesting.

"Tell me about your brother. Is he as weak as I believe him to be?"

"Fuck you. Rafferty isn't weak, he's just well, successful."

"Successful men aren't weak, Allegra. They need their strength to reach their position. He must have natural ability and got lucky then."

"Damn you, Shade. He worked bloody hard for this, which is why he's freaking out that it could be taken from him."

I shrug. "The woman who was found murdered. Tell me about it."

I'm interested because I need to know the full story before I hand it over to Kyle to deal with.

"Her name was Taylor Sutherland. They met at a party."

"What party?"

"I don't know, he was invited to a party by one of the team and she was there. Anyway, they hit it off and ended up in a nearby hotel. You can guess the rest and they left soon after."

"Did he walk her home?" I say curiously, and she shakes her head. "No, he called her a cab, and they went their separate ways. That was the last he heard of her."

She gazes out on the sunrise and says sadly, "Two days later, she was found on the side of the road with her heart cut out. The cops obviously don't know about her night with Rafferty because nobody has been to see him. What do you think happened?"

A cold feeling creeps over me as I think about the way she died. It has a familiarity to it that alarms me.

Allegra carries on eating, but my mind is working hard. Something isn't adding up. I don't like it and need to talk to my brother fast.

* * *

AFTER BREAKFAST I show Allegra to the guest cabin to shower and change into something more comfortable. I have several generic items equipping the closet there because this isn't the first time I've entertained on this boat. I don't recall one as interesting as this one and I'm happy it's turning out to be as much a pleasure for me as it is for her.

I head to my den that I keep for business and waste no time in calling my brother, who answers immediately.

"Your plan is working, I see." His low chuckle momentarily makes me smile.

"I'm guessing you follow Allegra on Instagram then."

He laughs. *"One of my personalities does."*

We all have fake media accounts to stalk our enemies, and to my knowledge, my brother has many, male and female.

"Yes, my plan is working well. Her father should be receiving the evidence any time now."

He chuckles again and then stops when I say urgently,

"Taylor Sutherland. I need answers."

"The girl minus her heart." He says cagily and I growl, "Something doesn't add up. She was with Allegra's brother before she died, and now he is being blackmailed."

"Explain."

I fill him in on what she told me and the long silence on the other end of the line tells me he's as disturbed as I am.

"Leave it with me. I'll make some investigations." He says with a sigh.

"Keep me informed."

"Stick with the plan, Shade. This changes nothing."

"I hoped you'd say that." I laugh softly and he says with an irritated growl, *"Remember, she's business, not pleasure. Ruin the woman and document every sordid step. Bring her father to his knees and expect retaliation."*

"What about Jefferson?"

I remind him of his part of the revenge because Killian is to destroy Judge Stevenson's legitimate son as part of our revenge on his father.

"I've got Gina Di Angelo on the case as a spy. She's feeding back intelligence that I will use against him."

"He won't know what hit him."

I laugh softly as Killian sighs heavily. *"I could do without this fucking shit. I want to take Purity on an overdue honeymoon before the baby arrives."*

"You've got eight months, brother."

"I didn't tell you how long the vacation would be."

He laughs into the phone, and I reply, "Tell that to Don Vieri. I'm sure he would have something to say about your wish for an extended vacation."

In our family, business is everything and any talk of walking away, even for a fucking vacation, is frowned upon. That's why I chose my boat for this particular pastime. Combining business with pleasure is the smart thing to do.

Everyone's happy, except my victim at the end of it but at least she will have fun in the meantime.

As I think about her currently in the shower, I say with a sigh, "Anyway, duty calls, brother. I have an angel to break. I'll keep you posted."

"Spare me the details. Just make sure her father suffers."

He cuts the call, leaving me safe in the knowledge he will have all the details we need before we head back to the city. Whoever is attempting to blackmail my victim had better watch their back because we don't like to share. She's mine to break, and I will enjoy every second of it.

CHAPTER 13

ALLEGRA

This is pure heaven. As the power shower hits the spot, it washes away the night of sin I wallowed in. I loved it. Every single moment and if you told me this time yesterday, I would be here today, I would never have believed it. I wonder what Cecilia is thinking. I left her at Gyration and for all she knows I'm missing, presumed dead. She must be out of her mind with worry. I should call her, but what would I say?

Sorry I left you, but I was whisked away to a mafia yacht and wined and dined before being fucked senseless. How was your night?

It makes me giggle and I jump when I hear an amused, "Somebody's happy."

I turn to see Shade leaning against the doorjamb, casting his appreciative gaze over the length of my body as I rub the soap all over me. He looks so deliciously hot I just gawp at him, and then as he enters the bathroom, he closes the door firmly behind him, shrugging out of his polo shirt and stepping out of his shorts.

My eyes widen at the sight before me because I never did

get to appreciate the body of a man who apparently enjoys the gym as a hobby.

His tanned skin is ripped, and the smattering of hair on his chest leads down to a very tantalizing cock that is primed and ready for more action.

I am weak with lust as he joins me in the shower and pushes me hard against the marble and grips both my wrists, dipping his mouth to my neck and biting down hard.

"Fuck!" I gasp as the pain shoots through me and then he massages my clit, causing a different kind of sensation. It feels so good as he plays hot and cold, pain one minute and pleasure the next. I don't know what is coming first as he leaves bite marks over my entire body, alternating between pleasure and pain, causing me to scream and pant as if I can't make up my mind.

Then he pushes in hard, nailing me to the shower wall and as my back slides against the tiles, the water rains down on the burn.

He is relentless as he hammers me to the wall and my feet slip, and yet he holds me up with one hand, pinning me to the side of the shower as he pounds into me. He is so big. As if he consumes me and there is nowhere left to hide. His hands grip my wrists, causing them to sting and his teeth bite my skin, driving intense pain through my entire body. He fucks hard and fast, playing with my clit one minute and biting me the next.

My mind is fucked because I can't deal with the emotions switching up as they change on his whim. It's too many sensations for my body to cope with and as he grips my hair and smashes his lips to mine, I come all over his cock as he takes over my entire body. I belong to him now. I am part of him and everything he does is to demonstrate that. My body is no longer my own. He controls it now and far from worrying about that, I welcome every single second of it because with him I can lose control, abandon any sense of morality and give in to temptation.

With him, I am free.

When he finishes, he steps back and almost appraises his work as I slouch against the shower wall, too exhausted to care.

The water is still flowing as if the morality angel is weeping for me because I have sunk lower than I ever thought possible. Who is this girl allowing herself to be used like this? I'm in no doubt that's his plan. He gets off on victim control, obviously. There can be no other explanation for his actions, although I have an inkling that there is a hidden agenda concerning my uncle, or should I say, father.

It all comes back to haunt me when I come back down to earth, and as the horror of my situation hits, I say gruffly, "What am I going to tell Rafferty?"

"Do you tell him about all of your sexual experiences?"

He smirks as he towels off, watching me with a predator's eyes.

"Our uncle." I gulp. "I'm talking about serious life shit stuff here and all you can do is joke about it."

My eyes flash as I stare at him, and he openly laughs in my face.

"Of course you are concerned about that. How refreshing."

He shrugs as he fixes the towel around his waist and runs his fingers through his damp hair.

He holds out a towel to me in a sweet show of chivalry, although chivalrous is not really a term I'd use to describe this man.

As he wraps it around me, he says gently, "It must have been a shock. Forgive me. I forget that not everybody deals with shit like that daily. So, the question is, what are you going to do with the knowledge now you have it?"

If anything, he appears interested but not concerned, and I sigh. "I don't know. I'm still figuring that one out."

I stare up into his velvet eyes and whisper, "I don't know who I am anymore."

His thumb brushes against my lips and he whispers, "For the next six nights and seven days, you are mine. You don't need to think, just do what I tell you."

"And if I disagree with what you, um, want me to do?"

This is a question I really should have asked before agreeing to his demands and I'm nervous about the answer.

"You could try, I guess." He shrugs and then grins, the spark in his eyes strangely exciting. "It's more fun for me if you do."

My eyes flash. "Is this how you get your get your kicks? Corrupting innocent women and controlling them?"

My breath hitches at the deepening passion in his eyes and he whispers against my lips, "My kicks come in many forms, Allegra. I intend on educating you about life on the dark side. Have you ever done something morally wrong but loved every fucking delicious second of it?"

I swear my whole body vibrates with excitement at his words and I whisper back, "I'm here with you, aren't I."

He laughs softly and whispers, "That's a very good answer, princess. I will enjoy educating you."

"And then I can leave?"

I hitch my breath as he licks a trail down my face like an over eager puppy and I swear every part of me is aching for him again. I can't believe it's possible after the orgasm I just experienced and he says huskily, "Of course. I am a man of my word."

"And I will never see you again." I press, unsure why I need that to be a condition. If anything, I'm hoping he says no, but he nips my neck and whispers, "Never."

He rubs my nipple between his fingers and whispers, "So

whatever we do stays between us. No judge and jury and no repercussions. Out here you are free and if you can live with the memory, I can show you how extreme life can be when you ditch your principles and step into the darkness."

I am so fucking turned on because he is promising me something I really need right now. Oblivion.

CHAPTER 14

SHADE

I have her exactly where I want her. She will do everything I say and won't even realize it's all in the name of revenge. She believes this is how I get my kicks. It is, but usually with whores, not decent women who deserve better. I'm not interested in them. I'm not my brother and definitely don't want to hitch myself to one woman. I am too far gone for that. My depravity has overtaken my common sense and I am sexually out of control.

Luckily for me, my business ensures a steady stream of willing companions and no comeback. I can do what the fuck I want with who I want. Killian will be my Don, which means I have none of the duty he is expected to show. He was told to clean up his act and be respectable. To marry and to paint a picture of domestic bliss and security. The fact he fell in love was a bonus but me-my instructions were very different.

Make sure there are no leaks in our organization and tear down our enemies.

Business as usual for a Vieri. I fucking love my life.

I pull away from Allegra and grin.

"Ever ridden a jet ski, baby?"

"A few times."

"Then let's go."

"But I have no costume." She says with disappointment, and I shrug. "So go naked. You'll have a life vest. What's the problem?"

"But everyone will see."

"Who?"

"Your staff."

"They're used to it. They won't care."

I'm feeling deliciously evil today, so I add, "I insist."

She visibly gulps and then, to my surprise, says with a shy smile, "Okay, but only if you join me."

"You're telling *me* what to do now?"

I raise my eyes and she giggles. "What can I say? I'm learning from the master. Don't blame me if being an asshole rubs off on me."

It makes me smile and so I grab her wrist and tear the towel off, loving the heightened color in her cheeks as I drag her from the bathroom.

We head to the rear of the boat where my toys are kept, and it amuses me that she hides behind my body as I instruct the steward to launch two of my jet skis. It's unusually calm today and as the sun beats down, I know it's the perfect conditions for some fun, although the ocean won't be so warm because it never seems to heat up in the Atlantic.

Once she is wearing the life vest, secured by me because the thought of the steward anywhere near her body is a definite red card and as she sits astride the ski, I gain a delightful view of her pert ass as she launches into the ocean with a delighted squeal.

I waste no time in joining her and as we head off at speed, I am assured of the photographs taken on her phone by my steward that will make it onto Instagram for all her family to see.

By the time the week is up, Allegra's reputation will be in tatters, her parents humiliated, and her father, Judge Stevenson so incensed he will probably physically boil with rage. Then we will blow his secret out of the water and watch the scandal ruin his life and his reputation, making him no longer suitable to hold the title of a Dark Lord. His son will soon follow when Killian reveals his own skeletons in his cupboard, and we will turn our attention to the next bastard on the list.

As I tear after her, I'm impressed by her skills. She is fast and has obviously done this before and artfully dodges my ski, almost running rings around me. Her infectious giggle travels high on the waves she dominates, and it appears I have underestimated my protected princess.

I finally catch up with her and point to a buoy and as she pulls alongside, I love the flushed excitement on her face and the wet spray clinging to her hair.

"You're good." I say, impressed, and she grins.

"Rafferty made it his hobby one summer, and we spent the entire time honing our skills."

I lean on the bars of the ski and say with interest. "Are you close to him?"

"Yes." She smiles sweetly. "I love him. I suppose it's unusual to get on with your younger brother, but I've always adored him. We look out for one another, as I'm sure you've already discovered."

"What would he say if he saw you now?"

A shadow passes across her face and she says nervously, "He would be afraid for me."

I nod. "He should be."

"Is that right?"

She fixes me with a cheeky grin. "Why do I like what you just said?"

It makes me laugh and as she joins me, I love hearing her

infectious giggle and the cheeky wink she throws in my direction.

"Fancy a swim?" I say casually.

"What here?"

She gazes around at the expanse of ocean surrounding us and even my boat is a small speck on the horizon.

"It's the perfect place."

I secure my ski to the buoy and with a shrug, she does the same and with a crafty wink dives into the ocean like a mermaid. As she surfaces, she resembles a goddess, and I swear I want her more right now than I have ever wanted anything in life.

I waste no time and dive in after her and love how she doesn't make it easy for me and starts swimming power strokes that cut through the water.

It doesn't take me long and I emerge in front of her, and she falls into my arms, our mouths clashing together with a hunger that surprises me.

As we tread water, we kiss, and it feels fucking amazing being naked and free in the middle of the ocean. Why have I never done this before?

We head for the buoy, and I press her against the side, instructing her to grip the handles that are conveniently placed.

She is shivering and not from the cold and I love her adventurous spirit, that appears to match my own.

I move between her legs and say roughly, "Stare at me, princess. Watch me own your body."

Her eyes flash as I press into her, spearing her against the buoy, loving the impish grin she flashes me that quickly changes to heated lust as she bites her bottom lip as I fill her drenched pussy.

The water laps against our bodies as I move slowly, in no hurry to end this experience that is a first for me too.

The sun beats down on our naked bodies as we fuck in the middle of the ocean, two free spirits testing morality. She groans as I own her, loving the sense of freedom out here and for some reason I can't tear my eyes from hers. I am drowning in the green eyes of a goddess. They reflect the sea almost as if she owns it. She is the queen of the waves, an ethereal creature that I have discovered against the odds, and she appears more at home here–with me than I ever believed possible.

This is the first day of her damnation. The first of many tests I will throw in her path. She will resist them, but I have a feeling she will try them all and it will be interesting to discover where she will draw the line.

Imagining the crazy things I will do to this woman causes me to cum so hard I roar, the breeze capturing the sound and dancing it across the breaking waves. Her own ragged moans join mine and I love how she clenches my cock and milks it hard, her wet heat at odds with the cool ocean waves.

As I stare into her eyes, she laughs softly and impulsively presses a light kiss to my lips, whispering, "What's next?"

Something moves inside me I'm not used to being there. An alien sensation that confuses me for a second. I still and try to figure it out but I can't place it. My heart is beating fast, faster than normal, and I wonder if I'm experiencing a mild heart attack. Then the sensation leaves me, and I shake the feeling away, not really liking what it did to me.

I pull out abruptly and say over my shoulder, "I'll race you back to the boat."

As I untie my ride, I'm conscious she is in no hurry and as I sit astride my ski, I note she hasn't even moved. She is just staring out to sea with a small smile on her face and I say abruptly, "You're going to lose if you don't shift your ass."

She fixes me with a wistful smile and says softly, "Then why do I feel as if I already won?"

CHAPTER 15

ALLEGRA

I watch him head off with an inner glow of peace that I'm keen to hang onto. Out here, clinging to the buoy, I am free. No responsibilities, no family to lie to me, and no inhibitions. I never realized being naked was so freeing. I love it. The fact I've fucked a man who was a stranger to me a few short weeks ago doesn't seem as bad now as when he first requested my company. For the next seven days and six nights, I am guaranteed freedom which is strange when I'm his sex prisoner.

It makes me giggle as I turn my face to the sun, knowing that he isn't making me do anything I'm not hungry for. I enjoy the moment for a little longer before I reluctantly slide into the cool sea and take a gentle swim, floating on my back and letting the waves wash over my heated body. I have never had sex like this before. It's always been a disappointing experience with dates that never really make the grade. A frantic act courtesy of a drunken stupor most nights and the odd encounter with a guy who catches my eye at a party. Not this premeditated assault that I still don't really understand the meaning of.

Who cares though, because my life isn't what I thought it was, anyway.

With a sigh, I haul myself back on the ski and head back the way I came. This time enjoying a solitary ride at leisure rather than speed and letting Shade win the race was an easy one. You don't have to win every game, just the ones that count. I wanted my solitude and my freedom far more than I wanted to beat him back to the boat and so I got what I wanted, as did he.

The ship gains in size as I approach, and I admire the sleek bow of a super-yacht. It's amazing, much like its owner, and I still can't believe what has happened to my life since I met him.

Mafia. Is this how they live? Blood money spent on decadence. How can he live with what he does? Murdering a man with no consequences and no dent in his conscience, either. I have never met a man like Shade Vieri in my life and yet from what he told me I've been surrounded by them. Unlike him, they don't announce it to the world. They don't revel in it, and they hide a don't give a fuck attitude where he wears his as a badge of honor.

I know what criminal I prefer and it's the one who doesn't pretend otherwise.

The anger boils away inside me, waiting to explode and I have a feeling the man watching me approach can help with that.

He has changed already and is wearing a black t-shirt and denim shorts, his expression hidden behind mirrored shades. My heart beats faster as I stare at a man who intrigues me. I love his attitude, as if nothing can drag him down. It's addictive—he's addictive, and it's no hardship to be his guest for a while.

Then I can walk away.

Why doesn't that sound as appealing as it did yesterday?

The steward helps bring the ski in and as my fingers attempt to unfasten the life vest, Shade appears by my side and says irritably, "Where the fuck were you?"

"Chilling." I shrug as his fingers inch inside the vest and twists one of my nipples—hard.

It brings tears to my eyes, and he growls, "I don't like to be kept waiting. Come."

He tears off my vest and grabs my wrist, not caring that I am naked for anyone to see and as we move through the boat, I sigh inside because I've angered him. He obviously issues orders and expects them to be obeyed and I suppose I must now face the consequences of that.

He tugs me down into the cabin area and thrusts me through a door that opens into a bedroom.

Then he drags me over to the bed and pulls me over his lap and I shriek when he lands a hard blow on my ass.

"Stop. What's that for?" I cry out and he hisses. "When I tell you to do something, you do it."

"Fuck you." I say through gritted teeth, causing him to add another sharp blow by way of a response.

"You're a fucking sadist, asshole."

I yell and he rewards me with another.

I struggle, but the more I do, the more he responds, and it becomes a contest as to who will win.

I'm not sure how many times he strikes my ass, but for some reason I am numb to it. Perhaps I've lost the ability to feel. It certainly seems like that and so I fall silent and let him vent his anger with no response.

It has the desired effect and with a low growl, he pushes me onto the floor and says roughly, "You disobey me, and I punish you. Get used to it."

"What do I care?"

I shift so my back is against the wall and draw my knees to my chest, peering at him through tear encrusted eyes. My ass is stinging, but my blood is heated, and I say sadly, "Whatever you do doesn't matter."

He appears shocked at that and says quickly, "Why?"

"Because I don't care anymore, Shade. To be honest, you could toss me overboard and I would welcome it. My life isn't what I thought it was, and I'm kind of searching for a new one."

He just stares at me, and I expect he'll leave the crazy woman to her own crappy conversation, but instead he comes and sits beside me, striking the same pose and laces his fingers with mine.

"I kind of understand what that's like, princess."

"You do?"

He nods. "I've questioned my own life thousands of times. Growing up was a life lesson no child should learn."

I say nothing because I don't want to interrupt him. He is unlocking a little window into his soul, and I am curious to peer inside.

He sighs. "I'm wild because I know no different. I suppose I've always been searching for something, but I don't know what it looks like. So, if you want assurances from me that it gets better. It doesn't. You just learn to live with it and make it part of you."

He squeezes my fingers tightly and says huskily, "You must have many questions for your mom and your uncle. They lied to you your entire life, and that's not easily forgiven."

"I kind of think you're going to do something about that yourself, Shade." I sigh. "I'm guessing that was your motive in bringing me here in the first place."

"You are very astute, princess. Congratulations."

He turns and smiles and I say with curiosity.

"Tell me. Maybe I can help."

"To bring your uncle down. I doubt it."

"Is that what you want? Why?"

"I have my reasons."

His eyes are dark and gleam with malevolence, making me shiver.

"I'm sure you do." I smile softly and turn my head away from him, resting it against the wall of the cabin and say with a sigh.

"It sucks."

"What does?"

"Knowledge. I wish I didn't know their secret, then I could pretend I was happy."

"Aren't you?" He adds with a soft whisper.

"I haven't been happy for a while now, Shade, but I can't tell you why."

"You can try." He probes, appearing concerned, although I doubt that very much.

"I could, but possibly I don't want to face it. Perhaps I want you to corrupt me even more and distract my attention and to ruin me. Have you even considered that?"

He falls silent and I wince as my ass starts protesting at the treatment it just received.

"You pack a mean punch, honey. I'm impressed."

For some reason that makes him laugh and I'm surprised when he grips my face and turns it to face him, whispering, "Then allow me to kiss it better."

CHAPTER 16

SHADE

Something has happened that I didn't count on. I like her. The more time I spend with Allegra Powell, the more I discover we have in common.

I love that she isn't afraid of me. She's the first woman outside of family who isn't.

It's refreshing, almost as if I have a partner in crime who craves the same things I do.

I wonder how low she will sink. How low she will let *me* sink, because what I have planned for her is nothing short of evil. I am going easy on her now, but what happens when I crank up the pressure? Will she break then? Do I want her to?

It disturbs me a little and so I shake any compassion I have for her away and say quickly, "Come. We must eat. You have surely worked up an appetite by now."

"Now you mention it." She grins and then says with amusement, "I don't suppose I can trouble you for a robe or something. This nudity thing you've got going on is thrilling and all that, but this sun is hot, and I may burn if I'm careful."

I toss her a robe from the back of the door and grin. "You'll burn baby. I promise you that."

All she does is roll her eyes and tear the robe from my hands.

"You really are an asshole, Shade Vieri."

"What did you call me?" I'm astonished because only my siblings call me that and she giggles as she ties the belt around her.

"I can say what I like because I don't give a fuck, remember? I'm learning from the master, so take your complaint to him."

She blows me a kiss and nods at the door.

"Come on then. Feed me, you bastard, because in your own words, we've got to eat."

I walk away without another word because I'm not comfortable with the direction our relationship is going in. Why isn't she afraid of me?

All the others are. Nobody calls me an asshole, bastard, definitely, but asshole—no, they wouldn't dare. Then why do I like it that she does? Playing me at my own game and knowing there isn't much I can do about that. Well, if she wants to believe that, it will be fun to watch the terror build in her eyes when she realizes just how much of an asshole I really am.

* * *

Lunch is a barbeque on the rear of the boat. Steak and skewers of vegetables, all dressed in interesting spices and marinades.

Soft music is playing, and we sit on the edge, eating our food, our legs dangling over the side and as the sun warms my face, I take a deep breath of fresh sea air.

I've always loved this boat. I'd live on it if I could, but

business always comes first to a Vieri and it's just lucky I can combine the two this time.

I'm feeling good and, unlike me, I start an actual conversation. "So, tell me about your new position with The Social Queen. Are you looking for a role in PR?"

I don't know why I'm interested, but I am.

"It's something that interests me for sure." She shrugs as she picks a cube of vegetable off the skewer.

"To be honest, Shade, I've never really known what I wanted to do before. Does that shock you?"

"Why should it? Nothing shocks me anymore, baby girl."

"I guess."

She giggles and says thoughtfully, "Everything shocks me. I've always been *that* girl. Too scared to step out of line in case I upset my folks. I once smoked a cigarette at a party and fully expected the sirens to go off and the cops to arrive. I was that straight I feared stepping out of line."

"What would your folks say if they could see you now?"

I laugh softly as she rolls her eyes.

"You can probably guess. You think locking me away for seven days is bad? I would get life imprisonment if they knew of this."

Thinking of the building messages on her phone, I'm guessing she's right. When I returned from our excursion, my steward handed me Allegra's phone and it was lit with messages from her mom, dad and brother to name only three. It appears my little princess is quite the internet star, and I will deal with those messages with a cruel heart later.

I wonder what she would think if she saw them. By the time she does, it will be too late, and the damage will be done.

Do I feel sorry for her? The fuck I do. This is what I do best, so why would I suddenly grow a conscience now?

To prove that more to myself than her, I reach for a pack of cigarettes in my pocket and light one.

"It's time to upset your parents, princess."

I smirk, holding it out to her, and she stares at me through those glorious eyes and grins.

I'm surprised when she takes it and as she takes a long drag, I'm amazed when she blows rings of smoke into the air and as I shake my head, she shrugs. "What? The story I told was the first time. I didn't say I stopped."

I take the cigarette from her fingers and take a long drag, handing it back to her as I blow my own rings of smoke. It becomes a game between us and when the cigarette is finished, I toss the butt into the ocean and, turning, slip the robe from her shoulders and ease her back onto the wooden deck.

"What again?" She teases, her eyes heavy with lust and I nod. "It's time for dessert."

I kiss her deeply, loving the taste of smoke and decadence. Ruining the sorority girl isn't uncommon for me, but she is way more than that. She could well be the better part of my soul. We are so alike it intrigues me. Grabbing one of the skewers, I drag the point down her naked body, and she shivers with a mixture of trepidation and desire.

"What are you going to do with that?"

Her eyes are wide, and I say huskily, "Have you ever experienced real fear, Allegra?"

"I believe you already know the answer to that." She gasps as the skewer reaches her drenched pussy.

I run the point against her clit, and she freezes because one wrong move would hurt very badly and I whisper, "I could draw blood with this. Would you like that?"

"No thank you." She gasps and I grin wickedly as I run the point up to her breast and hold it against her nipple.

"Some people are turned on by pain. They get piercings, tattoos and allow knife to play. I *love* knife play."

"In sex?"

Her eyes are wide, and I nod. "Yes. However, in the absence of an actual knife that deserves its title, this will have to do."

I drag the point in deeper, just above her left breast, and love the deep scratch that appears as it cuts into her skin.

"Fuck!" she yelps, and I press down hard on her clit and her attention is distracted, causing her to gasp, "That's not fair!"

Once again, I mark her skin with the pointed skewer and she yelps before I push three fingers into her wet heat, curling my finger around her G-spot, causing her hips to buck and her breath to pant.

As she closes her eyes, I run my fingers around them, pressing them closed and with the other hand, I set her phone to the video. Propped up beside us, just out of her eye-line and as it records, I bend my mouth to her clit and give it the attention it deserves.

She groans with desire and whispers, "Fuck, Shade, that's so good."

As I increase the pressure, I hold the steel against her hip and dig in deeper, bringing her pain, then as I bite softly on her clit, her orgasm crashes through her, causing her to scream into the ocean as she comes so hard a neighboring seagull takes offense and heads off at speed.

My hand closes around the phone and I pocket it before she is even aware she starred in a private porno and as she lies spent on the wooden deck, I whisper, "Come, it's siesta time."

"Thank God." She groans and I smirk as I pull her up, loving the flush of pleasure on her face that I put there.

* * *

I show her to one of the bedrooms and as she falls onto the crisp white sheets, I say casually, "You'll need your rest. Take it while you can."

"Are you still here?" She says sleepily and, as I turn away, I'm shocked that there's a smile on my face. I don't know what it is about Allegra that brings out the best and the beast in me. I want to corrupt her, but I want to discover her. To find out what makes her tick and dive into her soul to learn all her secrets. There's also the part of me that wants to protect her and as I head to my den, I wonder if this time I've taken things too far.

CHAPTER 17

SHADE

As soon as I take my seat at my desk, I pull out Allegra's phone. It's lit brighter than a firework display and it amuses me to see the number of messages from her family. I open them and scroll through.

> Mom
>
> Call me at once.

> Mom
>
> Please, Allegra, I need to know you're safe.

> Mom
>
> You've had your fun, now call me. I'm angry now.

> **Rafferty**
>
> What the fuck is going on, Ally? Call me NOW!

> **Cessy**
>
> Just so you know, I'm in the mafia now. Scrub that the mafia is in me.

That one makes me laugh out loud. At least Kyle had a good time.

> **Dad**
>
> Please call us, honey. You're not in any trouble.

> **Mom**
>
> If you blow this internship, Ally, I swear you're on your own.

There are so many more, but it's the one on my own phone that amuses me the most.

> **Unknown**

> I swear to God, Shade Vieri, by the time I've finished with you, you'll be sewing mailbags for the rest of your life.

The fact it's from Judge Stevenson makes me laugh out loud.

There is also one from my brother.

> Kill
>
> Gina reported back. Call me.

I pick up the phone and he answers immediately.

"Still having fun, I see." He sighs. *"Lucky bastard. What I wouldn't give to be on that boat, with my wife, before you get the wrong idea."*

It makes me laugh.

"I'm sad for you, brother, being the boss sucks."

"You can say that again."

There's a small pause, and he growls, *"Gina got hold of Jefferson's phone while he was in the shower. If you think you've got it bad, spare a thought for the hell she's going through."*

I tease. "If she wasn't so in love with you, she wouldn't put herself through torture like this."

"She has no business loving me. I'm a married man." He sighs causing me to smile.

My brother doesn't give a fuck about anyone, especially a past fuck that got attached. The only person he cares about is his wife and their unborn child. Like me, he cares for family but not in the same all-consuming way, and I wonder what that must feel like.

I get my mind back into the business at hand and say with interest, "What did she find?"

"That it wasn't his phone."

I sit up and pay attention.

"Who's phone was it?"

"A burner."

"Any details?"

I'm intrigued and Kill says roughly, *"There is only one number on the contact list and it belongs to your current victim."*

"Is that right?"

My mood suddenly switches to dark mode, and I hiss, "Any history?"

"Creepy as fuck texts. Stalker type things. Pictures of her taken when she's around town. Some of her at the gym, out running and on the town."

"Send them to me." I'm enraged and Killian says firmly, *"I'll send you the screen shots, but it appears her cousin Jefferson either has an unhealthy interest in her or knows someone who does."*

"What's the plan?"

"Wrap up your business, go in for the kill, and then send her home. Watch what happens when the shit hits the fan and who knows, we may even kill two birds with one shot."

"Fuck!"

I sink back in my seat, my earlier good mood evaporating rapidly. "I hate this shit."

Killian chuckles. *"What's the matter bro? Are you having too much fun?"*

"Fuck you, boss." I say sarcastically and he rewards me by cutting the call.

As I stare at the texts on Allegra's phone, I am livid inside. I'm not sure why I'm angry, but I am.

The thought of wrapping this up isn't sitting well with me because the grand finale isn't something I want anymore. When I think of the final degradation that should be days away, I can't even bring myself to make the call.

More to distract my mind, I reach for her phone and type in a response to her mom's texts.

> Allegra
>
> Fuck you!

I smile at the phone, imagining her expression when she receives it.

I replay the video and love watching Allegra's pretty face full of desire for what I am doing. She is so amazing and so gorgeous. Like a rare butterfly unusually seen in the wild.

I experience a surge of longing to be inside her. To stroke that soft skin and inhale her sweet scent. There is so much I want to do with her—to her and being told to wrap this up isn't helping with that.

Ruin and return. That was my mission. So, why don't I want to finish what I started?

CHAPTER 18

ALLEGRA

The bed dips, which is the only indication I'm not alone. It appears that Shade can creep up on you when you least expect it and I should know, he has a habit of doing that with me.

I keep my eyes tightly closed as the sheets are pulled back, exposing my body to the cool air conditioning, loving how his hand slides against my skin, causing flutters inside that only he can create.

His lips replace his fingers and I sigh with contentment as he presses light kisses all over my body, soft and sweet, unlike his usual preferred method, and I can't decide what I like the most.

I open my eyes as he reaches my lips and for some reason, the turbulent expression in his eyes is at odds with his touch.

"Something has happened." I whisper against his lips, and he sighs.

"I'm afraid it has."

He cups his hand around the back of my head and pulls it off the pillows to gain deeper access. He holds me as if he is afraid of letting go and I wonder what has disturbed him so much.

So many thoughts are running through my mind, but I can't deal with them now. I want to prolong this pleasure, because from the sound of it, this could be the last time.

I'm not sure why I'm sad about that and this time I kiss him with a difference. It's softer, as if I mean it, a lover's kiss definitely because this isn't just sex anymore.

He groans into my mouth, and I feel him hard against me, which sends ripples of expectation through my entire body.

Why is it different now?

I like it.

He wastes no time and slides inside, stretching me, filling me and almost loving me.

His kisses are deep but loaded with passion. His ownership of my body more reverent than before.

As he moves inside, it's slow and unhurried. He is taking his time, making a memory I cherish more than the other ones.

In here we are alone. No eyes on us, secure in our own little world. It's more intimate. Deliciously so and I moan his name as he strips away any doubts I ever had.

He says nothing in return and it's as if he is trapped among his own torturous thoughts, and I wonder how to reach him. Is this what he does, lock himself away with the madness, afraid to let anyone in out of fear of being destroyed?

Reaching up, I lie my hand flat against his face and whisper, "Look at me."

His eyes stare into mine with a dark stormy gaze and I smile, "I've got you." I whisper as he moves slowly inside me. "Do what you must. It's fine."

He increases the speed and I sense the power return. The darkness in his eyes taking over again. This conflicted, beautiful man who keeps his heart well protected is doing what he does best. Dominate.

With a low growl, he grips my face hard and whispers, "I do what the fuck I like, and we have an agreement. Seven days and nights and I have only just got started."

He thrusts harder, deeper and with so much force, I swear he is tearing me open from the inside out.

It burns, but I like it. It excites me and I feel the orgasm fast and hard, almost from out of nowhere as it tears through my body, causing me to lose the ability to breathe. I just lie under him convulsing, as if I'm having a seizure and his roar of release sounds a million miles away as I float on a cloud of euphoria, back down to earth, with a gigantic bump.

"We're leaving."

He pulls out while I'm still throbbing from the effects of him inside me and I gasp, "Why?"

"Shit happens and things have changed."

I stare across the room at him and see a stranger before me. He is angry, I can tell, and he dresses at speed without even looking in my direction.

I shift onto my side and stare at him in confusion.

"So, that's it then. I'm free."

I'm not sure why that is bringing me so much misery and he shrugs.

"You may be returning home sooner than expected princess, but one thing I can guarantee."

He turns and I should be afraid right now because the expression on his face promises a hard road ahead.

"You still owe me six days and six nights, and I will make certain you honor every single fucking one of them."

He leaves before I can reply to that, and I'm not sure what to do now.

For a moment, I lie still, processing the changes and then with a sigh, I edge out of the bed, his cum dripping down my thighs and for some reason it makes me smile. I don't know why. I suppose because I have claimed a part of him. Evidence that he was mine for a moment in time. A man like Shade Vieri wouldn't look twice at me unless there was something he wanted. I'm not a fool. I know the score and even if he ruins me forever, at least I had my moment with him.

He can never take that away from me. The pure romance of this kidnapping, the candlelit dinner, the jet ski safari and the way he held me so tenderly in his arms and pretended he didn't care. Even the beating is a memory I will keep close because there is not a minute of my time with him that I haven't enjoyed every fucked-up minute of.

* * *

I SHOWER and dress in the outfit I arrived in and as walks of shame go, I'd take this one every single time.

My hair is washed and my eyes bright as I head into the sunlight, every nerve in my body heightened from the experience.

Normal life will never be the same again now I have experienced the exhilaration of the dark side. But I still have six days and six nights to enjoy, which is why I have a smile on my face as I join him on the forward deck.

"What are you so happy about?" He seems tetchy and I lean with my arms on the rail looking out to sea.

"I had a good time. Is it a crime to be happy about that?"

He shakes his head. "You're as fucked as I am, princess. Most women would be afraid of this experience, not treasuring it."

"I'm not most women, Shade. I actually couldn't give a fuck about my life right now. It's not the same one I thought I was living. You changed it."

"Your big secret coming out, I guess." He shrugs and leans with his back to the rail beside me, taking out a cigarette and lighting it, then taking a huge drag before offering it to me.

I accept and as the toxic smoke enters my lungs, I savor the sense of corruption.

I hand it back to him and sigh. "I haven't smoked since college. You are a bad influence on me, Shade Vieri. Maybe I should leave for my own self-preservation."

"You are only leaving because I am allowing it, princess. Remember, you belong to me until your debt is paid."

"Whatever." I roll my eyes because I really couldn't give a fuck about that and only the sound of the helicopter approaching makes my heart beat a little faster.

It's over.

I watch the bird land and feel a sense of loss already. This boat, this magical boat, was an experience I will never forget. I feel cheated somehow and yet I still have time. It's not the end, it's just the beginning, so I follow Shade to the open door and try to accept we are merely changing our surroundings and nothing else.

CHAPTER 19

SHADE

I am irrationally pissed. I hate that we're leaving my beloved boat and I had so much more planned for my hostage. Fuck Killian and fuck Jefferson, because now he has prodded the beast and I have sharp claws.

I have thought of little else since the call. Is Jefferson the one making the threats, or is it somebody else? Does he even know Allegra and Rafferty aren't his cousins at all, but his half siblings?

I hope Gina is as good as Killian thinks she is, because we need answers and fast. I am taking Allegra back to possible danger, and that is not sitting well with me. She will be a target; we are using her to drag our enemies into full sight. She is hurting already, but this could push her over the edge and why do I even care?

I am silent because I'm brooding on a situation that is out of my control and I don't like it. So, as we fly away from my favorite place in the world, I switch my mind back to bastard.

We don't speak for the entire journey and as the helicopter lands back on the roof of Gyration, with a heavy heart I say roughly, "Party's over, princess. I'll call you a cab."

Ignoring the hurtful expression in her eyes, I nod to Kyle, who is waiting, and as we head to the door leading down to the club, Allegra follows in silence.

At the bottom of the stairs, I jerk my thumb at her and say to Kyle, "Miss Powell needs a cab home. There's probably one in the street you can hail."

He hides his expression well and says in his husky voice, "Follow me, Miss Powell."

I don't even look at her until she says sharply, "My phone, please."

I'd almost forgotten I had it and as I pull it from my pocket, I toss it into her hand and turn and walk away.

* * *

I HEAD STRAIGHT to my office and the whiskey bottle. I know I'm being cruel, heartless and all the things I'm associated with, but I'm trying to deal with something unexpected. I don't like how I'm feeling inside. The sense of loss I'm experiencing. It's not something I'm used to, so I take a swig and can't help taking the bottle over to the window.

As I stare at the ground outside, I notice a yellow cab outside my building. The figure is too small to make out, but a flash of green tells me it's her.

I chuck back some more of the whiskey and lean my head against the glass, watching the cab until it disappears from view. I fucking hate my brother. If he was here now, I would power my fist through his smug face because of how I'm feeling now. Six more days would have been enough to tire of her. To use and abuse her and move onto the next one. It wasn't enough time and I'm pissed at that. She has gotten off lightly and I'm angry. Surely, that must be the reason for this emptiness inside.

The door opens and Kyle enters.

"Fuck, Shade. What happened?"

I turn and nod toward the tray holding the drinks.

"Grab a glass. We're celebrating."

"It doesn't look like that."

He does as I say, and I fill his glass, the liquid spilling over the sides onto the wooden floor below.

"I can tell it's gonna be one of those days." He sighs and sinks down onto the couch as I chug from the bottle and say roughly, "Killian discovered Jefferson has a burner phone he is either using to threaten Allegra, or he took it from the person who is."

"And?"

Kyle sits forward and I snarl, "She's being placed in a trap. Whoever is doing this must believe it's business as usual and then, if they make their move, we've got them."

"So, what's the plan?" he says, ever practical, which I sure need right now.

"Set up eyes on her. Monitor her every move. Become the hunter of the hunter if you like. Discover who is responsible for this and why?"

"Consider it done."

He stands and yet before he leaves to take care of that, he places his hand on my shoulder and says with concern, "Are you ok?"

I set the bottle down and run my fingers through my hair, before saying with no emotion, "I'm always okay."

"Are you sure about that?" Kyle knows me too well, so I force a wicked grin and reply, "I'm just pissed I never got to the good part. It's nothing a fuck with a whore or two won't cure. Let's get to business."

He nods and leaves me to wallow in my own misery and as I retreat to my desk, I try desperately hard to push Allegra Powell out of my mind.

* * *

Two hours later and it didn't work. I am still pissed, and the bottle is almost empty. I just can't make the switch from pleasure to business, so I decide to fuck her out of my mind instead and head downstairs to the lap dancing club I own in the same building as Gyration.

As I push through the door, the stench of alcohol and sex is a welcome home I could sure use. It's slow today judging from the number of empty seats, which doesn't improve my mood. Come to think of it, business has been dipping a little lately and my profits are down. Not that it matters, I earn way more than I will ever spend, but I hate seeing that fucking downward graph my accountant waves in my face demanding answers.

I head to the booth I always use when I come here. It's reserved for VIPs and me.

No sooner have I sat down than Cadence materializes and purrs, "Mr. Vieri, what an honor. Please allow me to get you anything you desire."

"Bourbon and make it a double." I snap and lean back, closing my eyes, trying to shift this mood I'm wearing like a bad smell.

It doesn't take her long, and she's soon back with the order and as she sets it down, her cleavage dances before my eyes as she whispers, "I'm free for a dance if you're interested."

I glance past her to see who else is working because Cadence makes no secret of her desire to be my 'go to' girl, and I am definitely not interested in that.

"No. Send Polly over."

I dismiss her, noting her sullen expression as she turns, but I couldn't give a fuck about her feelings.

Polly wastes no time in heading over, dressed in the gold

uniform most of the dancers wear. Sultry, sexy and revealing. The dress that has a zip down the front is figure hugging and far too short. The high gold heels causing her legs to reach to the heavens and the gold thong underneath, the receptacle of the dollar bills they earn depending on how good they are.

The music is loud, which suits my mood, and as she stands astride my legs, she begins to sway to the music, her eyes half closed as she gazes at me through heavy lashes.

She's an attractive woman. Her long black hair is sleek and hangs to her tits. Her dark brown eyes are sultry and lustful, and her red painted lips are ready for just about anything.

My club sells dances, but the girls sell a lot more than that if the customer pays high enough. The hotel in this building is also owned by me and we keep a suite of rooms, especially for those occasions. The men pay for the room and tip the dancer, and everyone is happy.

She wiggles her hips and pouts in my direction and slowly eases the zipper down on her dress, her tits spilling out and dangling in my face.

She sucks her finger slowly and then drags it down her breasts, groaning as she edges closer, inches from my participation.

"Enough." I snap, causing her to say quickly, "I'm sorry…"

"I said, enough." I hand her a hundred-dollar bill and wave her away.

"Leave."

She moves away, zipping up her dress, probably wondering if she did something wrong. She didn't. I'm just not in the mood to play. Not with her. Not with a whore. There is only one woman I want to play with, and she is currently probably creating a voodoo doll in my image after what I've done.

"Problem?" Kyle slides in opposite, and I sigh heavily.

"There's always a problem, Kyle. Distract me and tell me about Allegra's friend. What did you find out?"

"That she fucks like a pro," Kyle grins. "Man, I've got to thank you for that. I almost couldn't keep up. That woman is a machine."

"Then offer her a job." I laugh at the anger on his face.

"She's not a whore, in fact…"

"You like her." I state the obvious because Kyle has that look in his eye that dares me to fuck with him and I've only ever seen that once before when he met the love of his life Astrid who left him because she couldn't deal with this life."

"I do." He shrugs. "She's good company, as well as being a fucking genius in bed. I'm just as sorry as you it's game over."

"It doesn't have to be." I laugh softly and he leans forward with interest.

"Why, what's your plan?"

"Maybe you should arrange a little double date for this evening. Invite …"

"Cecilia."

"Invite her to dinner and tell her to bring her friend."

He shakes his head. "It won't work."

"Why not?"

"She left for Washington. She's a trainee attorney and has work tomorrow. She's coming back on Friday and is staying the weekend."

"Fuck, Kyle, I leave you for five minutes and you become domesticated."

He shrugs and I stare past him at the almost empty club, an idea forming in my mind.

"What are you smiling about?" He says roughly, and I grin.

"Business, Kyle. It's always business. You should know that."

I nod toward the exit.

"We should go. I have a call to make."

He rolls his eyes as we head out of the bar and back to my office to set things in place.

The venue may have changed, but the game continues. My little victim won't know what hit her.

CHAPTER 20

ALLEGRA

I am never leaving this apartment again. Ever. In fact, I'm not leaving this room because my brother will be home soon, and I can't look him in the face. I can never look anyone in the face ever again because what the fucking hell was Shade thinking?

As soon as I got home, I fled to the shower to scrub that man from my skin. How could he treat me like that after being so amazing? It was as if I was no longer required, and he dismissed me like a common whore. Then I get home and there was a parcel waiting for me with ten thousand dollars inside. The note merely saying,

To replace the blood money. I hope it was worth it.

I feel so cheap. So used and so worthless. It's as if this is payment for services rendered and not the most beautiful experience of my life.

As I sob on the bed surrounded by thousands of dollar

bills, I wonder if I should snap a shot and post this to my fucking Instagram feed because it can't be much worse than the photos staring back at me.

I am so angry I could take his gun and murder him in cold blood like he did that gruesome man.

I look like a fucking whore for the whole world to see. I appear wrecked and the hickies on my neck and down my front disgust me. My hair is all over the place and my mascara is streaked down my face.

There's the one at the meal where I appear happy and excited. Obviously smiling for the camera before the storm hit. Then there are the messages from my mom and my apparent response.

I scream into my pillow with mortification.

Fuck you.

I can't believe he sent that.

I was almost afraid to listen to her voicemail, and I was right. She is apoplectic and told me to call her immediately because she, *'has a lot to say young lady.'*

Those were her words, but what the hell am I going to say to her?

The door slams and I hear footsteps beating a path to my door. Before I can jump up and lock it, it bursts open and my brother roars, "Fuck, Ally! What the hell are you on?"

I lift my tear-streaked face from the pillow and catch his amazed expression as he stares at the money all over my bed.

"Please don't tell me that's what I think it is." He sounds horrified, and I snap, "For services rendered. Is that what you think?"

I am so angry and sit up and yell, "Don't you fucking lecture me because this, asshole, is my life's savings that I withdrew to save your ass and look where it got me."

His eyes widen and he turns ashen as he sits heavily on the edge of the bed and says, "What are you talking about?"

Between sobs, I tell him about the threats and what happened in the alley, and he says wretchedly, "Fuck, Ally. Why didn't you tell me?"

"How could I?" I sob on his shoulder as his strong arms wrap around me.

"You were the big star; the man of the hour and any hint of scandal could have destroyed it all. I dealt with it. I'm still dealing with it, and I don't need your judgmental attitude right now."

He strokes my hair and hugs me hard and whispers, "I'm so sorry, conker."

"Don't fucking call me that!" I yell, dissolving into tears and giggles at the same time.

He shakes his head and mutters, "The fuck I know what to do." Which makes me laugh before crying even harder, causing him to say in alarm, "Maybe you should go home to mom. She'll know what to do."

"Oh yes. Mom."

My heart hardens and yet when I see his perplexed expression, I can't bring myself to tell him. I'm still hoping it's all a big mistake, but those photographs are still playing on repeat in my mind.

"Just make me a coffee, Rafe, please."

I take a deep breath and attempt to get my shit together. My life may be in the toilet right now, but his definitely isn't and I will not be the one responsible for sending it there.

As he leaves, grateful for the instruction, I slowly gather the money into a bundle and place it back in the box.

I'll give it back. I'll march into that club and demand to see him and throw it in his face and make him feel as small as I do now. Fucking Shade Vieri. Who the hell does he think he is?

When Rafferty comes back with the coffee and an apologetic smile, I accept both with relief. We will need one another because the shit will soon hit the fan. I am in two minds about telling him and I should prepare him for the inevitable, but I note the weariness in his expression.

My protective instinct takes over as I say with concern, "Is everything ok, Rafe?"

He sits on the bed, that is now minus the money, and runs his fingers through his hair with distraction.

"It's that Taylor shit, Ally. I just can't get it out of my head. One minute she was here and the next a corpse. Who did that and why?"

I reach out and link my arm in his and say softly, "There are some sick people in this world and who knows how their mind's work. The only thing we can do is protect ourselves. Tell me what happened, without the gruesome details about how you met and what happened next."

He sighs heavily. "It was at a party. One of the team invited me to some rich kids' house outside Brooklyn. Most of the team were there and because it was pre-season, we were getting tanked. We were the untouchables, at least it felt like that, and the women were up for anything."

"I said spare me the details." I shake my head and he says with a groan.

"Taylor came onto me, and I thought she was kinda sweet. The other women wore more make-up, had bleached hair, fake tits, that kind of thing. Taylor was natural and seemed an okay kind of girl. Anyway, we hit it off and decided to continue the evening at a nearby hotel."

"Was that your idea?"

I probe carefully and he shakes his head. "No. I was beat and ready to head home, but she persuaded me to extend our evening somewhere quiet. I had a lot to drink, and it seemed a good idea at the time and so I went with it. I hadn't been laid in months and I thought it was a good time to relieve the built-up tension inside me and she was offering."

"Gross."

I say sharply, "So, what happened after you well, relieved your tension?"

"She changed, Ally. Almost as soon as I came, she was pulling on her clothes and heading for the door. I was confused and asked her to wait up, but all she said was it was a mistake and not to think badly of her. She left, and it made me feel like shit, if I'm honest. Almost as if I forced her into doing something she didn't want to, but she made all the moves, not me. I swear."

"Then you got the threats."

He nods. "As soon as the news reported her murder, I received a text from an unknown number. It contained photographs of us in that hotel room and it wasn't pretty. She appeared upset, as if I was raping her but I swear she came onto me and instigated the whole thing."

"What did the text say again?" I take a deep breath and try to establish the facts because my brother needs me to be strong.

I know we've already been through this, but I was in shock the first time and couldn't really take it all in at the time.

He shrugs. "That the photographs would be posted on the internet along with the headline, 'the Jets' new signing implicated in rape and murder' and I panicked."

"Which is where I came in and said I'd handle it."

He shakes his head. "That makes me feel like shit." He stares at me with concern. "What did you do, Ally, because something is telling me this isn't over, and we should just go to the cops and tell them everything?"

"Are you crazy, Rafferty?"

The panic grips me hard and I lower my voice to a whisper.

"That ship has long sailed. We are in so deep we're drowning right now, and you must let me deal with this."

"No, Ally. I don't want to see you destroyed because of me. I've been going out of my fucking mind when I saw those photos on your Instagram. Mom's been lighting up my phone, blaming me for not taking care of you, and now I find you surrounded in money and sobbing like a baby. We have no choice. We must call the cops."

"Leave it twenty-four hours." I say in a blind panic. "I'll deal with it. I have, um, connections now."

"You mean that fucking mafia yacht you spent the night on?" He shakes his head. "Walk away, Ally. Don't get involved with guys like that. They're bad news."

"I know." I say miserably. Hell, if anyone knows that it's me but I have unfinished business with Shade Vieri and he owes *me* now, not the other way around and I intend on making him pay in full.

He makes my problem go away and I play along with his revenge because why the hell should I care about an uncle who has lied to his entire family and worse, his own brother?

I have no love left for Uncle Lucas, whoever he is now and Shade's revenge is now aligned with my own and I have six more days to persuade him to help me.

CHAPTER 21

SHADE

The car pulls up outside The Social Queen offices in Manhattan at ten am and as my door opens, I step into the sunlight, covering my eyes with my customary shade. I am dressed for business in a black suit and silk shirt and tie, every inch the successful bastard whose life has become an easy ride.

I am flanked on either side by two identical cars, the men inside them dressed the same. With my trusted second in command by side, we head into the reception area as a black wall of menace. Yes, as entrances go, this one is a fucking statement and I love the anxious glances in my direction as we cross the vast expanse of space, the security guards remaining in position, knowing there is fuck all they can do to prevent our business here.

The receptionist is nervous as I stand before her and say huskily, "I have a meeting with Evangeline Solomon."

She nods, her lower lip trembling as she whispers into the phone and says softly, "Miss. Solomon will be down for you personally, Mr. Vieri."

I nod and remove my shades, fixing her with a dark look

that has her reaching out to steady herself. It always amuses me that people like her believe they are in danger just breathing the same air as me.

It takes Evangeline a few minutes to surface, and she clicks across the marble floor in haste, her smile larger than the fake tits she has enhanced yearly, never apparently satisfied with the size.

"Shade, this is an unexpected pleasure. I'm honored."

She makes to kiss me but Kyle steps between us, causing her to stop and say quickly, "Oh, um, well, if you will follow me to the boardroom, I have refreshments organized." She glances around her nervously and my men fall back and take their positions around the reception area and only Kyle accompanies me to the elevator with the queen herself.

I wasn't kidding when I told Allegra I knew her boss. This woman has been on her knees before me several times, usually at parties we both attend. I say parties, more like fucking orgies because Evangeline Solomon likes to play hard and dirty.

It's why she's so successful. Most of her clients come from those parties. She takes networking to a whole new level and rather than face any awkward conversations with their wives, many of the men that attend them give Evangeline their business just to keep her mouth on their dick and not spilling their secrets.

We head to the boardroom and as we take our seats, I glance around at the glass and mirrors, and feel as if I'm in a goldfish bowl.

She pours us both a glass of champagne and says with a suggestive smile.

"You asked for this meeting to discuss a campaign."

"I did." I leave my champagne untouched, as does Kyle, and she says nervously, "Would you like a different refreshment?"

"No."

I stare at her with a brooding expression.

"I like to keep a clear head when I discuss business. That way there can be no misunderstandings."

She sets her own glass down and takes a deep breath.

"May I ask what campaign you wish us to run?"

"My lap dancing club, Angelz."

She nods, but I can tell she's not ecstatic about it. Having a campaign like that on her books won't sit well with her other customers, but I don't give a shit about her business, only mine and my money is too attractive for her to refuse.

"I will deal with it personally." She gazes into my eyes with the promise of an extremely intimate working partnership, and I raise my hand and say firmly, "No. I have a different person in mind to assist me."

"You do?" Her eyes are wide and widen even further when I say evenly, "Allegra Powell. I believe she started here today."

"My intern!" She gasps, and adds quickly, "But she's new and has no experience. It would be a car crash."

"Are you questioning my choices, Evangeline?"

She backs down under my ferocious gaze and shakes her head. "Of course not. I only want to provide you with the best service there is and no offense, but Miss Powell has a lot to learn."

"I'll be the judge of that. Bring her to me and I'll discuss the campaign with her, and she will report back to you."

For a moment, I think she's going to argue with me because her eyes narrow and her mouth disappears into a thin line.

I know she's pissed. I've disregarded her authority in her own business, and she will look foolish with her staff when she offers an extremely lucrative assignment to an intern on her first day that would ordinarily take years of proving themselves to attain.

In asking for Allegra, I have alienated her from her new workmates and incurred the wrath of her boss, who will want her to fail to prove a point.

I watch her changing emotions with interest as they play out across her face before she sighs heavily and nods.

"If you insist, but don't blame me if your campaign fails. There will be no refunds, just to make that clear. We also insist on fifty percent up front."

"Insist, Evangeline?"

I raise my eyes and she has the sense to blush and lick her lips nervously.

However, she holds her ground and says defiantly, "Come on, Shade, you know how it works. It's obvious Miss. Powell is of interest to you in another way. I'm not a fool and you are using my company to make some kind of point. It's fine. Go ahead with my blessing, but you must give me something back. It's only fair."

I shake my head. "I'm not a fair man, Evangeline. Surely you already know that."

"I know exactly the kind of man you are, Shade, which is why we are even having this conversation. As I said, I'll agree to your demands, but you must meet me half way."

I nod. "Fine. I will pay the entire fee upfront on one condition."

I lean forward and say darkly, "That Allegra Powell works solely on my campaign. She reports to me every fucking morning and again when she finishes at night. She will get her own office to work in private with all your resources at her disposal, and she is given six days to complete it."

Evangeline shakes her head and sighs. "I have given up trying to figure you out, Shade, but you obviously have your reasons, so yes, I'll agree to your demands and will have the contract drawn up."

"No need." I nod to Kyle, who removes a file from his briefcase and as I slide it across the desk, I say with a wicked grin, "Contracts are my speciality, Evangeline, all you have to do is sign on the dotted line."

"But..." She attempts to disagree, and I harden my voice and growl, "Now and then send in Miss Powell."

With a deep sigh, she grasps her pen and signs her name with a flourish and stands.

"If you wait here, I'll send her in."

As we watch her leave, Kyle laughs softly. "Well played, Shade. She had no choice."

"They never do." I grin and switch my mind to another woman who has no choice where I'm concerned, and I can't wait to see the expression on her face when she realizes just what she has signed up for.

CHAPTER 22

ALLEGRA

I hate being an intern already. I've only been here for two hours and all I've done is make coffee for people who don't even say thank you. I may as well be invisible. I know I must start at the bottom, but this is seriously scraping the bottom of the barrel.

My neck is itching, courtesy of the scarf I wound around it to disguise the freaking bite marks, and I had to wear my hair long to hide the ones higher up. It's baking hot in here and I am shrouded like an Egyptian Mummy, all because of one man and his sick games.

I reported for duty and instead of the induction I expected, I was issued a pass and told to report to a woman called Simone Wilder, who I already hate with a passion.

She shook her head when she saw me standing there and sighed. "Darling, you really should dress to impress on your first day. You are seriously mixing colors there."

I said, "I'm sorry, I…" and she didn't even let me finish and just pointed to the door and told me to fetch her a coffee and then ask everyone in the entire building if they wanted one too.

It has taken me two hours and the only thing I've learned is that every single fucking person here likes their coffee different. I never knew there were so many variations on a drink, and the dismissive way they supped the beverage and then pulled a face didn't make me feel good about my barista credentials.

I make my way back to Simone's office in the hope that was just the initiation and now she will show me exactly what I'll be doing.

I tap nervously on her door, and she barks, "Wait outside."

I catch the eye of her assistant, who offers me a small smile and a slight roll of her eyes. I smile and take a seat to wait, and it must be twenty minutes later her assistant says apologetically, "She will see you now."

As I make to pass, she whispers, "Listen, if it's any help, she made the last one wait until past lunchtime. She must like you."

"I'm honored." I grin and head to the door and open it tentatively.

Simone is poised, elegant and dressed in designer brands and her sleek blonde hair is styled in a sharp bob and her red painted lips are set permanently in a downward curve. She could be pretty I suppose but is ugly inside and it obviously affects her outward appearance.

I'm a little unnerved when she raises her eyes and stares at me long and hard and I detect disapproval in her eyes as she snaps, "Miss. Solomon has requested your attendance in the boardroom. Don't keep her waiting."

I'm a little surprised but expect it's common practice to welcome the new staff and so I nod politely and leave, stopping only by her assistant's desk to whisper, "Where is the boardroom?"

She says in surprise, "Wow. That's unusual. I'll show you if you like. I'm due my break."

She holds up her hand and presses her intercom and says sweetly, "I'm taking my ten-minute break. Can I get you anything?"

She rolls her eyes and scribbles down the order and as she grabs her purse, she nods toward the elevator.

We step inside in silence and as the door closes, she says angrily, "Simone is a fucking bitch, and we have lost more good people because of her than anyone else."

She grins and holds out her hand. "I'm Alice, by the way. Alice Springs and you will immediately realize that my parents hated me from birth."

It makes me laugh and I shake her hand and say with a grateful smile. "Allegra Powell. Newest coffee making dogsbody at your service."

She says sympathetically. "It gets better. She tries but can't keep the act up for long. She'll soon get bored and move you onto envelope stuffing or photocopying duty. It sucks being new."

"How long have you worked here?"

"Five years. I was the lucky one. I joined when they were new, and Simone wasn't here then. I worked for a great guy, Thomas O Malley, but he returned to Ireland and set up on his own. Simone replaced him and relied on me to make her look good. She still does."

"Is she bad at her job?"

"I wouldn't say that, but she's the kind of woman who takes other's ideas as her own. It's why she's still here. She saps all the good ideas from her staff and takes all the glory. Plus, she's a good friend of Evangeline and makes certain that is one friendship she doesn't mess with."

She stares at me with interest.

"So, what brings you to this place of Hell?"

I shrug. "I've always been interested in public relations and thought this was the perfect training ground, although I may only be qualified to work in the coffee shop next door if it carries on like this."

"It gets better, trust me."

The elevator stops and she smiles. "Come, it's down the hall. I'll leave you at the door, but if you need anything, you know where to find me."

She points to a door at the end of the corridor, and I smile gratefully.

"Thanks. I wonder what's waiting for me."

I make a joke, but inside my nerves are dancing because what if the great Evangeline Solomon hates me as much as her friend does?

* * *

I approach the door nervously and wonder if I should wait to be collected. There is nobody here and so she must be waiting inside.

I knock tentatively on the wooden door and when I hear nothing, I inch it open and peer inside.

My eyes scan the room and then my heart almost gives out on me because watching me with a hungry glint in his eye is the man I hate most in the world. Shade Vieri.

I make to slam the door, but an arm reaches out and pulls me inside and I say angrily, "Let go of me."

I glare at the man who hailed me the cab yesterday, and he shrugs and moves to block my exit.

So, I turn my anger on his boss and say furiously, "What the fuck are you doing here?"

"Allegra." He shakes his head slowly, his voice sliding through my body like the most delicious narcotic.

"I am here purely on business to help you in your chosen career."

"I'm sorry—what?"

I stare around the room, expecting to see Miss Solomon and it soon becomes apparent it's just us.

He points to the seat opposite him, and I drop down into it with an evil glare in his direction, causing him to smirk.

"You're angry."

"Too right I'm fucking angry, you asshole. You have ruined my life."

"A slight exaggeration, but I accept I pushed things too far."

He shrugs. "It was fun, though."

"Fun!" I glare at him. "You trashed my reputation and told my mom to fuck herself. I can't even speak to her I'm so ashamed."

He leans forward and stares at me with a dark gleam in his eye. "You have nothing to be embarrassed about, princess. If anyone has, it's your fucking mom, so can the attitude, shut the fuck up and let me help you."

"I don't want your help. In fact…" I reach into my purse and pull out the money I have been guarding like a security guard all day, intent on delivering it back to him personally when my day ends here.

I toss it on the table and say angrily, "You can take your freaking money, too. How dare you treat me like a cheap whore!"

The notes on the table stare up defiantly and he says with amusement, "Not so cheap, judging by the stack of bills."

"Ten thousand dollars and a note telling me it's to replace the blood money and enjoy. How could you make a joke out of something so, well, evil?"

I am gratified when his smug expression changes into one of concern and his eyes flick to his henchman standing guarding the door, and then he turns his attention back to me. "I never sent this money."

"But…" I open my mouth, but no words join the but and I close it again and then open it again in shock.

"Have you got the note?" He says with a sudden urgency, and I shake my head. "It's in the trash, where it belongs." I add and he stares at the money and says to the man by the door, "Dust it for prints."

He says to me, "Retrieve the note and give it to me. I repeat, this did not come from me, and the question remains, who sent it?"

I gaze around me in fear because nothing in my life is making sense anymore and I say in a whisper, "Do you think it's the blackmailer? But why would he pay me when he wants money for his silence? What if it's someone else? Does the whole fucking world know about this?"

I am creeped out beyond belief but Shade merely shrugs as if it's of no consequence.

"I'll deal with it. You have more important things to worry about."

"What can be more important than this?" I snap, and his swagger returns as he shrugs, leaning back in his seat.

"I have paid for your services. You are to be my personal PR consultant on a campaign for my lap dancing club." He leans forward and stares at me long and hard. "This is your big shot, Allegra, and you have six days to make it happen."

"I'm sorry—what?"

I must be in a parallel universe because what on God's earth is happening?

He laughs softly. "Miss. Solomon agreed to my terms. You work for me for six days and I pay her a lot of money for your services."

"My public relations services, are you freaking kidding me?"

I shake my head. "You're a shit businessman, Shade, because I haven't got a clue where to start. Why me?"

He actually winks and whispers, "Because you owe me six days, Allegra and I'm going to enjoy every single fucking minute of it. Now…" He adjusts his sleeves and rubs his thumb against his chin as if he's thinking hard.

"You are to report to me at six am every morning at my office to brief me on your progress. Then again at six pm every evening. During that time, you make my club shine and the hottest place to be in town. At the end of the six days, our business contract ends, along with our, shall we say, more personal one."

"But I hate you." I say it as if we are discussing the weather, and then shrug and lean back in my seat as if I couldn't give a shit.

"You see, Shade, I have discovered something since you dismissed me into a cab. I have discovered that you want to use me to bring my uncle down. This is all a big game to you, and my problem was a little too convenient."

I lean forward and hiss, "I believe you sent those notes, you made those calls, and you were there to heroically save me. You are the man I should avoid, and I'm guessing there is no other person involved at all."

I cross my legs and lean forward and stare him right in the eye and snap, "Six days to work on your campaign is a small price to pay to get you out of my life and if you want my help in bringing Lucas Stevenson down, I'll throw that in for free."

I offer him my hand and say tightly, "Do we have a deal?"

He grasps my hand and squeezes it so hard I think he's going to break it and the expression in his eyes should scare the panties off me. I am drowning in decadence and deprivation, and I hate to admit it—lust and before he replies, he glances at the man behind me who heads across and scoops up the money with a gloved hand, before turning and leaving the room, closing the door behind him.

Then Shade grips my hand hard and says huskily, "We have a deal, princess, but just for the record, you're wrong. I am *not* the person you should fear the most. He is lingering in the shadows, waiting for the first opportunity to bring you down. Do you think I would go to all this trouble to keep my eyes on you if that wasn't the case? So, shut the fuck up and do what I tell you if you want to survive because I'm not the big bad wolf in this fairy tale, I'm your fucking hero. So, whether you like that or not, you're stuck with me until we figure this shit out."

His eyes are lit with lust and it's taking my breath away. I can't look away and when he says in that husky voice, "Now get over here and let me finish what we started." I can't get there quickly enough.

CHAPTER 23

SHADE

The moment she walks in, I am hard. Seeing her beautiful face twisted in anger is like Viagra to me. Her long chestnut hair gleams against her pale skin and the fucking tight skirt she is wearing, paired with the highest heels, is every fantasy I have come to life.

She reaches me in an instant, her own lust plain to see and as I grip the scarf at her throat, I pull her sharply toward me and punish her mouth for ever doubting me.

As I kiss her like a wild animal, I untie her scarf and, pulling back, growl, "Give me your hands."

She holds them in front of her and I bind them tightly, causing her to gasp, "What are you doing?"

"Teaching you not to fuck with me."

I pull her over my knee, her wrists bound before her, and run my hand up her legs, inching her skirt around her waist, loving the silk panties she's wearing as I run my hand over her ass.

I whisper, "I wouldn't scream if I were you. There is no one coming."

She tenses. "Why do I need help?"

It makes me laugh because if only she knew how deep she has fallen.

I tear off her panties, causing her to say furiously, "Fuck, Shade, now what am I going to wear?"

"Nothing."

I grip her hair tightly and she gasps with pain as I bring my hand hard down on her ass, causing her to jump."

"Fuck! Stop!" she says through her tears, and I growl, "Never doubt me again, princess. I am all you have right now, so show me some respect."

I run my hand over her ass as she sobs, "I hate you."

"You're not the only one, princess. I can live with that."

I pull her up and spin her around, so she is straddling me, and I whisper, "I'm guessing that greedy little pussy is missing my hard cock."

"You're disgusting." She hisses and as I reach down and free my cock, I lift her slightly and pull her down hard onto it. Her eyes widen but her low moan betrays her and as her pussy clenches my cock, I thrust up hard, gripping her hair in one hand and using her like a whore.

She has never looked so beautiful to me as she glares at me with a mixture of lust and hate, my favorite blend of emotion and as I fuck her hard, the flush on her face is a magnificent sight to behold.

"You're beautiful, princess." I really mean that because I I've never seen such a beauty in my life.

She closes her eyes and moans softly and I tighten my hold, causing her to groan even louder and as I fuck her deep, I sense her orgasm isn't far away.

For some reason, being inside her is like coming home. This is what I've been waiting for since we left the boat in such a hurry. I needed more time. More time inside this woman and I now have six days to fuck her out of my system.

As she milks my cock, I explode inside her, the release soothing my anger far more than alcohol or any business deal.

I allow the ecstasy to flood my body, bathing it in a sweet balm that calms me the fuck down. She is what I needed, which is a big problem for me because in six days' time, I promised to set her free.

As she slumps against my body, my arms wrap around her. I bury my face in her hair and take a deep breath as I close my eyes, wanting nothing to disturb this moment. She smells so delicious, like all my favorite scents bottled in one package. This is what I came for. *She* is what I came for and just like that, everything rights with my world.

"Untie me." She says with a low whisper, and I tighten my hold and say softly, "On one condition."

She tenses and says angrily, "For fuck's sake, Shade. This could be my first day and my last if Miss. Solomon pays us a visit. What were you thinking?"

I smile against her hair and chuckle softly. "Relax, princess. Kyle is acting as security outside the door. Nobody will get past him, guaranteed."

She pulls back and the look she throws me could wither a freshly bloomed flower and I love it. Stroking her face lightly, I whisper, "You look so beautiful, with my cum dripping between your legs."

"You're a fucking animal. You disgust me." She growls, and it's so sexy I'm in no hurry to release her.

"Careful, princess, you still owe me, and I have a plan to make all your problems go away."

Now I have her attention and her eyes light up as she whispers, "How?"

Keeping her close, I whisper against her ear, "All will be revealed at six pm. A cab will be waiting just outside and there is only one passenger booked. The driver will take you to my offices, where you will report to me under the terms of my contract with Evangeline. Then, at exactly six-thirty, another cab will take you back to your apartment. In the morning, another cab will collect you at six am and bring you back to my office for an early morning meeting before delivering you to The Social Queen to work on my campaign."

"What if I don't want to report to you? What if I prefer to email you my progress instead? To be honest, that is my preferred method, despite what agreement you have with my boss."

She glares at me fiercely and I laugh softly, loving how angry she is that I'm the one pulling her strings.

I shake my head, watching eagerly for her reaction as I say casually, "You will have no choice because I will not be content with a few snatched hours. You see…" I brush my lips against hers and whisper huskily, "You will be spending the next six nights with me, and my campaign is a very different one where it concerns you. We will pick up where we left off on the boat and when your debt is repaid in full, you will be free of blackmail and of me."

She stares at me in astonishment and a light flush creeps across her face and her eyes sparkle. She is so beautiful to watch, like a force of nature that has yet to be discovered and I really believe I have my met my match in Allegra Powell because it appears that just like me, she gets off on the game.

As her breath hitches and her eyes sparkle, I know I've won before we've even played. She craves this as much I do and as I grab her chin and pull her plump lips roughly to mine, I can't wait for this day to be over because what I have planned for my little princess is nothing short of evil.

CHAPTER 24

ALLEGRA

Miss Solomon is pissed. I can tell by her expression, but she is trying not to show it.

I am sitting in her office after the most frustrating hour of my life, knowing I've been manipulated and there is nothing I can do about that.

When Shade left, I ran straight to the restroom to clean up before facing my boss because one look in my direction would tell her everything that went on in that boardroom.

When I saw my reflection in the mirror, I could have wept because there are even more fucking bite marks on my neck and my make-up was smeared across my face. It was a complete disaster between my legs, and I cleaned up as best I could before anyone walked in.

Despite my anger, I left with a smile on my face because as much as I hate Shade Vieri, I am also addicted to him.

Miss. Solomon drags my attention back to her with a firm, "This is highly unusual, Miss. Powell. I'm sure you realize that, but for some reason Mr. Vieri wants you to run his campaign, which tells me there is something going on between you."

She fixes me with a hard stare and leans forward. "I don't care what that is, but I *do* care about my reputation and that of the company I built up from scratch. You are inexperienced and liable to fail and only have six days to deliver a passable campaign."

I am so miserable because everything she is saying is right. I can't disagree. I'm as lousy as she says I am, and it's all because I'm fucking the client and he wants to control my life.

For a moment, a hint of concern sparkles in her eyes and she says with a small smile. "Listen. I know Shade Vieri and his brother, too. That family doesn't follow the same rules as the rest of us and it can be intoxicating and a little wild. Just don't get sucked into their world, Allegra. Resist it at all costs because a young vulnerable woman like you wouldn't last two hours when they play hard."

She is looking at me with so much concern I almost crumble. I never realized just how stressful my life has become lately and a little kindness is going a long way. I almost consider confiding in her, but there is something stopping me. I don't know what it is about Shade that has me hating him one minute with a passion and then wanting him back when he's gone.

Miss. Solomon sighs heavily. "You will be assigned your own office and an assistant. I will be allocating one of my more experienced ones to this campaign to guide you through it."

She shakes her head. "The client has paid a lot of money to get this moving and you only have six days to make it all happen. Your new assistant will be here soon, and I suggest listening to everything she says because time is against us. Run everything past me when you leave at five-thirty to head across town to meet with the client. That is the conditions of their contract and if you encounter any problems, my door is always open."

She fixes me with a hard stare. "Don't let me down, Miss. Powell. Your future career with The Social Queen is riding on this."

A tentative knock to the door causes me to turn, and I'm delighted and extremely relieved when Alice heads inside. A vision of capability.

"Miss. Solomon. Miss. Powell." She greets us both respectfully and Miss. Solomon says with a sigh. "It's up to you now, girls. Spend that bastard's money wisely and make this work because he is the last person I want to explain any failure to. Do I make myself clear?"

"Yes, Miss. Solomon." We dutifully answer and as we turn to go, it's as if I'm carrying a huge burden of responsibility on my already loaded shoulders.

* * *

As soon as we are out of earshot, Alice whispers her concern.

"Are you okay, Allegra?"

"I don't think so."

She stares at me with wide eyes. "I can't believe this is happening. You should have seen Simone's expression when she told me to report to you. I wish I had taken a photograph. I think it was the best moment of my life."

We giggle like a couple of schoolgirls and as we take the elevator, she says with an excited grin. "Opportunities don't come up like this very often. Let's make this one count for something amazing."

I really don't want to burst her bubble because I am definitely *not* excited about this, but I realize my future career is riding on my success, so I push my anger aside and into the job at hand.

* * *

Alice shows me to a bright office overlooking the skyline and as she closes the door, she claps her hands with excitement.

"Okay, this is the plan. If you need me any hour of the day or night, call me. I don't know if you have anything in mind, but I took the liberty of swiping some files from my computer. They are blueprints for campaigns similar to the one we must create, and it will provide us with a checklist if nothing else."

I could kiss her because she has probably saved my life and as she fires up the computer, I say tentatively, "Should I fetch us some coffee?"

She rolls her eyes. "Your coffee making days are over. We'll call for takeout because this is going to be a long six days."

* * *

The day passes so quickly, I'm surprised when Alice glances up from her computer screen and sighs. "It's time for you to report to Miss. Solomon. She told me you must take your ideas to the client at six thirty, so you will need to clear it with her first."

"What shall I say?" I stare with horror at my life saver of an assistant and Alice sighs. "You don't need to go into details. Just show her the mock up boards and the bullet point list. Ask her advice. She's always delighted when she's made to feel valued. Don't pretend to know it all because she'll suss that out in record time. Just show her what we've got so far and ask for her advice. It's all you can do."

The fact we worked solidly on this all day doesn't show because we are no further forward with an idea than when we first started.

It's a freaking lap-dancing club. What the hell do I know about them and so with a deep sigh, I gather the folder Alice has prepared and grabbing my purse say miserably, "Wish me luck."

As I head to the door, I turn back and smile gratefully. "Thanks for your help, Alice. I wouldn't know where to begin."

She smiles reassuringly. "We'll do this, Ally. I'll work on it some more and see if I can come up with something. Leave it with me."

"But I don't want to be another Simone and pass your ideas off as my own." I say with desperation, and she shakes her head.

"This is an emergency, honey. We'll figure it out when we have something to offer. You may come up with something overnight. Who knows?"

"Okay. Wish me luck then."

As I make the journey to Miss. Solomon's office, I knew I should *never* have left Rafferty's apartment and *never* gone to Gyration and then I would *never* have met Shade Vieri. My life was so uneventful until he walked into it and murdered a man in front of me. Now I'm caught up in the craziest time of my life and it's all because of him.

Fucking mafia. Who do they think they are?

CHAPTER 25

SHADE

Kyle stares at me in disbelief.

"That's your plan. Are you serious?"

I shrug, feeling very good about it as it happens.

"It will work. I don't see what the problem is."

"Your guest might." Kyle says with a slight shake of his head, and I grin.

"She'll love it. It will be fine."

I settle back in my chair after a very stressful day with my accountant. I'm not sure why we still use that guy, but he's an old friend of my grandfather who trusts him with our business and has done for several years. He thinks I'm reckless, out of control and nowhere near as astute as my brother, or even my grandfather. It pisses me off and now I'm in need of something to relieve my stress.

I glance at my Rolex and smile inside. Six twenty-five. Any minute now.

My phone lights up with a text from reception and I say with smug satisfaction. "It appears my next appointment is here."

Kyle sighs and stands and as he heads to the door, I say quickly, "Is Heather on standby?"

"Of course." He shakes his head and I nod with satisfaction.

"This is going to be a pleasure."

"For you maybe." He laughs softly. "You're fucking evil, Shade."

I shrug. "Tell me something I don't already know."

* * *

WE HEAD DOWNSTAIRS and I wish we had been there to see the look on her face when she was shown into my club. Angelz is emblazoned in gold on the neon sign that hangs above the door and as we head inside, I sigh inside when I note it's almost empty. There are a few guys enjoying a dance and some watching the pole dancer on the stage. However, there is one sight that gets my attention more than any other when I see Allegra sitting on a bar stool, straight backed and clutching a folder to her chest. She is staring around her in disbelief, and I love how her skirt has risen a little, revealing a long and shapely leg.

She is sipping a glass of something and as we approach, she faces me with an enigmatic expression and yet from the spark in her eye, she is reacting just as I thought she would.

"Shade." She nods as I approach, and I grin lazily, looking her up and down with a smirk on my face.

"It's good to see you, Miss. Powell. I decided our meeting should be conducted here because how can you promote a business if you know nothing about it?"

"That's a fair point, sir."

Why does my cock twitch at that? In fact, my cock is always twitching when she's around, which can only mean one thing. It isn't bored with her yet.

I jerk my thumb toward my usual booth. "Follow me. We have much to discuss."

She slides off the bar stool and reaches for her drink and I say, "Leave it. There will be a fresh one waiting."

Ignoring me, she grabs the glass and drains it with a defiant smirk on her face, and right at this moment, I fucking love this woman. It's almost as if we're two souls reunited. She appears to be the female version of me because I recognize my own defiance in her. It's just what I would have done, so I chuckle softly and head toward my booth, leaving Kyle to make sure she joins me.

We slide into our seats, and I insist she sit beside me and as I said, there is already a bucket of champagne waiting, along with a bottle of bourbon and three glasses.

Kyle sits opposite and her eyes widen as three of my men close in a circle around us.

"What's this?" She says, glancing around her nervously and I shrug. "We need our privacy. We are doing business, Allegra, and I require no interruptions."

"Of course."

She spreads the contents of the folder on the table and says with a deep breath, "These are the preliminary outlines. We have devised a blueprint to follow and just need to agree on a theme. A unique selling point that will guarantee the customers to flood through the doors. I was thinking along the lines of The Greatest Showman, the movie."

Her eyes light up as she speaks with animation. "We will dress the girls as circus performers and they can entertain the crowds with snakes, perhaps. Exotic dancing, possibly a magician, you know, more than just a sleazy sex show, something of a performance."

I daren't look at Kyle because what the fuck? She is deluded and so I lean back, bored already, and decide to play with my new toy instead.

"Think again princess, that idea is shit."

Her furious glance in my direction makes me laugh inside and I nod to Kyle, who whispers to one of the men guarding us.

"Shit!" She glares at me as if I've personally insulted her child's artworks on the first day of school and, to be honest, this idea feels like that.

I lean in and lower my voice. "Forget the campaign. We need to move onto our other business."

Immediately she tenses and leaning forward, whispers, "Is that why you've increased security? Have you heard something?"

"No." I shrug. "I'm talking about your debt to me. You owe me six days and six nights because our trip was cut short. So, for the duration of the campaign you will work for me in the day, taking care of that part of the deal, but your nights are mine. However, we have a problem."

"What problem?"

I lower my voice. "Somebody knows about the money. Your blackmailer is still out there, despite the unfortunate demise of River. To flush them out, we need to place you in their sight, which means your routine must remain unchanged."

"You are using me to set a trap!" She glares at me, and I nod. "Of course. We need to know who it is, and the best way of flushing them out is to wait for them to come to you."

"You bastard." She makes to stand, and I grip her hand tightly and pull her down sharply, hissing, "Don't be stupid. It's your best chance at surviving this because there will be eyes on you the entire time. We will be watching and waiting to strike, but you *must* cooperate."

"And if I don't?" She sneers defiantly, causing me to growl, "Then I'll pray for your soul at your funeral."

"Are you threatening me?" Her eyes are wide, and I say

impatiently, "I'm not interested in removing you from life, but we can't rule out that somebody else might."

For the first time, she realizes the seriousness of her situation and her lower lip trembles as she sinks back against the seat and whispers, "So, I'm fucked either way."

I reach for the champagne and pour three glasses and as I hand one to her and one to Kyle, I raise mine in a toast.

"To surrendering control to me and staying alive."

She knocks the drink back in two gulps, and I can almost touch her thoughts as they race for cover. Yes, my little princess has just discovered there's a big bad world out there and it eats girls like her up for breakfast.

CHAPTER 26

SHADE

*I*t's going well. Better than expected because now Allegra is so terrified, she will do anything I ask.

As the sea of menace parts, a flash of gold enters the circle and I watch with anticipation as the woman drops into the seat beside Kyle.

Allegra peers with surprise at the dancer sitting opposite and I say pleasantly, "Allegra, may I introduce Heather Cardine."

"I'm pleased to meet you." She says politely and Heather nods. "I'm glad to be of service."

I sense the disapproval coming from Allegra, who has probably never been anywhere near a whore before. At least that's what she thinks Heather is and I say softly, "Heather has agreed to help with our problem."

I glance at my watch and say casually. "In fifteen minutes' time your cab will leave, taking you home and will return here twelve hours later. However, the person traveling in it is currently sitting opposite you."

"Excuse me." Allegra stares at me in shock and I smile wickedly. "You will swap places. Heather will accompany you to a private room where you will swap clothes. She will wear a wig and carry your folder and head back to your apartment. You will re-join me here and nobody will be any wiser."

Allegra's mouth drops open and she stutters, "But…"

She gulps. "My brother will know."

"Who is away for the next seven days on tour with his club." I remind her and she stutters, "It won't work. People know me there. They will realize she isn't me and what if I get visitors?"

"You won't." I laugh softly. "You won't answer when they call, and any texts will be telling them you are busy working and arrange to meet next week instead."

"But the doorman will. We always chat."

"Who has been paid to assure anyone asking that you are currently tucked up in bed."

"You're mad." She shakes her head, staring at Heather in confusion. "But we don't even look alike." She says, almost to herself, and Heather speaks up. "Not now, but we soon will. Come on honey, this will be a fun game."

As if on autopilot, Allegra stands and follows her through the wall of guards and toward the back room without saying another word or even looking in my direction.

Kyle shakes his head as we watch them go and whispers, "Do you think this will work?"

"Of course. People believe what their eyes tell them. Heather will play her part and I'm really hoping Allegra will play hers."

I laugh at the amusement on his face as he chuckles, "I wouldn't miss this for the world."

* * *

TEN MINUTES later and every wish I had regarding her comes true as the men part and an angel appears before me.

She is dressed in the gold costume that molds to her body like a silk glove, the zipper revealing a cleavage I can't wait to bury my face into, wearing high stilettos that make her legs appear even longer. Her face is painted professionally, and her ruby red lips are fixed in a pout and her black-lined eyes glitter as she tosses her new long blonde hair over her shoulder. Her eyes flash behind the gold mask she is wearing that covers half her face, and she heads toward me with purpose.

I swear I am so hard right now as she leans down and whispers in my ear, "Is this what you want? A cheap whore."

Reaching out, I grab her hips and pull her so she is straddling my lap, and I tip her face to mine and whisper, "Come on baby, it's dress up time. Dance for me and lose yourself in fantasy."

"In your dreams, asshole."

I grip her face tightly and hiss, "You will do what I fucking tell you because I own you, remember? You will dance for me in my club, and only then will you be qualified to dream up a campaign in its name. Think of it as research and putting everything into your job. Show me what you're made of, baby girl, and then I'll show you what happens next."

I almost believe she'll bail on me. The tight fury in her eyes makes that a distinct possibility, but she surprises me by twisting her mouth into a wicked grin and then slowly moves her hips before my eyes. As she loses herself in the music, she runs her hands over her body and moans softly, owning the role she has been given and I stare in shock as she sucks in her bottom lip and sighs, pushing her breasts up with her hands and swinging her hips.

My hands are on either side of her thighs and she feels so good in them. She commands my complete attention, and it's as if we are the only ones in the room. I even black out my men as she swings her hips from side to side, teasing me by lowering her zip just enough to test my resolve. Her tits are fucking amazing as they swell against the fabric and as she leans forward, my face is in touching distance, and I am so hard right now I could fuck her with no care for who's watching.

"Let me through." I hear a loud voice behind one of my men who is doing a very good job of keeping someone out and as Kyle stands, I instinctively reach for Allegra and pull her onto my lap, her face against my chest as Kyle turns and from the expression in his eye, I'm not going to like this.

"Lucas Stevenson wants a word, boss."

"Fuck." Allegra hisses in my arms and stiffens and I say roughly, "I'm a little busy here."

Kyle shrugs and in a moment of pure wickedness, I sigh and say with resignation, "Let him through."

Allegra pinches my arm and it damn well hurts, so I tighten my hold and say pleasantly, "Judge Stevenson, this is an unexpected pleasure. I'm sorry, as you can see, I'm a little busy right now."

The expression on his face is priceless and I really wish Allegra could see it, but she lies frozen in my arms and has almost stopped breathing as he says roughly, "You are fucking finished, Shade. What the fuck are you playing at with my niece?"

"Your niece?" I say with a puzzled frown.

I stare at Kyle, who shrugs, and I address him, saying, "I didn't know the Judge has a niece. Did you Kyle?"

Kyle shakes his head. "Not to my knowledge."

The Judge says angrily. "Cut the crap, Vieri. We both know I have a niece and you sent me that pornographic video of you fucking her to prove a point."

Allegra pinches me hard again and I swear her fingers are

inching toward my gun right now, so I shift her slightly and grip her wrists behind her back and say pleasantly, "Oh, you mean the one I sent you when I fucked your daughter. Is that the one you're talking about?"

I swear he ages right before my eyes as he whispers, "What did you say?"

"Your daughter, Lucas. Allegra Powell. I believe you also have another son, Rafferty Powell. I wonder if your brother knows his wife has been fucking his brother for close to twenty-five years already?"

"You're wrong. You're spreading false lies." He tries to protest, but his voice shakes, revealing his guilt in a far more devastating way than admitting it.

I sigh theatrically. "I would hate to be there when he does. Imagine the headlines. Respected Judge had an affair with his brother's wife for twenty-five years. Fathering two bastard children behind his brother's back."

I shake my head. "That wouldn't be good for your career, would it, Lucas? I'm guessing your marriage wouldn't survive either, and what about your brother? I'm almost positive he will have something to say about that." I shake my head. "Goodness me." I say in mock alarm. "What if the other Dark Lords get to hear of it? Tainting our respectable organization with scandal. You could lose everything."

Allegra is panting against my chest, and I feel wet tears on my neck and for some reason it angers me that she's upset. The man staring at me with mounting anger mixed with shock is the one responsible for that, and I snarl, "So, if you have any sense, you will turn around and walk away. Head back the way you came and keep as far away from me and my family as you can because I don't take kindly to threats against me, in my own fucking club."

Kyle moves to his side and one of my other guards does the same on his other one and I hiss, "Now if you don't mind,

I was enjoying a pleasant evening before you so rudely interrupted me. Next time, call my office and make an appointment. You may leave."

He has no choice as my men grab one arm each and effectively pull him away and as the circle closes once again, I drop a kiss on Allegra's head and whisper, "He's gone. It's okay, baby girl, I've got you."

To my surprise, her arms tighten around my waist, and she sobs in my arms, something I definitely wasn't expecting, which causes something sharp to pierce my heart.

I tighten my hold and kiss her soft cheek and whisper, "Let it all out. Take as long as you need."

As I hold the broken woman in my arms, a murderous rage consumes me. I almost wish the Judge was still here so I could take my anger out on him. I want to kill him and make it long, slow and painful and I want it to count. He has destroyed this woman's life and I will never be okay with that.

CHAPTER 27

ALLEGRA

So many emotions have assaulted my mind today, and this one has pushed me over the edge. I can't take anymore. I am officially broken because what just happened confirmed everything.

Lucas Stevenson is my father.

It was obvious. He tried to deny it, but I could tell he was bluffing. Shade was right. My mom has been cheating on my dad my entire life and I hate her so much is burns inside.

How could they?

My childhood has been destroyed and it's all because of the man holding me so tenderly in his arms and kissing my head while whispering words of comfort in my ear. He is all I have right now, which is a freaking car crash because a mafia bad boy isn't really someone you can trust.

But I do.

For some strange reason, I do trust him. He has humiliated me, ridiculed me and made me the star of a porno movie, and yet I still trust him. He has killed for me. He is helping me and right now, as I sob in his arms, he is loving me.

I'm not even sure how long we sit in the club, the music playing around us serenading my misery. It's as if we are alone, though. The men remain in their positions, and nobody can see in. We are in the eye of the storm, and it is breaking all around us.

Then something happens that shocks me. It's as if a cold resolve settles over my soul and any emotion in me is slowly draining away. Perhaps I'm losing my mind. I've already lost everything else, nothing really matters anymore, so I push back and, taking a deep breath, smile weakly.

"So…" His expression is full of concern as I attempt a small but shaky laugh.

"Where were we?"

He makes to speak, but I place my lips against his and kiss him slowly. My tongue edging inside and taking its time to savor something it needs more than anything right now. I'm hurting, but at least I'm feeling something. It's time to replace this emptiness inside me. To chase it away and leave me with a different kind of memory.

His low groan makes me feel so powerful at this moment. It's as if I can do anything and so I carry on dancing. His own private show from the lady well-hidden behind the mask. A disguise of sorts. Like the men around us, shutting the entire world out and I wiggle my hips and leaning back, lower the zipper on my dress just enough to get his attention.

The gleam in his eyes excites me because this is so liberating. So wrong and yet the right thing to do—for me. I am free. This is my choice now. I call the shots and so I lean forward and whisper, "What happens when you take the dancer to the hotel room?"

His eyes are heavy with lust and yet his face is a picture of concern as he whispers, "You don't have to…"

I place my finger on his lips and say quickly, "What's the matter, sir? Didn't I please you?"

I shrug. "Maybe I'll go and find someone else to play with."

I straighten up and attempt to turn, but his hand grips my wrist, and he growls, "Not fucking likely."

He stands and as the guards part, allowing us our freedom, he nods to Kyle, who is standing chatting to one of them. "I may be some time"

It's slightly amusing that we leave as a pack. Men are behind and in front of us as we walk through the club, curious glances thrown in our direction.

I bask in their interest. I could be anyone right now because they don't see Allegra Powell, the spoilt bastard of a despicable man. They see a lap-dancing whore and expect nothing less.

We move fast and end up in a corridor outside the club, and as we move down it toward a door at the end, Shade says nothing at all. He walks with a grim determination and as we reach a set of stairs, he pulls me up one flight where an elevator is waiting.

This is where the men remain and as soon as the doors close, he pushes me hard against the wall and says huskily, "God knows what's going on in your mind, Allegra, but I like it."

I smile up at him and whisper, "I only want to do my job. To learn about your business and pay a little of my debt that you say I owe at the same time."

I stroke his face lightly and say huskily, "I want to forget. Who I am, what's happening in my life and what's waiting for me when I get home. I just want you Shade Vieri because for some reason, you are the only person in my life who tells me straight and even though I fucking hate you right now for sending a sex tape to my um...well, you know who I'm talking about, I kind of got turned on about that at the same time."

His eyes are flashing and his expression one of intense darkness that causes my blood to heat to dangerous levels. We are so bad for one another. He is bad for me, but I can't help it. I crave this like a drug. All of it. The danger, the excitement and the unknown and he is the man who can give it to me, so in my new liberated mindset, I reach for my zipper and tug it down, exposing my breasts to his greedy eyes and I lean back against the wall of the elevator and pout suggestively, "So, what happens now?"

No sooner than I speak, his lips crash onto mine with alarming speed, rough, relentless and passionate. A lot like the man himself, and he pushes me hard against the wall, tugging the zipper all the way down and kicking my legs apart. The elevator comes to a halt, and I say in alarm, "What's happening?"

"I'm going to fuck this greedy whore in the elevator." He says, unfastening his pants and releasing his hard cock, palming it in his hand, rubbing it with a dirty gleam in his eye.

"Now spread your legs and earn your money."

I am so turned on there must be something morally wrong with me as he tears down my ridiculous underwear, and with his hand pinning my throat to the wall, he pushes inside with a feral gleam in his eye. It's not pretty. Rather rough, and yet it's the perfect blend of aggression I am looking for.

He uses me for his own pleasure, which is all I want. I don't want soft kisses and words of love. I want it rough to drive the demons away. A giant fuck you to my respectable life, doing something my parents would be devastated about.

Angry sex is amazing and the power I'm experiencing is at odds with how it must look. He is ripping me apart, standing before me fully dressed, raging war on my body for a cheap thrill.

I love it.

The disguise enables me to let go of any inhibitions I have because Allegra Powell has ceased to exist. I'm an Angel now. A woman who works in a club, desperate to make money using her only asset. Her body.

I gasp as he almost cuts off my air supply and as I hover between life and death, I feel a euphoria I wasn't expecting. It's as if I'm floating high above my old life toward my new one. I never want to leave this place and as the orgasm crashes through my body, I scream so loud, the echo bouncing off the walls of the elevator.

As he releases my breath, my entire body shakes, my mind scrambled and the most intense pleasure pushing away the pain.

I'm conscious of Shade's own savage release inside me. His roar causing a ripple of pleasure through my entire body. I don't even care that he fills me with his hot salty cum. I love knowing there is a part of him inside me. Unprotected sex is yet another risk I'm taking because, even though I'm on birth control, this man is probably riddled with shit. I suppose it goes with the job and if he passes it onto me, I may just ask my mom to accompany me to the clinic.

Picturing the horror on her face causes me to laugh so hard, Shade says with concern, "Are you okay, princess?"

His expression causes me to half laugh and half cry, and I slide down the wall of the elevator and shake my head.

"What's happening to me, Shade?"

To my surprise, he joins me, and we must look a strange pair as we sit on the floor of the elevator, him fully dressed and me with my tits out and the dress hanging by a thread.

He laces his fingers with mine and says softly, "You're hurting, princess. It's causing you to rebel against it."

"You appear to know a lot about that." I turn and study his expression and he nods, a storm breaking in his eyes as he says roughly, "I've been a rebel my entire life. Searching for the next high, not through drugs, but adrenalin."

He laughs softly. "It kind of comes with the territory. Power is an aphrodisiac that's hard to control. People do what the fuck I tell them and it's addictive."

"Like me."

He nods, with no hint of apology in his eye.

"Yes." He shrugs. "You see, it's all about knowledge. Discover a person's secrets and they will do anything to protect them. They don't realize I'm not an honorable man and will use them for my own gain, not theirs."

"Is that what you're doing now? Using my secret to destroy my family?"

It's as if we're discussing the weather and I have no personal interest in what he is doing.

"Of course." He shrugs and grins, a wicked twist to his mouth that causes me to smile. Then he reaches out and pushes my hair away from my face and, resting his hand on my cheek, says fiercely, "I love corrupting you. I never realized it would be so…"

He leans across and tugs my bottom lip into his mouth and sucks it slowly, before pulling back a little and whispering, "Delicious."

Before I can respond to that, he reaches up and pounds his fist on the red button, causing the elevator to jerk into motion and with a wink, he growls, "Now, let me show you what happens when a dancer lures a man to depravity."

CHAPTER 28

SHADE

I share a lot in common with Allegra. I recognize the yearning in her expression and the pain in her eyes when she thinks no one is looking. The sense of spinning out of control with nothing to hang onto.

It surprises me that I want to be the one she reaches out to steady her. The man who protects her from the storm even though I created it. I expect it's because I feel responsible for breaking her. I have gone in hard and all to prove a point. I do what the fuck I like and to hell with the consequences.

This has always been my life. I've lost count of the souls I have broken just for my own pleasure. However, this time, I don't like watching her break.

We head to the upper floor of the hotel via the private elevator I had installed for this purpose. Nobody gets to see the seedier part of my business. The hotel operates as normal, and this floor is only accessed from Angelz. It offers a degree of privacy for my customers. Nobody watches them walk on the wild side and at the end of it they return the same way and head out of my club with nobody any wiser.

We enter a vacant room, and I lock the door, placing the 'do not disturb' sign outside, notifying my dancers that this room is occupied.

Allegra peers around her with interest at the rather stark functional bedroom that has none of the luxuries of the rest of the hotel.

"It's pretty basic, isn't it?"

She shakes her head, glancing at the bed with no sheets with a disparaging gaze.

"It suits its purpose." I shrug out of my jacket. "It's a fuck room. What do you expect?"

She shrugs and wanders around the small space, heading over to the window and gazing down on the street below.

"Normal life goes on." She mutters almost to herself, and I nod. "If you say so. Life can be anything but normal. Normal is overrated."

She turns and seeing her in the blonde wig disturbs me a little. She is still wearing the mask and I don't like it. I want my princess back. To stare into her beautiful eyes as I ruin her. To watch the emotions flickering like a dancing flame, powerful and bright; so hot it burns.

I head toward her, and she licks her lips, her smile a slight tremble and I reach up and remove her mask, loving her heightened color and the sparkle in her eyes.

I ease the wig off, almost groaning as her luxurious hair tumbles down around her shoulders, causing me to run my fingers through it and whisper, "You are so beautiful, Ally."

Her eyes widen at my choice of name because this is the first time I have addressed her more as a friend than my victim. It's more intimate somehow, almost as if we share a close bond rather than me forcing her into a situation she has no choice of.

I grip her face and force it to my greedy lips, and tentatively brush them against hers. She smells of innocence dripping in depravity which is my most favorite scent in the world.

As I kiss her, I drown in purity. Something I'm not used to. She is an innocent dragged into a toxic world. A truer angel than any other I have fucked in this room.

She deserves more. Strangely, I want to give her more and ease away her troubles with a gentle touch rather than cruelty.

I step back and ease the dress off her shoulders, loving her faint gasp as she shivers in the air conditioning. I push down her G-string, ridding her of vulgarity and leaving her standing beautiful before my eyes.

Stepping back, I gaze upon her body as I remove my shirt, unbuckling my belt and allowing my pants to drop to the floor. Her lustful gaze runs the length of my body, and she whispers, "Why do I want you so badly?"

I shake my head, my finger pressed to my lips, causing her to smile softly as I set the tone for this seduction. Because that is exactly what I have in mind. Not rough sex. Not a quick fix. Allegra deserves something special. A sweet memory to replace the bitter ones that must be destroying her inside.

The moment I'm naked, I advance like a predator about to strike and as I drop to my knees before my goddess, I part her thighs and bury my face deep inside her center. She smells of woman. So sweet, dripping in honey, and I'm the lucky bastard who gets to sample it.

I swipe her from front to back, groaning at the sweet nectar on my tongue and she moans softly as I gently bite her clit, loving how she grips my hair and gasps, "That's so good, Shade."

Hearing my name on her lips is the sweetest sound and as I pleasure my woman, I only just register that I now think of her this way.

Her entire body trembles as she feels my touch and to prolong the enjoyment, I pull back and plant sticky kisses across her abdomen and then stand, sweeping her into my arms and offering her a taste of her own desire as I kiss her deep and hard.

She is so good in my arms. As light as a feather. So fragile, almost as if she will break if I don't handle with care, and as I lower her back onto the unmade bed, I curse myself for not taking her to my penthouse instead. She deserves the best I can offer her, and yet this is a fitting end to our evening. She wanted the full experience, but that changed somewhere along the journey here because it's a completely different one I want to give her now.

She lies before me, spread out as a feast for my enjoyment and I take full advantage of that. There is not one inch of her skin that doesn't experience my touch as I kiss, lick and suck every part of it, leaving my mark and bringing back to the life the ones that are starting to fade. I want the whole world to see that she belongs to me. I am the bastard controlling this woman and nobody gets to go anywhere near her all the time she is mine.

She gasps and moans as I bring her body to life, edging away the bitter memories and replacing them with sweet pleasure. I am uncharacteristically gentle, which is a surprising turn on for me too. This is soft, sweet loving, and I underestimated its power. My entire attention is focused on making her happy, not my own gratification, which is unusual for a man who takes rather than gives.

But I'm giving now, one hundred percent and as she gasps my name, I love how it sounds against her sweet lips.

"That is so good, Shade, but it's not enough."

I smile inside because she must hate how much she wants me right now.

I grip her face and force her to look up at me and whisper, "Eyes on me, princess. Watch me own every part of you."

As I slide in slowly, I feel every muscle in her pussy contract against my cock. Holding it, welcoming it in, and it's a rush I wasn't expecting. It appears that my princess knows a lot about owning someone herself as she draws me in while staring deep into my eyes, the passion dancing in hers matching my own.

I reach my limit. I am consuming her and there is nowhere else to go, but it's not enough. It's as if I don't have the whole of her yet. I want her to be wrecked by me. To only see me and to only want me.

I push in faster, harder, determined to leave my mark. To show her she can't survive without me. To show her who's boss. As she grips my cock hard, she squeezes it almost painfully. As if she can't let go, she has trapped me inside her, and I only get out when she says so.

"What are you doing to me?" I whisper against her sweet lips, and she replies huskily, "I am inviting you to ruin me, Shade. It obviously turns you on."

She gazes at me seductively and I can't help allow the beast in me to take over as I grip her wrists hard and raise them over her head, punishing her as I thrust so hard inside her the bed rocks. I want to dominate, to put her firmly back in her place, but she won't comply. She has turned the master into the servant as I drive her pleasure rather than mine.

I pull out, confused by what's happening inside me. I want to own her, to bring her under my control, but it's not working. It's not enough because I promised to let her go and so I shake myself and spin her onto her front and say roughly, "You want to know how hard I play?"

"God, yeah." Is her muffled response and I grip her hips and pull her ass in the air, delivering a sharp stinging blow to it, causing her to scream. "Yes! That's what I need."

I waste no time in plunging into her from behind, causing her to face plant the mattress as I fuck her doggie style. The sweat is dripping down my body and her screams turn me on as I ride her hard, punishing her for making me weak.

I deny her an orgasm and pulling out, come hard over her ass, marking her on the outside, making her dirty with my cum.

"Oh, God." She groans as the cum drips down her body and I give her no warning and gripping her hair, pull her head up and slap her ass hard.

Her grunts of pain are mixed with pleasure as she sobs, "Make it hurt, Shade. Fucking make it burn."

I am out of control as I roar with frustration, slapping her ass while I pull her hair hard.

Her screams are laced with pain as she cums so hard her entire body shakes and I don't believe I have ever seen such a beautiful sight in my life as she falls apart in front of me. Her ass is red, her sobs inconsolable, and I know that has nothing to do with what happened here.

She is broken.

I have cracked the shell, and she is bleeding emotion on this fucking bed used by whores.

This is the photograph I should be posting online.

This is the one I should have framed and sent to her parents wrapped in a pretty red bow.

This is the moment when my job is done because I have destroyed their princess and there is probably no way back for her now.

I stand, leaving her sobbing on the bed, running my hand through my hair as I look at what I've done. This is what I wanted. I would have taken it further. I had so much depravity planned for Allegra Powell, and I still have five more days to make it happen.

The trouble is, I know she will let me. She will be eager

for every sordid part of it and that strips away the fun. I don't want to play anymore, so I say roughly, "Get dressed. We're leaving."

Her tear-stained face gazes in my direction with a mixture of hurt and hope. A strange mixture of vulnerability that doesn't help my mood.

"I said we're leaving." I growl as I dress quickly, tossing her gold dress at her with no attempt to sugar coat my fury.

"What?" she whispers nervously, and I snap, "I have business to attend to. I'll show you to your room. You'll sleep there tonight."

"My room?" She sits up and grabs the dress, attempting to cover her body, and I watch the pain light in her eyes as she feels cheap and used.

"You wanted the full experience, baby girl. I hope I didn't disappoint. Now, get dressed. I'm done with you for now. Tomorrow will be a demanding day, followed by an equally demanding night."

The hatred in her expression rights my world. There it is. The look I expect, telling me I'm back where I belong. I'm the bastard calling the shots and she is my fuck toy to break at my leisure. Nothing else, no more, just a fucking hole to fill.

As I turn to leave, I'm conscious she's dressing quickly and as soon as she is standing, I open the door and without looking back, expect her to keep up.

CHAPTER 29

ALLEGRA

Wow. One minute I hate the bastard and the next I believe I'm falling in love with him. Then he does something so appalling I hate him all over again. It's as if I have whiplash and as I struggle to keep up with him as he strides down the hallway, I can't help loving every minute of this sadistic game he is playing.

Why am I so mentally disturbed?

I follow him back the way we came and this time our elevator ride is in silence. I don't really care if I'm honest. He's the one making the rules and I'm merely following his lead. I pull the wig back over my head and set the mask in place and his brooding stare that is fixed on me tells me he's unhappy about that. Well, fuck him because he made the rules and I'm just the gullible fool following them.

We pick up his entourage at the foot of the steps and, as I follow him, they press around me like a black cloak. I feel strangely protected in this vicious circle. As if they are keeping the whole world out and, in this moment, I wish he was also out there.

I don't know why he turned on me so suddenly. One

minute he was almost caring and, dare I say it, loving. Then he switched and became the brutal bastard I'm used to. Who knows what goes on inside that turbulent mind of his, but I am past caring? I've had the day from hell, and I just want to eat and fall into a hot bath before bed.

We arrive at another elevator and as we step inside, once again we are alone.

He says gruffly, "You can take off the wig and mask now. Nobody will see you."

"Where are we going?" I ask, as I remove the obviously offending items and he says with a sigh. "Home."

He leans against the elevator wall and runs his fingers through his hair.

"You can sleep in the guest room. Just order room service and then do what the fuck you usually do when you get home at night."

"You're not joining me?" I say hopefully because he is draining my energy in so many ways with his mood swings and demands on my body.

"I must work."

"In the club?" I can't shake the surge of jealously that races through me at the thought of him repeating our performance with one of the dancers. For a moment he appears happy about my reaction and shrugs, a wicked glint in his eye as he whispers, "Maybe two this time, or three. That makes for an interesting experience."

I don't even reply because really, a foursome! What planet does this guy live on?

I stare at him in apparent disgust, and he crosses the elevator and reaches for my face, cupping it between his hands and whispering against my lips, "Don't knock it until you've tried it." His eyes flash as he whispers huskily, "Have you ever wondered what it's like to have three people work your body? Assaulting you from all angles, their sole aim to give you pleasure but damage your morality and send you down a path there is no way back from. Kissing you, fucking you, making you do unspeakable things to their bodies while they fuck yours in all ways. A mass of tangled limbs and panting bodies. Sweat joining you all together, hungry for the taste of sin. I can offer you that, princess. I can give you an experience that would be one middle finger to your family and if you ask nicely, I may even let them watch."

I push him away and snap, "You're disgusting. I hate you."

"Is that a no?" He cocks his brow and smirks.

"Of course it's a no. I've fallen low enough just by associating myself with you. That's as far as I'll go, asshole."

He laughs out loud as the elevator arrives at its destination and as we leave, I stare around in impressed awe.

"This place is amazing." I say, my bad mood evaporating in an instant.

"It's okay." He shrugs. "Anyway, make yourself at home. I may be late."

He laughs as if he's a fucking comedian and heads back the way he came, and I really couldn't care less. I need space between us to process what happened. My whole day turned to shit the minute he was waiting for me in that boardroom, and I honestly need this time to gather my dignity back around my soul.

I drop the wig and mask and prowl through his apartment, loving how tasteful it is. Chrome, mirrors, and fur, all blend together in a show of wealth only a man like him has the balls to flaunt.

I am high above the city, and I gaze down at the lights below, mindful of the people going about their business, oblivious to the sin and corruption surrounding them.

I take the opportunity to explore this space because I have never been in a penthouse before.

Much like its owner, the place is impersonal. No homey touches, just designed elegance that I'm guessing he had no part in.

As I wander through the rooms, I stare in wonder at a space so elegant I could die happy in here. I reach a bedroom that reeks of its owner and for some reason my heart flutters as I detect the aftershave that suits him so well.

I poke around in every drawer and cupboard, wandering into his closet and inhaling the masculine scent. It's all around me. Power, influence, and decadence, mixed with sin and corruption. It smells like Shade Vieri.

I make my way into his bathroom and can't resist stepping into the walk-in shower, turning on the jets and allowing myself to lose myself in pleasure. This place is a dream and I deserve it after the nightmare I stumbled into and, as I scrub my body, I note the evidence he's planted on me. Angry red marks that pucker the white skin. Scratches and bruises from his rough handling. My pussy is throbbing both from overuse and desire and I hate that I can't shake his description from my mind.

What would it be like to be part of a fantasy like that? He made it sound so appealing, even though I'd rather die than do something so shameless.

As I rub my body, I fantasize about it instead, loving how this is my own personal dream that will never be discovered.

This time I orgasm at my own hand, and it makes me laugh as I clean up, knowing he has lost control of me.

I must be delirious, high on adrenalin and so hungry food is my number one priority right now. It appears that you can't live on hot sex alone, so I towel myself off and head back into the main living area and spying a phone, I lift the receiver.

"How may I assist you?"

The voice on the other end is quick to respond and I say

falteringly, "Um, may I order a Caesar salad please and a bottle of red? Perhaps a steak too, medium and some fries. Oh, do you have any cheesecake? That would be good, possibly a pie even. Cherry perhaps."

"Anything else, madam?"

"What do you suggest?"

I'm interested in what's on offer and she says without missing a beat, *"A service perhaps. Massage, nails, or a facial. We have an experienced team on hand to cater for anything."*

I bet they do. I roll my eyes and say with a wicked smile, "A massage sounds good. You could send them up before I eat. Say, deliver the food in one hour when I'll be completely relaxed."

"Of course. Anything else, madam?"

"No. Oh, and please charge it to Mr. Vieri."

"Of course." She says, as if that was a given and as I drop the phone, I feel a shiver of devilish delight pass through me.

I may be here against my will, but I'm going to make the most of every single second of it.

CHAPTER 30

SHADE

I had to get away from her. She is confusing me, and I need to get my head straight.

Kyle is waiting and we head to my office, and I pour us both a shot of bourbon and groan.

"Fuck. What a day."

"Trouble?" He raises his eyes and I down the whiskey in one gulp and refill it immediately.

"Women."

His smirk does little for my temper, which doesn't get any better when his phone rings and his expression darkens in an instant.

"I'll get back to you," he says abruptly, cutting the call and fixing me with a worried frown.

"What?"

"That was Heather." He shakes his head in apparent disgust.

"She went to Allegra's apartment as arranged and all was good. Nobody got in her way and she used the key you had made. The apartment was empty, as promised, except for one thing."

"What?"

"A box was waiting. It was inside the apartment placed on the kitchen counter." He says with concern.

"So, it could have been delivered yesterday, and she hasn't opened it yet."

"No." He sighs heavily. "There was a note on top of it. Handwritten in blood."

"In blood! What the hell!"

I stare at him in shock, and he says in disgust. "It told her to be careful. She has blood on her hands and if she wants to avoid a similar fate, to take twenty-thousand dollars to the alley off third street tomorrow at seven pm. To leave it in a black holdall in a dumpster and if she tells anyone, the next victim will be her brother."

"What was in the box?"

I dread to think, and he hisses, "A heart. A festering, disgusting, rank heart that must have been dead for a while. Heather said she can't stay there. It's unsafe and too vile and now she's waiting for your instruction."

"Fuck!" I run my fingers through my hair and wonder what the fuck is going on. Just imagining Allegra coming home to that makes my blood boil and I start to pace behind my desk before saying roughly, "Heather stays. Tell her to call it in. This shit is spiraling out of our control. She knows what to do."

"Call it in?"

"Yes, Kyle. She's a fucking cop, isn't she? I know she's a bent one, but she's still a fucking cop. Tell her to call the goddamned precinct and let them fucking deal with this."

"Don't you want to check with your brother first?"

Kyle's words are like gasoline on a flame, and I yell, "No, I don't want to run it by my fucking brother, grandfather, or God himself! I make the decisions in this part of the business and I'm deciding to call the fucking cops! Got it!"

He nods and calls her back, relaying my instructions with a firm tone and as I pour another shot of whiskey, my mind fills with murderous rage.

Grabbing my phone, I call my brother, despite my outburst and when he answers, I say roughly, "We have a problem, and you are *not* going to like it."

"Tell me." As always, he is calm and undeterred and as I tell him everything, the Judge's visit, the switch I made and the subsequent discovery, he makes me wait with a long pause before he speaks.

"Fuck, Shade, you have been busy."

"I aways am," I remind him because while Killian is dealing with one part of my grandfather's plan, I am left to shovel the shit as always.

"That's a good plan, Shade." He says after a while, and it shocks me a little into silence.

"Keep the doppelganger in place and continue. Build a case against her uncle, father, call him what you like, and I'll get the cops on our payroll to investigate this blackmail attempt." He says practically. *"Keep her safe until I tell you otherwise."*

"Until what, Killian?" I know my brother and, like me, he isn't averse to using anyone to further our interests at the expense of their own, and he sighs. *"Until I discover a way to use her to our advantage. All the time she's under your control, she's safe. To a point, that is."* He laughs, but I'm not returning it.

"We'll cut her free when the time is right and leave her to tear her family apart from the inside out. Meanwhile, I'll increase the pressure on Jefferson and see where that takes us."

His tone lightens. *"I have a good feeling about this one, Shade. It appears that Judge Stevenson's fall from grace is just around the corner, and I can't fucking wait to see that smug bastard crumble."*

He laughs darkly and whispers, *"I've got to go. We have dinner reservations with the man himself."*

"Judge Stevenson?"

"Yes. I wonder if his wife, Mary, knows. It was arranged so he can strike a deal with me for our silence. It's obvious he got nowhere with you, and I received the call a couple of hours ago. He seemed mighty pissed. It was quite amusing, and he demanded a meeting tonight."

"It's not like you to give into demands." I say tartly, and his voice settles over me like a demon's breath. *"Only when it suits me, brother. You should know that more than most. I'm interested in what he wants and prepared to give him nothing. My perfect kind of evening. Enjoy yours."*

He cuts the call and for some reason, it's as if a huge burden has left me. I can leave that with him and leave the cops to him, which only leaves me with one job to do. The woman currently pampering herself in my apartment.

I turn to Kyle and say with a deep sigh.

"I'm heading off to bed. Tomorrow is another day."

He nods. "Any instructions?"

"Just sleep, Kyle. Sleep or fuck, I don't care what you do to relax. I'll see you in the morning."

As I leave my right-hand man, I almost envy him his position. He gets to enjoy a certain kind of freedom. I do not. I am part of the well-oiled Vieri machine and there is always something or someone wanting to mess with it.

CHAPTER 31

ALLEGRA

I'm relaxed for the first time in forever. As the masseuse rubs oil all over my body, I almost groan with pleasure. I could live like this. Secured away in a penthouse with a wall of menace protecting me. Enjoying sessions like this one and a hot man to fulfill my fantasies.

That is how I view Shade Vieri. He is my dark side. The part of me I hide from respectable people. He pushes me over a cliff every single time and I just pick myself up and run back to the top so he can do it all over again.

I'm not even sure what we have going on. I know I'm only here because of the hatred he has against Judge Stevenson. I can only think of him in that way now. He is no longer family. Not my uncle and definitely not…

"Relax." The calm voice of Ingrid, the masseuse, chase away my disturbing thoughts and she says softly, "Try to empty your mind. Search for your happy place and hide out there for a while. You are so tense. It's not good for you."

She sounds disapproving, and she probably is. My body must resemble a battle scene with all the marks and scratches that decorate it. I'm guessing she's not shocked, though. She's probably seen it all before because of the man in charge around here.

Is he my happy place? I certainly can't stop thinking about him, but it's with a mixture of helplessness and desire. Hatred and venom. One minute he is everything I ever wanted and the next everything I didn't want. He is a man of multiple personalities and I never know which one I'm getting.

I kind of like that. Maybe he is my happy place because I can't stop thinking about him.

I try so hard not to. To think about a life without him where everything is normal. I am successful in public relations. I have my own agency that knocks The Social Queen off the top spot. I am rich and have a hot boyfriend. An actor perhaps, successful in his own right, or a model. Somebody who adores me. Who makes me happy. *Who is boring.*

It's no use. Shade Vieri has crept under my skin and is attacking my immune system from within. He is slowly destroying me, and I don't have an antidote.

Ingrid steps in and drags my mind back to relaxation and says softly, "I'll play some music. That may distract you."

I nod and attempt to clear my mind. It's easier said than done though because wild dark eyes stare at me from my subconscious. That insanely handsome face with a dark shadow to his jaw, his dark flashing eyes promising to strip me of my dignity. His hair is unruly, much like the man himself, and hangs just above his neckline, wild and unkempt, exactly like him.

That body tempts me every single time, from the tanned skin and rippling muscles, his biceps decorated with tribal ink. He is all man and all-encompassing, and I desire him almost as much as I hate him. What's that song? I hate myself for loving you. That's playing on repeat in my mind when he is around. Love may be a strong word to use when it concerns him, but he's a man who drags out strong words and strong emotions. There really is no other kind where it concerns him.

The hands that push against my skin are now different somehow. Harder, rougher, and less careful. I stiffen as the scent of mischief and my downfall flood my senses and I hate the shiver of desire that passes through me as a husky whisper disturbs my solitude, "Honey, I'm home."

He drags his rough lips against my neck and bites softly, sucking the skin that apparently exists only for his pleasure.

A brutal man likes brutal pleasure, and he is more deserving of that title than most.

"I thought you were working." I whisper into the bench I am lying on and he laughs softly. "I decided to work on you instead."

"Again?" I grin and as his hand runs down my back and dips between my thighs, he says huskily, "You make me a workaholic."

"Or a sex addict." I reply as he spins me around and places his finger to his lips. "Shh, you're meant to be relaxing."

"Then leave." I smile, not really meaning a word of it.

He chuckles softly and then grasps an eye mask from the table and slips it across my eyes, saying huskily, "Now you can't see what I'm going to do. You are at my mercy, and I control every part of you."

"Still dreaming I see." I gasp as something cold presses against my left breast making me jump and then he replaces it with his hot lips, causing me to moan softly.

As he continues to kiss a light trail across my body, I whisper, "Um, Ingrid has gone, hasn't she?"

He chuckles against my left breast, "What if I said no?"

"Seriously!" I make to move, and he presses me down and says with amusement, "She's gone. It's just me and you and a whole night of fun before us."

"You're going to be the death of me, Shade." I groan as I lie back, loving his hands working my body with a firm pressure, interspersed with hot kisses and dirty touches.

As massages go, I am having the best one ever and I'm almost certain it's because of the man doing it.

His image fills my mind, and I can't get him out of my head. Knowing he is here is turning me on and the anticipation of what he can do is almost as delicious as when he's doing it.

There is not an inch of my body that doesn't feel his touch and I have never been as relaxed as I am in this moment. When his face dips between my thighs, I groan out loud as he coaxes me to an orgasm that ripples through my body, cleansing it of any stress and replacing the madness with euphoria.

I could be in my own little world. It's as if I am floating on a fluffy white cloud suspended above reality. There is no pain, no passion even, just complete and utter relaxation.

A gentle touch to my face makes me smile as he whispers, "You are so beautiful, baby girl. Has anyone ever told you that?"

I open my eyes and stare into two velvet pools of lustful desire, and it strikes me that I have never seen him like this. His guard has been dropped and the softer side of him emerges. It makes me reach up and cup his face in my hand, loving how he leans into it. I rub my thumb against his rough stubble and smile. "Why can't I stay mad at you?"

His hand covers mine and his expression is almost vulnerable as he says in the barest whisper, "I don't want to lose you, Ally."

I stare at him in shock, almost as if I misheard what he said and the light dies a little in his eye as he says huskily, "We need to talk."

The easy atmosphere is replaced by one of tension and I shift so I'm sitting up, concerned about what's happened.

He smiles ruefully and reaches for the gown I was wearing when Ingrid arrived.

"Here. The food will be here soon. We should talk and eat."

"How do you know I ordered food?" I'm mildly curious and he grins, a little of the old Shade returning.

"I know *everything*, Ally, especially when it concerns you. Don't ever try to hide anything from me because it won't work."

I'm not sure why I'm happy about that. Probably because I've lost my mind around him. He has made me into a weak puppet where he is concerned, and I really should buy a book on feminism to study because I am seriously letting the sisterhood down.

Cecilia would be outraged at the things I let him do, but I can't help it. It's him. The man with the ability to control my emotions. Who makes me want to do things I shouldn't and who lights up my world with one touch or a wicked grin in my direction.

My heart flutters when I'm near him and when he's not, he's in my head instead. How did this happen and so quickly? Why do I want him and why am I dreading what happens in a few days' time?

CHAPTER 32

SHADE

Allegra Powell has broken me. I know that now. I want to do cruel, wicked things to her for my amusement, but only me. The thought of anyone even near her is causing me an anxiety I haven't felt before. Knowing there is someone out there who wants to harm her makes the wild beast inside me feral. I want to hunt them down and rip them apart for having her name in their thoughts at all. I *will* find them, and I *will* use every tool at my disposable, even the legal ones.

Kyle was astonished I'm involving the cops. We *never* involve them. If anything, we do everything in our power not to. But Heather is well placed to discover the information I badly need because as soon as they have a suspect, I will remove them from life. I'm almost salivating at the idea of that, and I experienced an overwhelming need to get back to her. To protect her, to spend time with her because somehow Allegra Powell isn't my victim anymore. She is my world.

When I saw her lying on the massage bench, naked and covered in oil, I almost came on the spot. Ingrid was working her body which turned me on so much, I jerked my thumb at her to leave.

I wanted to touch her so badly it was overwhelming and as the masseuse tiptoed out of my suite, I replaced her soft hands with mine.

Nobody touches this woman but me. Only me and fuck our agreement. I have changed the rules because now I want her, Allegra Powell is going nowhere.

So, it's time to spell it out for her and to solve her problem so I can get on with the business of chaining her to me —forever.

As she takes her seat at the dining table by the window, there's a knock on the door and the waiter pushes the trolley into the room and averts his eyes as they are trained to do. A silent servant, which is the best kind there is.

I press one hundred dollars into his hand, and he exits immediately, leaving me to serve my lady with her choice of food.

"Are you really this hungry?" I laugh as I set more food before her than is humanly possible to eat.

"I must have known you'd be joining me." She shrugs and points to the seat opposite her.

"I hope you approve of my choices."

"It will do." I grin as I divide the dishes between the two of us and she giggles. "I never had you down as a waiter, Shade."

"There's a lot you don't know about me." I shrug as I heap salad on her plate. "I can cook. I can clean if I must and wash my own clothes. I make a mean coq-au-vin and my hobby is painting."

I stare at her with interest. "Your turn."

"Well." She pretends to think and looks so adorable I can't tear my eyes from her.

"I like to jet ski, obviously." She grins. "I like to dance, usually in clubs, and I like to fuck on boats so anyone can see. Some may call me an exhibitionist because of it."

She spears a cube of meat on her fork and says with a sparkle in her eye, "I love to travel and post photographs of myself in compromising positions and rebel against my parents. Then there's the darker side of me."

"The darker side. I'd like to know more about that." I say with amusement, and she leans forward, the robe falling open, offering me a feast of a different kind.

"There's the side of me who goes out in the dead of night and meets criminals in dark alleys. The wild, carefree side of me that jumps into helicopters with strange men and allows them to fuck me on the first date. That's the kind of woman I am Shade, and if you don't mind me saying, your hobbies are a lot lamer than mine."

For the first time in forever, I laugh out loud. It's as if the dark clouds lifted and everything's right with my world. We are two people enjoying one another's company, doing something millions of other people are doing right now. Having dinner together and talking and I like it—a lot.

I don't entertain in my home. I don't talk to women for pleasure. I don't even ask them anything about themselves that doesn't benefit me. Now I realize how much I missed out on. The closeness, the intimacy of two like-minded people, doesn't always have to involve sex. It's a meeting of minds too. An interest in what they are thinking and what makes them the person they are.

I almost consider carrying on our delightful evening and ditching the real reason I came home so early, but as Allegra reaches for her wine glass, I sigh heavily and stare at her with my usual dark expression.

"What?" Her glass hovers in mid-air as she senses the change in the atmosphere, and I say with a hint of anger.

"There is something I need to tell you, and you won't like it."

"Okay." She takes a long chug of her drink and sets the glass down. "Hit me with it."

"Your double who is currently pretending to be you in your brother's apartment has news."

"What happened?" She appears anxious and I reach out and grasp her hand tightly in mine and say carefully, "There was a package waiting, addressed to you."

She tenses and I say quickly, "On the counter in the kitchen."

"How?" Her eyes widen.

"Who put it there? Is Rafferty back, my mom even?"

"Are they the only ones with a key?" I ask and she nods, her eyes wide and filled with fear.

"Yes."

"Are you sure about that, baby girl? Think hard."

"I'm sure, unless Rafferty gave anyone else a key, but he never said."

I reach for my phone and type out a quick text to Kyle to question the doorman and check the cameras. Something I'm almost certain he would have done already by now.

"What was in the box?" She sounds afraid to ask and I tell her straight.

"A heart."

"As in…"

"A human heart. At least we think it was."

Her eyes fill with tears, and I hate that I've destroyed her perfect evening, and her eyes are bright as she whispers, "Do you think it was Taylor's?"

"Possibly, or they may want you to think it was."

She shakes her head, obviously struggling to deal with this.

"Was there anything else? A note perhaps?"

"Yes." I grip her hand tightly again and say carefully, "It appeared to be written in blood and asked for twenty-thousand dollars to be left at a location in a black holdall tomorrow evening. If you don't deliver, the next heart you receive will be your brothers."

"No!" Her face crumbles and the tears follow quickly. She is devastated, and fear is written over her entire face.

"Please, Shade, please stop this." She sobs and I say gently.

"I'm doing the best I can, baby. As I said, there is something you should know."

She wipes the tears away with the back of her hand and her voice shakes as she whispers, "What?"

"Heather is an undercover cop. She's not really a dancer at my club. I'm not saying she doesn't pretend to be, but she works for the cops and passes them information I want her to."

"I don't understand." She stares at me in confusion, and I shrug. "It's all about knowledge, princess, and knowing a person's limits. Heather's is money, not honor, and I pay her far more than she earns at the precinct. She has a sick mother in New Jersey, and we pay her nursing home fees. The cops don't know about her mom and that's why she works for me. Family is everything and always will be, and she does what she can to help hers."

"So, what will happen now?" Her lower lip trembles and I hate dragging her into this filthy world I inhabit and say with a sigh. "I protect you."

"How?"

My heart is hammering because there is no doubt in my mind that I will kill for her—again and she may not like what I am or what I represent but I'm not letting her go, so I say darkly, "You are moving in with me. Permanently."

CHAPTER 33

ALLEGRA

It's as if he is firing a machine gun loaded with shocks, not shot and the bullets are flying all around me.

"Move in?" Strange that's all I can think of when he has told me so many other more shocking things.

He shrugs, staring at me with an intensity that causes my breath to desert me.

"Our deal has changed. I'm not letting you leave — ever."

"I'm your prisoner." My eyes are wide, and he nods, those damned eyes drawing me into his dark and twisted world.

"Yes. You see, princess, your only chance of surviving this is with me fighting your corner. You need me to shield you and there is no one more qualified for the job."

"But you said forever." I stare at him in shock, and he nods. "I did."

"Forever is a long time."

"Forever is as long as I'm good at what I do, and don't let an assassin finish what many start."

For some reason, his words sadden me. I never considered his world, really. Never thought about what it must be like to live with constant threats. It kind of makes me understand him a little more and why he surrounds himself with protection. Why he is so reckless and living life to the extreme. He is fitting a lifetime of living into what time he is allowed, and that cuts me deeper than anything else I've heard. I kind of get it too. I am living under the same cloud. I am being threatened and realize how hard it is to deal with.

I don't even think and drop his hand and push back my chair, rounding the table to sit on his lap, wrapping my arms around him and pressing my face to his chest.

His arms lock around me and as he dips his face into my hair, I whisper, "We need each other."

This is the moment when my life changes forever. I am going nowhere. I realize that now. He has crashed into my life and *become* my life. He is my wild adventure that I am desperate to continue. We shouldn't be compatible, but we are. It appears that chalk and cheese do go together and make something wonderful.

I love being with him. He heightens every sense I possess and offers me some I don't. He is everything I've been searching for and everything I thought I didn't want. He is —everything.

We sit hugging for a while and then he whispers, "You need your sleep. It's close to one in the morning. Tomorrow will be a busy one."

I groan. "I must be at work at eight and I've done nothing for the campaign at all."

He laughs softly. "I wouldn't say that. The dance was pretty convincing, and I'm guessing you have a greater understanding of my business now."

"You thought I was good?" I raise my eyes and he kisses me softly and whispers, "Don't go getting any ideas about a career change, though. I'm happy with the one you have, although we may have to revisit that later."

"Why?"

"Because it will demand more of your time away from me, and I'm not sure I can live with that."

"Asshole." I smack his hand away and he grins.

"Come on baby, I'm taking you to bed—to sleep."

We walk from the room hand in hand, and it's kind of nice. As if we are a proper couple now. It makes me laugh, which is an odd reaction after I've been told that someone is out to get me, harm my family and I am now imprisoned by the mafia. Mind you, the way my life is going, this is just another day at the office.

"What's so funny?" he asks, a gentle smile on his face and I grin. "I was thinking we're like a proper couple now. Does that mean you are my boyfriend?"

It's almost ridiculous thinking of a man like Shade Vieri as boyfriend material and he raises my hand to his lips and whispers, "Get used to it baby, but not too used to it."

"Why not?" My heart falls, sensing this is just a temporary position, and he spins me around into his arms, his dark eyes heavy with lust, as he whispers, "The way I'm feeling now you won't be my girlfriend for long. You'll soon be my wife."

I stare at him in amazement, the dark night sky a backdrop to the most life-changing moment of my life. It's almost poetic as from the shadows emerged a man of such darkness, he is even named after them. My husband. My deliciously dark husband and I can't help the huge smile that reveals I am more than happy about that.

"You do realize my mom won't like you." I add, and he shrugs.

"I can live with that."

"My father will despise you."

He nods. "He'll come round."

"My brother will be fascinated by you."

"That goes without saying."

"Then there's my uncle." I laugh softly. "We both know what he thinks about you already."

He reaches up and drags my lips to his and whispers, "I don't give a fuck what any of them think. You are mine and there is fuck all they can do about that."

He kisses me long, leisurely, and slow. As if we have all the time in the world and I really hope we do. Any time I spend with him is worth a lifetime with someone else. He is the star in my darkest sky, showing me the way. He is bad to the bone, and I love every dark, jagged edge of his soul. I have fallen into depravity, and I am more than happy about that.

* * *

The alarm sounds and it's still dark outside.

"What?" I sit upright and stare around me in confusion, the unfamiliar room looming out of the shadows, slowly reminding me of where I am and who with.

A low groan beside me tells me I wasn't dreaming and the fact I'm still aching between my thighs reminds me of the hot sex we enjoyed until we passed out just an hour ago.

"You are kidding me." I stare at the clock illuminated on the bedside stand and groan loudly.

"We had one hour's sleep. I don't need a stalker to finish me off. You'll do that on your own."

He laughs softly and pulls me back against his chest.

"It was fun ruining you, baby girl. Now I get to do it for the rest of my life."

I smile against his chest because that's a promise I hope he keeps knowing I will die happy being ruined by him.

"What's the plan?" I ask, hoping he tells me to go back to sleep, but he tangles his fingers in my hair and says with a sigh, "We shower, dress, and eat. Then you head to your office and work on my campaign while I work on yours."

"Mine?"

"Finding the bastard who is doing this."

It reminds me of what's at stake and I say fearfully, "I don't want anything to happen to you." I groan. "Now I've got someone even more reckless to cause me anxiety."

He laughs as he kisses my head and whispers, "You know me, princess, I can take care of myself. Worry about the bastard who doesn't see me coming."

With reluctant acceptance, I do as he says, and we shower together, no time for anything but cleanliness and when we dry off, I'm surprised when he jerks his thumb toward the closet beside his and says, "There's an outfit in there you can change into for work."

"Since when?" I ask, my eyes wide, and he grins. "I kind of planned for you staying overnight, remember, and decided to indulge my fantasy a little."

"Dear God, what will Evangeline say? You've dressed me as a whore, haven't you?"

I'm not sure how many more of his games I can endure, and he laughs out loud.

"No. Quite the opposite, in fact. I like my women corruptible, as I'm sure you've discovered. I think you'll like it."

I'm like an eager puppy as I leave him standing there and head to the 'hers' closet beside his.

There is one outfit hanging up and my eyes sparkle as I lift it down from the rail. It's a beautiful white dress that hangs just above the knee. The top is cut in a low v, and it cinches around my waist, two splits on either side that show my thighs as I move but rest demurely above my knees when I'm standing. The sheer silk stockings fasten to a garter of silk lace and the soft white leather shoes have a sharp silver stiletto heel resembling a weapon. I will never admit this, but I love it.

The lacey white Basque makes my tits look amazing and holds them in place like a careful lover. The dress clings to my waist and flares at my hips, making me feel sexy and smart both at the same time. There is nothing I don't love about this outfit. It's business chic at its finest and as I apply subtle makeup and tie my long hair into a chic bun, I could conquer the world.

I head out into the bedroom and a burst of longing shoots through my entire body. There he is. My bad boy watching my approach with a dark, predatory gaze.

His hair is combed and the dark stubble on his face is sexy and rough. He is wearing his customary black business suit with a black shirt; this time open enough to see his toned body. He looks every inch mafia, and I never realized it has fast become my favorite look.

He watches me with an expression that tells me he likes what he sees. His eyes flash and it's as if I'm the only person in the world and his attention is focused solely on me. I love it. Some may say it's intimidating, but I crave his attention. Since I met him, I blossom under his lustful gaze and now our situation has changed I don't fear this ending. Last night changed our relationship. I should have been scared, resisted him, and told him to fuck off because why does he get to dictate my life? I don't care though because I only want to be with him anyway, so why fight something that is everything I want?

He nods his approval and says in his sexy, husky voice, "Come here."

I hate that I melt at the command in his voice. I hate the woman I become around him, but most of all I hate the fact I'm leaving him to go to work.

I can't get over there quickly enough and as he pulls me into his arms, I shake my head. "You know, if my friend Cessy could see me now, she would be so angry."

"Why?" He dusts his lips against my ear, and I sigh. "Because I am allowing you to control me."

"Would that be the same friend who spent the entire weekend tied up on Kyle's bed?" He says with amusement, and I pull back and stare at him in shock, "Excuse me."

He laughs softly. "He is quite taken with your wild friend. I've never seen him so obsessed and apparently, she feels the same. They are meeting up this weekend to carry on where they left off, so before you question your own choices, perhaps you should ask her about hers."

"Wow." I shake my head, wondering what was in the champagne that night at Gyration. Cessy is the strongest woman I've met and imagining her being told what to do by any man is a plot twist I definitely never saw coming.

Shade leans in and kisses me slowly, lighting the desire inside me almost on contact and so I pull away and say rather crossly, "No."

"No?"

He raises his eyes and I attempt to push him away.

"I am washed and wearing an amazing outfit and I don't have a change of underwear. I need to keep a cool head and a dry set of panties for the day ahead, so if you don't mind, can you ruin me later when I don't have to face the disapproving stare of Evangeline Solomon while I explain I have done fuck all about your campaign."

It makes him laugh out loud and as he releases me, I suffer the loss already, causing me to sigh heavily.

"Let's eat to distract my mind. You really shouldn't look so hot in the morning, Shade, it's just not fair."

He reaches for my hand and twists my fingers in his and says with a wicked smile.

"Then prepare to be ruined later when I fuck you in that dress bent over my desk."

He winks. "I will fantasize about that all day so don't be late home. Six thirty on the dot, or I'll punish you."

The fact that turns me on even more makes me wonder if I need therapy. I'm guessing I probably do because this can't be normal. Surely.

CHAPTER 34

SHADE

It was strange waking up with someone in my bed. What was even stranger was how much I liked it. Having someone to hold at night is a pleasure I never realized I'd enjoy and now as we head toward The Social Queen, I feel a strange sense of loss, knowing we will be apart for the entire day. I don't like it and I don't like not having eyes on her. Until the bastard responsible for blackmailing her is caught, she's not safe.

"I really could have taken a cab."

She squeezes my fingers, that have been firmly entwined with hers for the duration of the journey, and I say irritably, "And risk your safety. I don't think so."

"They're not that bad at driving." She laughs and I say roughly, "I'm not sure you've grasped how serious this is, Ally."

Her hold tightens on me, and I snap, "I live with threats to me twenty-four seven and I take steps to minimize them. Do you think I enjoy traveling with a dark army surrounding me? Do you think I enjoy watching my back and hoping the men I pay do a good job of protecting me? All my life I've lived not knowing if I'll see the sunrise and now I have twice the worry because you are now part of this world whether you like it or not. Someone is blackmailing you for Christ's sake, and you are now an attractive target for my enemies, so forgive me if I'm a little overprotective but deal with it."

Her silence tells me my words scored a direct hit and then she says with a sigh, "I'm sorry, Shade. I never really thought of it before."

"That's why I'm doing the thinking for both of us. Do me a favor and stay inside that office. Don't venture out for lunch, coffee, or any shit shopping you may need. Just do your job while I do mine."

I turn and hate the worry that now fills her expression and, grasping her face in my hands, I say with a groan. "I hate how much I want you, princess. I wish I didn't care, but I do. If I'm a bastard, it's because I must be, just to keep you safe."

"I know." She kisses me lightly on the lips and then sighs. "Make it go away, Shade. Tell me what I can do to help. I hate seeing you like this."

If anything, I'm shocked at how simple words hold so much power. The concern in her eyes and the soft, loving look she gives me makes me want to hold on to her and never let go. Nobody has ever feared for me before outside of family. Nobody really cares. They just want what I can give them. They don't see me as a person, not really, and it's only now I realize how incredibly lonely I've been until I met her.

Until I met my little spitfire. My princess. The woman I set out to ruin but has ruined me instead. I'm a different man around her, a better man perhaps, and so as I crush my lips to hers, I don't care if I've messed up her lipstick. I don't care that I mess up her hair and I hope to God I've messed up her panties.

* * *

Ten minutes later, I watch her run into The Social Queen's building with a flushed face and lipstick smeared all over it. I'm in no doubt at all she will head straight for the restroom to repair the damage of the ride over. I couldn't stop if I tried and a quick fuck on the way to work is to be recommended.

I watch my guard follow her in and know he is in for the day from hell babysitting my woman, because if she attempts to leave this building, he will stop her.

Kyle steps into the car from the passenger seat up front and only when she is inside the building does the car move away from the kerb, sandwiched between two similar ones.

"What's the plan?" he wastes no time in asking.

"I'm going to pay my brother a visit."

"Chicago?" Kyle doesn't sound shocked about that because we fly between states like we're taking a cab and I shake my head. "Not this time. He's in New York on business and I'm interested in how it went."

"The Judge?"

I nod. "He requested a meeting with him last night. I'm guessing it has a lot to do with Allegra."

"He did seem pissed." Kyle chuckles.

"The plan worked." I reply and shrug as if it's just another day at the office.

He grins and I note a text flash up on his phone that he quickly swipes away.

"Who was that?"

He sighs, leaning back in his seat.

"Allegra's friend."

"I thought you found your one." I tease him and he rolls his eyes.

"It's only a bit of fun."

"So, she's not arriving this weekend as planned."

"I didn't say that."

"Then what?"

"Women like Cecilia like to grip a man by the balls. They want to bring him in line and start calling the shots, regardless of the reasons that attracted them in the first place."

"Now I get it." I roll my eyes.

"So, you're teaching her who's in control?"

"Of course. No woman is going to make me jump. She needs to learn how I operate."

"Good luck with that."

He shrugs. "It's fun playing the game, but only if I'm assured of winning."

"And they call me an asshole." It makes me laugh and I picture Allegra frantically making herself look respectable and know where he's coming from. She told me not to mess her up, but I went there anyway, and she loved every fucking minute of it. I understand Kyle, because playing the game is what we thrive on. How long that game lasts is up to us because there is nowhere to hide in the world if we want something and right now, what I want the most is the fucker threatening my woman.

* * *

WE ARRIVE at Killian's apartment and head for the underground parking lot. We have a pass and security knows we are coming in advance with a protected password that changes every visit. Once again, it reminds me of the lengths we go to keep alive, and I'm weary of it.

Kyle joins me in the private elevator to Kill's penthouse and he will meet with Saint, my brother's right-hand man. They swap intelligence and work together. We are a close-knit team and trust one another with our lives.

The door opens and Saint is waiting with a nod of respect.

"Mr. Vieri. Your brother is waiting on the terrace."

"Thanks."

I leave them to disappear and head up the staircase toward the top of the building, which enjoys one of the finest views in New York.

I step into the sunshine and see Kill enjoying breakfast, overlooking the skyline along with Purity, his wife. She smiles happily when she sees me and stands, heading toward me and kissing me three times.

"It's good to see you, Shade."

I catch Kill's expression and smirk because I have never met anyone so overprotective in my life as he is with her. Even family get the death stare when she transfers her attention to them and I play up to it by saying, "You are a vision, Purity. The sun is no comparison to such a beauty."

"Sit the fuck down." Kill growls and shakes his head as I drop her a wink and shrug out of my jacket, rolling up my sleeves to enjoy the warm sunshine.

Purity remains standing and heads to her husband's side, dropping a light kiss on his lips before saying in her sweet voice, "I must go. I have a charity event to attend before we leave."

I watch with amusement the irritation in his eyes as he says roughly, "How long will you be?"

"Two hours. I'm meeting Adelaide Southgate to discuss the donation for the shelter."

Kill says harshly, "Two hours at the most. Julian will accompany you."

She smiles and then turns, rolling her eyes and dropping me a cheeky wink as she leaves.

I'm not sure how he managed it, but Killian scored big when he met Purity. I've never met a woman like her in my life. So unspoiled, so innocent and yet incredibly brave and able to put up with Kill's shit. She deserves a fucking medal for it, but I can tell she is happy. Especially now she is carrying his child.

It's a sobering thought and once again my mind switches to Allegra. I wonder what she will look like swollen with my child. It shocks me a little because I always vowed never to marry—until her. In fact, it's as if my life was on hold until she walked into that alley and stole my heart.

"Lucas Stevenson." Killian drags my mind to business, and I lean forward, desperate for information.

He chuckles softly. "It was an interesting evening. You have pissed him off so much it was enjoyable watching him lose his shit."

"I wonder what his wife thought of that?" I pour myself a coffee and Kill grins.

"I could tell she was confused. He was on edge the entire time and kept snapping at her. Luckily, Purity managed the situation and took her off to the restroom, leaving me with her extremely irate husband."

"I wish I had been there." I really mean that, and Killian nods.

"Yes, it was enjoyable and to cut a long story short, he wants your head on a platter."

"I'm sure." I shrug and I love how Kill's eyes gleam with vindictive rage as he hisses, "He dared threaten me. He told me that unless you are brought in line, he would call a meeting of the Dark Lords and bring our exclusion forward. He would have you up on a murder charge and make sure you get life with no hope of parole. He will ruin our operation and put word out that Gold Hawk Enterprises is finished, and any contracts I have will be withdrawn."

"And his conditions?" I'm mildly interested, knowing how my brother will have reacted to those demands and Kill growls, "Our silence. Return his daughter to her family and walk away. To keep the hell out of his way and his family and, how did he put it, crawl back into the gutter where we belong."

Killian is angry. I see it in his eyes, and I almost pity Lucas Stevenson for what he has unleashed. Kill is becoming the respectable face of our business but is still the don in waiting of the Vieri mafia and threats like those will not go well for the man making them.

"So, your plan is…?" I ask, spreading marmalade on a croissant and he sneers, "Destroy him, his family and his reputation."

"Business as usual then."

"Of course." He pours himself some more coffee, black as he likes it, and says with an evil glint in his eye.

"Saint has been investigating your problem."

Now he has my full attention and I fix him with a dark stare of my own.

"And?"

"Do you remember a few months ago when Domenico Ortega was arrested on suspicion of murder? The victim was found outside his mansion with their heart cut out."

"I remember."

"Well, it appears it became a trend and was done in the name of the Dark Lords."

He sighs irritably. "Mario Bachini was going rogue and using our good name for rituals involving rape, torture, and murder. The Ortegas dealt with him and his miserable father, our uncle Carlos."

"So, you think someone is copying that? The heart thing is to prove a point. Someone who knows the history, someone who knew the Matassos."

"I do." He sips his drink and, as he sets it down, he shakes his head. "Gina reported back regarding Jefferson."

"And?"

"He's been talking to Freddie Connor."

"That two-bit villain. Risky."

"He's obviously desperate."

He smiles, a deliciously dark smile that makes me relax almost immediately. I can always rely on my brother to rise to the occasion, and it's obvious he has.

"Gina overheard a conversation with a man called Victor Gregory."

"The lawyer?"

"Apparently so. He was angry. He was yelling and neglected to close the door to his den, and didn't realize Gina had let herself in. Anyway, she recorded his side for my eager ears and the upshot was he was referring to your visitor."

"Allegra?" My blood runs cold as Killian nods.

"He was shouting that she gets a cut of his father's will over his dead body and there must be something they can do to change it. He called her and her brother bastards, who have no right to his inheritance."

I lean back as everything becomes clear and I shake my head and say thoughtfully, "Am I mistaken in thinking Jefferson was good friends with Mario Bachini? Such good friends that he wasn't averse to taking part in a few rituals himself?"

Killian grins. "You know, I heard that too. What a small world."

We share a look because Gina has outdone herself this time. We have our motive, and we have our man. Now we need to mess with his plan.

CHAPTER 35

ALLEGRA

Alice is a godsend. A miracle worker and a star. Somehow, I made myself look respectable and as soon as I arrived in my office, there was a coffee waiting for me and a broad smile on Alice's face.

"I've been working on the campaign." She says almost before I close the door.

"I figured we needed an angle. Something to draw the crowds in. An incentive even. Something with a short timeline, blink or you'll miss it kind of thing."

"That sounds great. What do you have in mind?"

Her face falls. "I don't know. I've tossed a few ideas around, but they've been done before. It needs to be something enticing. A must attend kind of evening."

"Evening?" I raise my eyes.

"Yes." She grins. "I don't pretend to know a lot about lap-dancing clubs, but I can guess. We need to understand the clientele. Discover what they like, why they go there and what makes them tick."

As I remember my own experience of that club, I wonder if I should tell her.

She taps her pen on the desk and appears thoughtful.

"An event perhaps. A golden ticket to something amazing. We have such a small window of opportunity we need to go all in on this."

"I've got it." I stare at her as the lightbulb goes off in my head.

"Fantasy."

"I don't understand." She looks puzzled as I stand up and begin pacing around the office, the dots connecting in my head as I speak.

"We could call it fantasy night. Be whoever you want to be."

"Fancy dress?" She looks doubtful, and I laugh.

"No. Masquerade. Everyone wears a mask concealing their identity. That way nobody need worry about being seen by their boss or their wife, husband, or whoever else they would prefer to avoid. Nobody knows who you are, and you get to enjoy the facilities anonymously. Tickets can be purchased online, and no personal details will be revealed. All they must do is turn up on the night and enjoy the show."

She stares at me thoughtfully as she processes the information, and I say with excitement. "We could call it the golden ticket night. Anonymity guaranteed. A night when you can step outside normality and be anyone you want to be."

"Do you think it will work?" she says doubtfully, and I nod.

"I *know* it will work." I grin, loving her surprised smile because if she had seen me last night dressed like a whore while I wiggled my hips on the owner's lap, she would be staring at me with a very different expression right now. The fact my uncle, father, it doesn't really matter now, walked in and didn't recognize me, tests my theory.

She appears to be deep in thought and then her eyes light

up and she grins. "Let's do it. We'll start work on it immediately."

* * *

THE DAY PASSES SO QUICKLY I'm surprised when she sighs and peers at her wristwatch. "It's nearly time for your meeting with Miss. Solomon. I'll assemble the file and wish you luck at the same time."

She rolls her eyes and heads outside to her desk, leaving me alone for the first time today.

I have been so involved in my work I even skipped lunch and now I'm hungry.

Hoping there's an old bar of something to keep me going in my purse, I open it and notice my phone is lit up like a Christmas tree.

Fuck! I forgot to check my phone.

Most of them are from my mom and a couple from my dad. Then there's a text from Cessy and I'm disappointed to notice none from Shade. Bastard. It makes me smile, loving the silent treatment. I've been out with clingy guys before and it makes me mad. Suffocates me and gives me the ick. Nothing about Shade gives me the ick. I hate him most of the time, but then he redeems himself and I fall harder the next time. It's an impossible situation.

Feeling quite brave for a moment, I decide to face the music and dial my mom's number, knowing I have ten minutes at the most before I must leave for my meeting, which will give me a good excuse to cut her off.

"Allegra." Her sharp voice radiates disapproval and I sigh inside.

"Mom. I'm sorry I missed your calls. I've been busy."

"Oh yes, Allegra. I can see exactly how busy you've been. Three days of doing things that have ruined your life. Three days of

staging a rebellion for God only knows what. How could you? Have you no self-respect?"

I let her rant, but I'm only half listening. Whatever she says means nothing because she's a fine one to talk and if anyone has let the side down, it's her.

I can't help firing back.

"At least I'm single. I'm not hurting anyone."

"What's that supposed to mean?" She says angrily. *"You're hurting your family and your reputation. Can't you see that?"*

"So, you'd rather I played under the radar. Is that what you're saying? Keep my shameful activities to myself. Is that what you would do?"

I just can't help myself and she yells, *"Don't you talk to me like that. It's obvious that person has corrupted you in more ways than I thought. You will speak to me with respect, and I expect you to come home on Friday and explain your behavior. God knows what Miss. Solomon would think if she discovered who you are keeping the company of."*

"You know nothing about my life here, mom." I bite back. So angry I just don't care anymore.

"You don't get to judge Shade and you definitely don't get to judge me. I'm an adult and no longer under your control. So, get used to it because for your information, I am moving in with Shade."

"You are not. I forbid it!" She almost screams down the phone and I say casually, "I'm sorry. Did I say you have a say in the matter? Get used to it mom because one day he could be the father of your grandkids. Anyway, I've got to report to Miss. Solomon. I'm working on a campaign and need to brief her. Speak soon, bye."

I cut the call, laughing as I picture her angry face all the way back in Washington. It's so liberating knowing there is nothing she can do. I was right. I am out of her control. Actually, I am out-of-control period and it's all because *she* started it.

I still have a few minutes, so I click on Cecilia's text.

> Are you okay, honey? We haven't spoken since, well, that night and even though my new guy has told me you're fine, I just need to hear that for myself. Call me.

I quickly dial and she answers immediately.

"Hey, about time."

"Sorry. I've been busy."

"I can see. Man, you know how to party, girl. I want a full report this weekend."

"This weekend?"

"Yes, I'm coming to stay with the hottest guy on the planet, otherwise known as Kyle. God the things that man can do with his, um, cock emoji."

It makes me laugh.

"You're such an idiot. So, Kyle, hey."

"Don't try to shift this onto me. What's with the big bad mafia don? Please tell me he's kinky. I want all the details. What did he make you do, and are you able to walk?"

"Well…" I take a deep breath and I can almost hear her panting on the other end of the line.

"I'll tell you when I see you. I have a meeting to attend

regarding the campaign I'm in charge of."

"Wait, what?" She says in disbelief.

"Wow, they get their money's worth from their interns in New York. I thought you'd be making the coffee. How come?"

"Shade came."

I giggle as she groans. *"Spare me the details of your love life. Actually, no, I want to know everything but preferably over a glass of champagne after I've exhausted his best friend."*

"Best friend?" I giggle at the idea of Shade having any actual friends. I can't quite imagine him having a beer with the guys in a bar on a night out.

Reluctantly, I groan and say with a sigh. "I really must go. I'm fine, so you can quit worrying and we will fully catch up on the weekend."

"I'll hold you to that. Take care, honey. Love you."

Alice comes in as I cut the call and hands me the folder with a rueful smile.

"Good luck, Allegra. Have a good evening."

"You too." She makes to leave, and I say with curiosity, "What are your plans?"

She shrugs. "To walk home, grab a takeout and watch a movie before bed. It doesn't get much better than that."

"Alone?" I know I'm prying into her private life, but I'm curious.

She shrugs. "Until I meet the billionaire the books I read promise me. Yes. Alone."

She grins and heads out of the door, and I understand exactly how she feels. That was my life a few days ago, but the man I read about never came for me. Luckily for me, he sent someone way more exciting, and I definitely wouldn't change a thing.

CHAPTER 36

SHADE

It's been an interesting day. As soon as we left Killian's penthouse, we came back to my office for an update. Kyle told me the plan Saint had formulated regarding Jefferson, and we discussed what to do about Freddie Connor.

As Kyle went to arrange it, I caught up with work regarding the Vieri empire.

Now I'm waiting in my office for my campaign manager and it's the one thing in my day I'm actually looking forward to.

Kyle shows her in at six-thirty on the dot and I lean forward and feast my eyes on the beauty who has been in my thoughts all day.

That outfit almost makes me salivate because business chic suits her.

As she walks, the skirt swings and the splits in the side offer me a tantalizing glimpse of her long legs and those heels are so sexy it makes me groan. Then there's knowing what lies underneath to fan the flames even higher and seeing her clutching the file with a sexy smile on her face makes me want to ditch business for a more personal kind.

"Miss. Powell." I arch my brow.

"Have you got something for me?"

She perches on the chair opposite and nods, pushing the folder across the desk and saying with a hint of undisguised excitement. "I have a plan, and it's a good one."

"I'll be the judge of that." I say, directing a dark stare her way, and I love the way she squirms on her seat.

"Miss. Solomon said it was an excellent one."

I can see the pleasure in her eyes as she says it, and I'm happy for her. Obviously, whatever she has come up with has passed the test of the great queen herself and I'm interested to hear it.

"Go on. Explain it to me."

The folder remains unopened, and she says with an excited sparkle in her eyes. "Fantasy. A masquerade evening where the customers purchase a golden ticket and hide behind masks. Tickets will be sold online and limited to your capacity and the ticket holder is guaranteed anonymity as they enjoy an evening without fear of being recognized."

I lean back and study her with a blank expression. She is waiting for my response, but I don't give her one.

My mind is working fast because this could be the opportunity we need. It's actually ingenious because it suits my plans and brings much needed revenue to my club. It's an opportunity to bring down my enemies and will require careful planning.

"What do you think?" She breaks the silence and I nod, slowly.

"It has potential."

"Really?"

She smiles like an eager puppy trying to please its master and points to the folder. "It's all in there. We have devised a

PR campaign to gain interest, adverts, internet posts, and a banner in Times Square. I just need you to sign it off and we will get to work. As I'm sure you realize, we don't have long and need to move fast."

"I don't need to see what's inside the folder, Miss. Powell."

She peers at me anxiously as I say lazily, "I need to see what's under your dress."

"Excuse me." Her eyes are wide, and I growl, "Face down on the desk, Miss. Powell. Then I will consider your proposal."

The way her eyes light up causes the blood to rush to my cock instantly and as I stand, she does too and while I head to the door and lock it with a satisfied smile on my face, she does as I say. When I turn, it's to the delectable sight of her ass waving in the air and I groan inside. This is what I've been fantasizing about all day, and it can't wait another minute.

I prowl across the room, reaching for the eye mask hidden in my pocket and as I reach her, I slip it over her eyes and whisper huskily, "As you are such a fan of masks, you may want to try this one out."

Her breathing is fast and as I lift her skirt, her low moan tells me exactly how compatible we are. I feast my eyes on the panties that caress her ass and tear them off, jealous they are even touching what's mine. She pants as I kick her legs apart and unfasten my pants, dropping them to allow my cock his freedom.

She says nothing, and the tension is thick in the room. I can almost taste expectation in the air and as I run my hand around her peachy ass, I growl, "I've been dreaming of this moment since you walked into my club."

"Fuck, Shade. You will be the death of me." She hisses as her whole body trembles, waiting for something that she desires more than anything at this moment.

I growl, "Lie on the desk and remain still. Arms flat on the desk, your face to one side."

I press my hand on her back so she can't move and as I enter her slowly from behind, she gasps as I inch inside, slowly, steadily, and with no urgency.

"That is so good." She groans as I fill her completely and, bending down, I whisper in her ear, "No talking."

The air is electric all around us as I possess my woman, mixing business with pleasure. She is not the first woman I've fucked over this desk, but I have a strong feeling she will be the last. Why would I want a whore when I have a woman like her? Beautiful, brave and interesting. Fearless and as chaotic as I am. She is my match, which makes this even more delicious as I slide in home, again and again. Loving the knowledge I am fucking my woman.

I increase my pace and watch her nailed to my desk. Faster, more frantically with an urgency that causes her to pant. Her low moans turn me on as I power in relentlessly and I sense her building orgasm about to hit her hard. It turns me on as she clenches my cock and squeezes it, milking it and causing me to roar. As my hot salty cum comes in waves, I fill her completely, loving that in this moment, nothing can come between us.

I own her, I possess her, and I really believe I love her. That can be the only reason I have such an insatiable need for her, and it's not just her body. It's her mind too. Now she is back where she belongs—under me, by my side and later in my bed. Now I understand why Killian is so possessive of his wife, because if anyone tries to take her from me, I'll kill the bastard.

She lies breathlessly on my desk and whispers, "So, is that a yes?"

It makes me laugh and spinning her around, I lift her

close to my chest and whisper against her luscious lips, "I think that was better than a handshake. Don't you?"

She grins and then shrugs, saying with a twinkle in her eye, "I'm not so sure."

As my lips silence her, she tastes better than any drug, any gourmet meal, or any business deal that makes me money. She tastes of hope, freedom, and fulfillment. She tastes of everything I ever want in life, and I pity the poor bastards who believe they stand a chance of taking her away from me.

CHAPTER 37

ALLEGRA

Shade makes me ditch any principles I have and any dignity. That was wild. I never realized meetings could be so much fun and as I enjoy being wrapped in his arms, I really don't believe I've been happier than I am now.

He pulls back and reaches for my hand and grins. "Let's go freshen up and eat. We have a lot to do if we're going to get this event off the ground."

"So, you like my idea?"

I really want his approval on this, and he nods. "Of course. It appeals to me. The mystery and the exclusive nature of it. I'll arrange the ticket sales; you just get the customers through the door."

"We make a good team." I say happily as I walk from his office with his hand in mine.

"I'm glad you think that, princess, because the deal has now changed."

My heart drops. "What do you mean, changed?"

He says casually, as if he's discussing the weather. "It means that seven days and seven nights have turned into the rest of your life. Non-negotiable."

I take a moment to process what he just said because when he mentioned making me his wife, I really thought he was kidding me.

"So, you were serious?"

Why can't I breathe all of a sudden?

"About marrying you. Of course." He shrugs and a shiver of excitement passes through me when I think of that.

Shade Vieri's wife. I can't believe it.

It makes me remember my childhood dreams of marriage. The big white wedding and my father giving me away. I'm not sure why, but that dream is nothing to what I want now. If Shade asked me to marry him on a desert island, I would. However, the disapproval that's sure to be on my parent's faces as I walk down the aisle makes me not want to invite them. I am protective of what we have because I know they will disapprove, and I don't want to see that disappointment in their eyes on the best day of my life. So, I say softly, "Promise me one thing."

"What?" He stops and stares at me with interest and I smile sadly. "Don't invite my parents."

"Why not?"

"Because they don't deserve to be there. You see, my mom called me at work and ranted about how bad you were for me. That I had made bad choices and to head home this weekend to discuss my wrongdoings."

"She said that?" He raises his eyes and I shake my head. "Not in those words, but her meaning was clear. I am so happy now, Shade, I don't want them to bring me down. They will try to talk me out of it. To make things difficult and I don't want to give them the chance."

I'm not sure I like the wicked gleam that lights up his eyes as he says evenly, "I think it's an excellent idea. We will head there this weekend and you don't need to worry because I'll be right beside you and I am more than a match for your mother, your father and even the man who pretends to be your uncle. Family gatherings can be so much fun."

He winks and my heart beats faster because I realize this will end in disaster. Shade Vieri in my family home. What could possibly go wrong?

* * *

It's only when we're eating that I remember a crucial detail I have obviously forgotten about, and I stare at Shade in dismay as the clock strikes seven.

"Oh my god."

"What?" He glances at me with concern, and I say fearfully, "The money. Wasn't I supposed to deposit twenty-thousand dollars into a dumpster right now? How could I have forgotten about that?"

"I wouldn't worry about that." He shrugs, taking another mouthful of food as if it's no concern.

"But I am. Really worried. If I don't show up, my brother will be…"

I can't even say the word and Shade drops his fork and reaches for my hand.

"You are making the drop, Abby."

"When?" I'm so nervous and he shrugs.

"Right on time. Currently, Heather is making her way into the alley and dropping the bag."

"Heather! The cop?"

I experience a sense of relief that tells me what a bad person I am, being happy that someone else is putting themselves in danger on my behalf.

Shade adds. "She'll do what they asked and the cops will be watching."

"I don't understand."

I'm missing some vital information here and he raises my

hand to his lips, kissing it softly, before saying, "I called the cops to deal with your problem."

"Isn't that against the code?" I say in disbelief, and he chuckles softly. "The code? I'm not a pirate, princess."

"Well, mafia law then. I didn't think you call the cops on anything."

"Ordinarily, no. We don't. But this concerns you, and I'm not taking any chances."

"You did it for me." I stare at him in shock.

Tears fill my eyes as I realize what he's done for me and he grips my hand, saying softly, "I will do *anything* for you, Ally. You are the most important person in my world, and I hate seeing you afraid. I could have dealt with it, but it would have had risks attached. Heather was already involved and so I decided to do things the right way for once. We should get a call anytime soon and see what they found."

"I can't believe it." I shake my head, a surge of love filling my heart as I gaze at the man who surprises me over and over again.

"I will do anything to protect you, princess. I may be a fucked up killer, but I will always do right by you."

This is the sweetest thing he's ever said to me and means so much. I drop his hand and head to his side of the table, planting myself in his lap and kissing him so fiercely my lips burn. It becomes the most important thing in my life right now to show him how much he means to me, and only the sound of his phone ringing makes us pull apart.

"Is that them?" I ask, my eyes wide, and he reaches for his phone and nods.

"It is."

I stay where I am, his arm around my waist while he answers the call.

"Heather."

He puts the call on speaker, and I listen to what she says.

"The money was delivered as arranged and the surveillance was tight. I walked into the alley with no disruptions and left just as easily. I made it out to the street and then I noticed two people heading my way. I don't know why, but they looked like trouble, so I turned and walked the other way. They followed me and I dodged into a nearby store, sure I'd lose them in there. I managed to get a photograph of them and sent it to the department. When I hid in the lingerie department, I received the ID. Does the name Constantine ring any bells because apparently, they're brothers?"

"Dimitri Constantine." He growls into the phone.

"They are his sons. Apollo and Adonis. Hit men for the Constantine mafia, enforcers if you like."

"What are they doing in New York?" Heather is breathless and Shade says quickly, "Where are you?"

"I'm still in the fucking lingerie changing rooms. Until I know they're taken care of, I'm staying in here all night."

"I'll send some guards. They'll get you safely out of there. Code word, princess." He winks at me, and I stare back, my eyes wide because in this moment Heather is pretending to me and I feel so guilty that she is in danger.

"Tell me what the cops find. Who lifts the money and what they're going to do about that?" He growls into the phone and says abruptly, "Stay where you are. I'm on it."

As he cuts the call, he types out a text to Kyle and sighs heavily.

"The Constantine's are trouble for us. They are here for a reason, and I don't like it."

"You know them?"

He nods. "Of them. They are Greek mafia and rarely step foot outside of their own country. Something has brought them to New York, and I want to know what."

He says with a deep sigh, "I must call Killian. He needs to be informed."

I slide off his lap as he stands, heading to the window and staring down at the city, his phone no longer on silent and pressed to his ear.

I hear him say, "The Constantines are involved."

I listen as he tells his brother everything he knows, and I have a sinking feeling inside when I sense my troubles are far from over.

They may have only just begun.

CHAPTER 38

SHADE

I leave Ally to change and relax in my penthouse, and I head off to find Kyle. Killian promised to investigate why the Constantine brothers are sniffing after Allegra, and I need to trust him. However, I'm not one to let others deal with my shit and especially not where it concerns her, so I head off to find Kyle and fill him in on Heather's call. He says at once. "I'll organize a team to pick her up."

He makes the call and as I splash two shots of bourbon in the glasses, my thoughts turn to this weekend.

When he finishes, I hand him the glass and say with deepening anger. "I'm tired of these threats. I hate not knowing what is going on in my city and I want answers."

He downs the shot in one and slams the glass on the desk. "Consider it done."

"Don't you have a guest this weekend?" I remember Ally's friend is coming to town, and he shrugs. "I can cancel. It's no big deal."

"I thought you liked her."

"I do but I always put business first."

"As it happens…" I grin wickedly.

"Our business is in Washington this weekend."

He raises his eyes and I laugh softly. "I want to get Ally out of town, and we are overdue a visit with her parents. Why don't you catch up with her friend there?"

"You're happy to leave town when shit is getting real?" Kyle asks, and I shrug. "They can't do anything if the woman they're after isn't here. Her brother is still out of State and my brother is causing heat on them. I'd say we can enjoy our weekend and when we return, we have a party to organize."

He shakes his head. "It will be an interesting one. I've already got the team on the tickets. They go live tomorrow."

I nod. "One call from Allegra and the promotion gets underway. She can get her assistant on it and Evangeline can earn the huge fee I'm paying her."

I stretch out and say with satisfaction.

"All we need is to fuel up the plane and pack a weekend bag. This should be fun."

* * *

"I CAN'T BELIEVE we are doing this." Allegra is nervous as we board the private jet.

"It's long overdue."

"I've only known you a week. How is it overdue?" She says incredulously and I laugh. "I move fast. Surely, you've realized that by now."

"I think I have."

She shakes her head. "You know they will be rude. Horrible, in fact."

"I'm used to it." I shrug. "I'm not really husband material, I get it. It doesn't matter anyway, because they will be too busy saving their own marriage to worry about yours."

She stares at me in alarm. "You're going to tell them, aren't you?"

"I'm bored with playing games, princess. It's Judgment Day."

She falls silent and I watch her bite her bottom lip with nerves and I feel a raw hatred for her mom. What she has done is far worse than anything her daughter has ever done and has shown no remorse, to my knowledge. They will be in no doubt of their position when we leave, and they will never treat their daughter with disrespect again.

Allegra is quiet for most of the journey, and I hate that I must talk business with Kyle rather than making her feel better about this. Luckily, the flight is a short one and we are soon touching down on the tarmac of the private airfield we use in Washington.

As we step out into the sunshine, I note the waiting black cavalcade and wonder what her mom will think when we show up at her door.

"This is a bit extreme, isn't it?" Allegra says in shock, her eyes wide.

"It's necessary. I'm taking no chances with your safety."

She visibly pales and I hate how scared she is.

When I picture her dealing with this bastard on her own my blood boils because I'm guessing if I hadn't stepped in, she would be a corpse right now.

It's all adding up that someone wants her gone, and I'm guessing that pleasure belongs to her sick and twisted half-brother, Jefferson Stevenson. I'm almost salivating at what I have planned for him, and as soon as we return, shit will get very real.

We take our positions in the car and speed off the short distance to her parent's home in a leafy suburb on the outskirts of the city.

* * *

WE SOON REACH the street where she grew up and I stare around me with interest at a place where the elite live. Meredith Powell married Richard Stevenson, but for reasons unknown she kept her name and so did her children. From what I know, Meredith's father was the last of his line and she wanted to continue their family name, so Rafferty became Powell and, to make it easier, so did Allegra. I suppose that shows what kind of man Richard is because he will do anything to please his wife. It's just a shame she doesn't return the favor.

We pull up outside their house, my cavalcade of cars making an intimidating sight in their neighborhood as they dominate the area. I'm guessing it will be a difficult one to explain over the lunches she enjoys, although I'm guessing there won't be many invitations when word gets out.

Allegra is nervous. She is quiet and pre-occupied and just before we leave the security of the car, I grip her hand and whisper with concern, "Are you okay, baby?"

"Not really." Her eyes are clouded with worry, and she says with a break in her voice. "Please don't let them change anything, Shade. I'm worried about us, and I'm worried about my father. He is innocent in all of this, and it will break him."

I say carefully, "I can't guarantee that, but I can guarantee I have your best interests at heart. Their secret isn't ours to keep. It's always there, hovering in the shadows. If we don't expose it, somebody else will. The fact you've been targeted at all is because of what your mom has done. Someone is causing trouble because of it, and it stops now."

"How can you be so sure? It may be nothing to do with her and more to do with the woman Rafferty met at the party. The blackmailer saw an opportunity to make some money because Rafe is a big star now."

"Nice thought, but you're wrong."

I sigh and pull her close, whispering, "I know who is doing this, and it's nothing to do with that girl who was murdered. Nothing to do with you and *everything* to do with your mom and that bastard who pretends he isn't your father."

"Who?" she says quickly, the hurt and pain in her expression agonizing to see.

"You'll know soon enough, princess. Just trust me. This is the beginning of the end."

I pull her from the car before she can ask any more questions and as we approach the front door, it swings open, revealing the disapproving stare of her mom. Meredith Powell.

"Allegra." She says sharply, stepping forward and gazing at me with derision.

"You can come in, but your friends must leave."

Ally grips my hand tighter and says angrily, "Now that's not very polite, mom. I came to introduce you to my fiancé."

Her mom's eyes are wide and full of anger, and she hisses, "We will discuss this in private. Follow me."

As we step inside her home, I peer around me with interest. Suburban life and the American dream in all its glory. I have visited many houses like this one and destroyed many families who live in them because they fell on hard times and got involved in my world just to maintain the illusion of winning at life. Allegra's family is no different. Her mother has hidden a devastating secret for so many years now I expect she believes it herself. It will be interesting to observe her reaction when she realizes its game over.

CHAPTER 39

ALLEGRA

It's so strange being home. I've only been gone for a few weeks and so much has happened. My entire life has changed.

When I left here, I was so excited about a new beginning. I was finally leaving home and although it was under the watchful eye of my brother, I was still guaranteed a freedom I had never had until then.

Suddenly, it all went to shit when the blackmail started. I tried to deal with it. I was a fool.

But I can't regret it happening because that's how I met Shade, and I'm amazed at how quickly and deeply I've fallen for him.

I cling onto his hand as we follow mom into the family room and my father appears through the French doors with a puzzled, "Meredith, have you seen…"

He stops and his brief expression of delight at seeing me is quickly replaced with one of concern when he notices who I've brought home.

"What's going on?" He says in confusion and mom snaps,

"Isn't it obvious, Richard? Your daughter has gone off the rails and got herself in a heap of trouble."

"Trouble?" He appears concerned and my heart breaks in two because despite everything, he is still my father—will always be my father and this is going to break him.

I step forward and say calmly. "Let's not get hysterical. I am merely bringing my boyfriend home to meet you. No big deal."

Mom explodes. "No big deal! Are you kidding me, Allegra? You disappear off the radar and your picture is all over the internet with him."

She points her finger at Shade and her lip curls. "How could you let him use you and humiliate you? Those images will live with me to my dying day of what he did to you, with no regard for your reputation or feelings."

My father appears confused and says softly, "They weren't that bad, Meredith. So, she had a wild night, many kids do and perhaps wasn't as polished as normal, but she was smiling at least."

"You fool!" Mom shouts, her face angrier than I have ever seen it.

"She didn't just have a wild night out with her friends, he…" She jabs her finger in Shade's direction, "Filmed her performing, well…"

My father looks shocked and glares at Shade, who appears amused by the whole spectacle.

"I take it you're referring to the video I sent to Judge Stevenson?" He says calmly.

I stare at my mother, who has suddenly turned a whiter shade of devastated.

"What video?" My father says in confusion and mom obviously realizes her mistake because she ignores his question entirely.

"It doesn't matter. What does is that Allegra's good name

has been dragged into the gutter and if she thinks we are ever going to accept that man into our family, she's got another thing coming."

Shade steps forward, glaring at her with derision.

"That man." He shakes his head. "You speak of me as if I'm beneath you. Not worthy to care for your daughter, to keep her safe and to make her happy. You know nothing at all about me and yet you have decided I am no good for her. What did you base that judgment on Mrs. Powell because if I'm not mistaken, we have never met?"

Mom's eyes are frantically scanning the room as if she's trapped and looking for a way out.

"I, I, well, I searched your name on the internet of course."

"I see." Shade appears thoughtful.

"Then may I ask how you came by the video I sent to Judge Stevenson? Especially as your husband doesn't appear to know anything about it."

I feel sick as mom struggles to answer him and above everything else, all I want to do is drag my father away, so he doesn't hear how the people he trusted most in the world betrayed him.

"I, well, Lucas sent it to me." She says quickly. "He thought I should be informed."

"To you?" Shade pretends to be surprised. "Why would he send it to you and not his brother? Speaking as a brother myself, I'm sure if I were in the same situation, I wouldn't be sending things to his wife. It doesn't make sense."

Dad says roughly, "Cut to the chase and tell me what the hell is going on here."

He is angry. I can tell from the expression in his eyes and mom's face drains of color as she falters, "I think you should go." She says to Shade, and I don't believe I have ever seen her so terrified.

"Now, why would we leave before we clear this mystery up?" Shade says with a slight shake of his head.

"Please." Mom folds before us. "Please, just go."

Shade steps forward and snarls, "You want us to leave to protect your secret. You are once again placing your own selfish needs above that of your family."

"Will somebody please tell me what the fuck is going on!" my father bellows and mom collapses into the nearby chair and places her head in her hands.

Shade turns to my father and says gently, "I'm sorry but your wife has been having an affair with your brother for the last twenty-five years."

I almost can't look at my father's expression and stare with hatred at my mom's broken figure.

"Meredith?" my father says in confusion. "What is he talking about?"

Mom shakes her head and I hate how weak she is. Even now she won't tell him the truth and Shade says gently, "I'm sorry, Mr. Stevenson. It has come to my attention that both Allegra and Rafferty are…"

"STOP!" Mom jumps up and screams, "Leave! For God's sake, just leave. Make them, Richard. Tell them to go."

"Sit down!" My father yells and she stares at him in shock as he says to Shade, "Tell me."

Shade turns to me with concern and whispers, "Are you okay, Ally?"

To be honest, I'm not sure I am, but I nod, frozen to the spot.

I'm touched when he gently pushes me down on the couch and sits beside me, holding my hand tenderly before turning to my father with a sympathetic smile.

"I'm sorry to be the one telling you this, but both Allegra and Rafferty are your brother's children."

To my surprise, my father sits down in the seat opposite and says gruffly, "I know."

I stare at him in shock, and he glances at his wife and whispers, "We should have told them."

"They're yours, Richard." Mom says with a break in her voice and dad says sadly. "When we married, I didn't realize at the time, but I can't father a child. We tried for many years and when we were unsuccessful, I sought help for my well, problem."

He stares at me with a desolate expression and says gently, "I'm sorry, angel. We tried every avenue going, but it was futile. Then we were told of a way through IVF. My sperm wasn't suitable, so my brother, your uncle Lucas, offered to help. At least that way we would be tied by blood. It was a great gift."

I am stunned and stare at Shade in horror as we completely got this wrong. This is a disaster.

Shade shakes his head and squeezing my hand says roughly, "So he donated his sperm, and it was artificially inseminated."

He rolls his eyes. "So, why has your wife been having an affair with him ever since?"

"You're lying!" Mom yells and as my father glares at Shade, I flinch as he slams the evidence down in front of them and says angrily, "Explain these photographs. I'd love to hear another fairy story. They were taken years apart in various hotel rooms booked for one reason only. Their affair."

Mom screams and tries to get to them first, but my father pushes her away and bellows, "Sit down!"

He grasps the evidence, and I swear he ages in seconds. He was once so strong and now appears vulnerable and broken.

"It's true." He shakes his head as he flips through the picture evidence no amount of denying can repair.

Then he turns to mom and sneers, "You lied to me."

He stares at the photographs again and roars. "You fucking lied to me all these years. Those business trips, lunches with the girls, and charity work were all a front. Weren't they?"

He is incensed and mom sobs in her seat, her head in her hands, broken beyond repair.

"I love him." Her voice shakes as she finally confesses and the pain in my father's eyes is too hard to witness, so I stand and say to Shade. "Take me home. I don't want to be here anymore. It's too painful."

I can't even look at my mother and instead, head toward my father and hug him hard, whispering, "You will always be daddy to me. I love you and this changes nothing. I'll be in touch."

"I'm sorry, angel. Please don't go." He whispers and I say sadly, "You have nothing to apologize for. I'll be in touch and…" My voice breaks. "I'm sorry, dad."

I make to leave and as I pass my mom, I say bitterly, "I never want to see you again."

As I leave, her pitiful cries follow me and yet I couldn't give a fuck. It will take a very long time for me to forgive her and right at this moment, I'm not sure if I ever will.

CHAPTER 40

SHADE

We waste no time and head to the finest hotel Washington offers, and I think Allegra is in a state of shock. She is rigid and unresponsive, merely staring out of the window, her small hand clasped firmly in mine.

I know better than to coax it out of her because I understand a little of what she is going through.

It's something I would do. Retreat to heal. I keep everything close and let nobody in. We are too alike in that respect and so I give her privacy and catch up with the texts coming in.

Killian is on the case for the Constantine brothers and his is short and sweet.

> I had a call with Dimitri. We have nothing to worry about and everything to gain. Relax, we'll talk on Monday.

The next is from Heather.

> "Forensics identified the heart as the missing one belonging to Taylor Sutherland. The man who retrieved the holdall was a homeless drunk who was paid fifty dollars to collect it. He has no leads and tells us it was a guy who stopped by the bridge and asked if anyone wanted to earn easy money. He couldn't remember anything about him except that he wore a pinstripe suit.

Fuck.

I lean back and hate the feeling of losing control. Whoever this man is, is always one step ahead of us and it's seriously pissing me off.

A text comes through from Kyle who is in the passenger seat ahead and he forwards a text from the agency we use for various business shit.

> The tickets for Tuesday's masquerade went on sale this morning. They are now sold out.

I stare at it in disbelief. We released two hundred tickets priced at five hundred dollars each. That's without drinks and extras. This night is a success on ticket sales alone.

I turn to Allegra and snap her out of her mood in an instant.

"Your event has sold out."

"Excuse me?" She turns sharply and stares at me with shock.

"Your ads have worked. God knows how you got them out so quickly, but we're sold out. Job done."

"But..." Her eyes are wide, and she tears her phone from her purse and scrolls through the texts.

"I don't believe it." She stares at me in shock.

"Alice placed a few ads that went viral. It appears this is the hottest ticket in town."

I love that her face breaks into a huge grin and the pain leaves her eyes and is quickly replaced by excitement.

"I only told her to run the ads last night after I got your approval. They must have only been out for a few hours. I never knew it would be this easy."

She shakes her head and quickly dials a number, her face flushed with pride.

"Alice." She says with excitement. "I've just heard we're sold out. What happened?"

She listens with delight as her assistant speaks and she squeals. "You're a genius. You really are the best. This is all down to you, and I'll make sure Miss. Solomon knows."

She giggles and then says happily, "I can't wait until Monday. We did it. Thank you so much."

As she cuts the call, she surprises me by kissing me so ferociously I forget my own name and then she pulls back, panting, her eyes shining as she says quickly, "April has a few bloggers on her contact list. They are connected to the entertainment industry, and it only took a couple of posts to go viral. It appears that everyone wants to be part of the masquerade, and there's already a waiting list for the next event."

She giggles with delight. "Oh my god, this is amazing. We could make it a monthly event. It will become the hottest ticket to get, and you could charge even more next time. April is a genius. A beautiful fucking genius and now Miss. Solomon won't be angry with me."

"She wouldn't dare, not when she discovers my plan for you. Nobody messes with my family and lives to do it again."

I laugh at the disbelief in her eyes as she whispers, "You will kill anyone who upsets me? That's a bit extreme, don't you think?"

It makes me laugh and I can't help myself and reach out and whisper huskily, "Have you forgotten who I am, princess? I'm not your average guy and I don't mess around. I am Shade Vieri and I do what the fuck I want and if anyone messes with my girl, they will suffer the consequences of that."

Her pupils dilate and her breathing is heavy, and she whispers breathlessly, "I am so freaking turned on right now."

I pull her roughly onto my lap and running my hand under her skirt I inch her panties aside, plunging three fingers into her wet heat and hitting that sweet spot.

I whisper, "Then let me help you with that."

She groans into my mouth as I finger fuck her pussy and as she comes hard all over my fingers, I watch every magical second of her release, not really understanding how such a beauty came into my life.

She is fearless, adventurous, and brave, and so beautiful I can't tear my eyes away. I love how she accepts me for who I am. Shade Vieri, the man, not the mafioso. She wants me, not the image, and I really believe I have found the other half of my soul.

* * *

As soon as we reach the hotel, I waste no time in grabbing the key to the penthouse and instruct Kyle to enjoy his weekend with his woman. I know he has arranged for her to meet him in his room and while the rest of my men settle in for a weekend of relaxation, I intend on spending the whole of it with my princess.

I waste no time either and as the elevator takes us to the top floor, I am going to wipe her memory of our visit to her home. She needs to forget. To replace it with excitement and I have the perfect activity in mind.

* * *

"Are you kidding me?" She is staring at me with so much horror it makes me laugh out loud.

"So, this is the worst thing I've done—seriously?"

I shake my head and hold out the outfit.

"Time to dress up, baby, and I'll take you on the ride of your life."

"What if I don't want to?"

She's nervous and bites her lip, causing me to say harshly, "Just do it princess, otherwise we head straight back to New York and no pleasure."

"Please, Shade. I, well, I can't. Not this."

I growl, "Are you still dressed, princess? Must I strip you myself?"

Her eyes are wide and her lower lip trembles, but I'm the bastard who doesn't fucking care and as I remove my own shirt with a wicked glare, she sighs and tentatively reaches for her zipper.

Ten minutes later we're good to go and hiding behind the anonymity of our outfits, we head down to the street below.

I grip her hand hard as Kyle stands to one side, shaking his head with a resigned smile.

"Enjoy."

"Right back at you, Kyle. Now go and spend time with your woman. We leave in the morning."

"His woman?" Allegra whispers and I nod. "Your friend. Cecilia, I think her name is."

"Oh my god, she's here." Allegra's voice changes in an

instant from worry to happiness and I whisper, "If you're a good girl and do everything I tell you, maybe we will catch up with them at dinner."

"You mean that?" Her eyes shine with excitement, and I glance at Kyle, who rolls his eyes. "I was going to order room service."

"That can be arranged." I say wickedly and he laughs at the outrage on Allegra's face as she hisses, "That will be a definite no, Shade. Way too far."

"Then be a good girl and do as I say."

I love the murderous rage in her eyes as she swings her leg over the Harley and sits fuming on the back of it, and I don't believe I have ever seen a more beautiful sight. She is dressed from head to toe in black leather and her cheeks are flushed and her eyes bright as she struggles to overcome her fear of what is about to happen.

Kyle hands me a helmet and I pull it down on her head and fasten it, whispering, "Trust me, princess. This is exactly what you need."

"Bastard." She says through gritted teeth, causing me to grin wickedly as I jam my own helmet down on my head.

I love this. The anonymity, the freedom and the rush speed gives me. Knowing Allegra will be clinging on for her life behind me will be a rush I don't normally experience. I usually ride alone. It's my passion, my escape and my freedom. The one time I can blend in with the rest of mankind and be Shade the man, not Shade, the murdering mafia bastard.

My men hate it. Especially Kyle, and at first, they attempted to keep up with me. They soon realized it was pointless and accept this is my rebellion against a life I never chose.

As I join Allegra on the bike, I relish the feeling of the steel between my legs and grip the handlebars with a sense of anticipation. This is what I love and is the perfect time to indulge my hobby because tonight, we have nowhere else we need to be.

I start the engine and as the beast roars into life, it fills the underground car park with raw power. It's as if they have unleashed a wild animal, and I waste no time in opening the throttle and heading for the exit.

Allegra is clinging on, her face buried behind my back, and I love the sensation of power rushing through my body like a shot.

We head out into the traffic and as I weave my way through it, I concentrate on the road ahead and not on the woman who is shit scared behind me.

We leave the city and head out on the freeway, and this is where I really open her up and deal with my love of speed. I ride fast and hard, it's what turns me on and as we cut through the traffic, I know exactly where I am heading.

* * *

Twenty minutes later, I pull to a stop in a place that satisfies my need for privacy. We are high on a ridge overlooking the town, and as the day turns to dusk, the lights twinkle below us.

I remove my helmet and help Allegra off with hers and her flushed face tells me everything I wanted to know.

"I hate you." She growls and then grins. "But I loved that."

It makes me laugh as she says with excitement, "At first I was so freaking scared but then I kind of settled into it and you were right, it was exactly what I needed."

"I'm always right." I smirk, causing her to roll her eyes and then her expression changes when I reach for her leathers and slowly unzip the jacket.

"What are you doing?" She hisses, glancing around her

nervously and as her beautiful tits spill out, I groan and dip my face to take my fill.

"Shade!" she says in shock, and I whisper, "Relax, nobody will see us."

"But anybody could stumble across us. A hiker perhaps."

"Then they will enjoy the show."

I bite down sharply on her nipple, causing her to squeal and I waste no time and ease her leathers off her shoulders along with her thin cotton tank.

She groans as I push her back against the metal and unzip the pants, lifting her hips so I can pull them over her ass.

"Please, Shade, it's too risky."

"That's why I'm doing it." I whisper, my lips brushing her sodden pussy, and she moans as I inch the fabric aside and suck gently on her clit.

Her fingers grasp my hair, and she gasps, "You're a wicked man."

"Get used to it." I laugh softly and suck her into my mouth, biting down gently on her clit, causing her to shiver and groan, "That is so good."

Reaching up, I thrust two fingers into her pussy as I pleasure her clit, causing her to groan, "Fuck."

I pump hard, bringing her pleasure and love how she is spread out naked on my bike. A feast for my own pleasure in the open air and an X-rated show for anyone who happens to pass by.

I've always loved living on the edge of danger. Battling against the unknown and testing how far my luck will run.

I am so turned on I can't even help myself and with a low growl, I pull her from the bike and onto the hard ground below.

She lies beneath me flushed and horny and as I unzip my pants, her eyes are wide and sparkle with excitement.

"Oh my god." She gasps as I settle between her legs and

say roughly, "I'm going to fuck you and you will love every minute of it."

"Shade!" Her eyes are wild, but her protestations fall off that ridge as I plunge into her wet heat and love how she clenches around my cock. She is the perfect fit for me, and I love knowing I am inside a woman like her. The only woman who makes me want to do it repeatedly. The only woman I can see myself still inside if I manage to dodge the odds and get old and gray.

CHAPTER 41

ALLEGRA

He has corrupted my mind, body and soul, and I'm lining up to do it again. I realize I wasn't living until I met this man who breathed new life into a soul that was going through the motions of life.

This is living.

This is making the most of life and as Shade fucks me on the hard, dirty ground in the open air, I feel wild and free. What happened back in that city earlier ceases to matter. That was my old life. This is my new and as he fucks me hard and fast, my back scraping against the stones, it's so deliciously dark I may never be content with a bed again.

The gentle breeze caresses the building heat inside me, its soft fingers of pleasure working in tune with his.

I can just about make out his expression in the darkening light, and the feral gleam in his eyes excites me.

I clench on his cock and milk it as I scream into the mountain air. I am an animal, wild and free and have found the perfect mate. He is my everything and I couldn't give a fuck what anyone thinks.

His own release is violent and explosive, and he grips my

face and stares into my eyes with a ferocious passion as he releases violently inside me, his roar of ecstasy carried away by the wind, informing everyone what's going on here.

I watch him with an awed passion because I have fallen so hard for a man who I should be repulsed by. He is everything I was warned about, but they didn't warn me against my own desires. The way reasoning is pushed to the side in the face of it, and it wins every single fucking time. This is wrong but so right for me and as Shade pulls out and wipes his hand across my pussy, he grins like the devil as he smears it all over my naked chest.

"The mark of Shade." He smirks, causing me to roll my eyes. "You're sick."

Leaning down, he licks our juices from my body with his wicked tongue, biting down hard on my nipple and whispering, "Lust sick for you."

"There's no such thing as lust sick?" I giggle as he sucks my skin, no doubt marking me as usual. I tease, "I think you love me. Lust doesn't even come into it. You have fallen madly in love with me, Shade, and I now control you."

I'm teasing, but as he pulls back, there is a deepening expression in his eyes that should terrify me. He looks possessed as he grips my face hard and growls, "I know that you're mine. I know that I am the only man who will ever fuck you again and I know you won't be walking away from me—ever."

I should be terrified, but his words cause my traitorous heart to flutter, and I say softly, "I'm going nowhere."

This time his kiss is surprisingly gentle, almost a lover's kiss and I'm not sure which one I prefer more. He is a man of many personalities and surprises, and I adore every single one of them.

He buries his face in my breasts and I tangle my fingers in his hair and commit this to memory. I have allowed him to do some wild things to me since we met, but this one is special. This time feelings are involved, and it means more somehow. I was high on adrenalin from the ride, and my senses were heightened. Now I'm high on Shade Vieri and it's an addiction I couldn't give up if I tried.

* * *

SOMEHOW, we make it back to the hotel parking lot, deep underground and guarded by his men. It's almost reassuring to see them and as we roll to a stop, I am disappointed this is over. As he tugs off his helmet, I love the wild man before me, dark, delicious, and sinful. Wicked, sexy and disturbed. There are too many adjectives to describe him, and he owns every single one of them.

He is everything.

He tosses the keys to his guard, and we head toward the private elevator leading to the penthouse.

As we make the journey, he pins me against the wall of the elevator and stares deep into my eyes.

"Are you okay, princess?" He strokes my face gently and I don't know how he does it. He treats me like a cheap whore one minute and his queen the next. I feel so protected with him and yet fearful at the same time. He confuses me and delights me, and I crave him and fear him. I am a mess of emotions where it concerns him and yet I have never been so happy.

"I'm good, more than good. Thank you."

I smile and love how his eyes deepen to dark pools of desire as he stares into my eyes with so much passion it makes me want him all over again.

"Tonight is our night, but first we eat with friends." He whispers against my lips and my heart leaps, knowing I'll see Cecilia again, even for a short time. I have missed her so much and we have a lot to talk about and so I smile softly and whisper, "Thanks, Shade."

"You're welcome, princess."

His mouth dusts against mine with slow temptation and I'm in no hurry to finish and intend on savoring every breath shared between us. I could kiss him all night which is a distinct possibility, and as the elevator arrives at our destination, I am sad that he pulls away.

"Come." He takes my hand, and we head into the apartment that makes me feel like a queen. It is so decadent, so palatial and I'm pinching myself that I am caught up in the best time of my life and also the worst.

We shed the leathers and, I pity whoever has the task of cleaning them because they reek of sex and deprivation.

We walk naked into the huge bathroom and Shade opens the faucet on the shower and pulls me under it with him, the power shower washing our sins away as he fills his hand with soap and gently rubs my heated skin.

"You are so beautiful." His eyes feast on my body and he gently touches the bruise on my breast.

"I love seeing my mark on you. I think we should make it permanent."

"What are you talking about?" I giggle as he strokes the skin reverently, and smirks. "I'll arrange a tattoo. Property of Shade."

"Fucking idiot." I giggle in the hope he is kidding me and as he traces a circle around my breast, he grins. "It will resemble a stamp, and it will be stamped over every inch of your skin. In red. I'll get someone on it tomorrow."

"You will not." I really hope the determination in his eye is a figment of my imagination because the fuck I'm letting him brand my body with a freaking name stamp. Hell no.

He pushes me up against the wall of the shower and his expression should terrify me, but it just excites me more as he growls, "I will do what the fuck I like with your body because I own it now."

"Asshole." I attempt to push him away, but his mouth lands on mine with a ferocious passion as he leaves me in no doubt of his desire for me. As he grips my hair hard, he nails me to the shower wall as if to prove a point, and I'm more than happy to let him. Shade is one big battle cry wrapped in deliciously dark behavior and I wouldn't change a thing.

CHAPTER 42

SHADE

I stare with interest at Allegra's friend as they sit gossiping in the corner, apparently not even stopping to take in air. The sound of their excited chatter fills the room, and Kyle hands me a bourbon and shakes his head.

"Is that normal?" he jerks his thumb as Cecilia squeals, and I shrug. "I guess. I bet a hundred they're talking about sex."

He reaches into his wallet and pulls out the bill and hands it to me with a resigned, "I'm not even going to attempt to deny it."

It makes me laugh as I pocket the cash and lower my voice.

"Have you heard from Freddie?"

"He's waiting at the warehouse on your return."

"Fuck! I've got a hard on."

He screws up his face in disgust. "Spare me your perversions and tell me the plan."

"We head back and persuade him to talk. Then prepare for an evening none of us will forget in a hurry."

Kyle nods, his eyes gleaming with danger. He loves this shit more than me and we make a good team. Freddie will be interrogated and every delicious secret he is hiding will be mine by the end of it.

"And Jefferson?" I ask casually.

"Has bought a ticket."

It makes me chuckle. "He can try to disguise his smug face, but I could pick him out in a room with no light. He's a dead man walking."

Kyle nods, in no doubt of our success. Yes, this masquerade is the perfect opportunity to remove him from our lives. To rid the Dark Lords of a fanatic and rid Allegra of any threat facing her.

* * *

We head to dinner at the exclusive roof top restaurant that is the talk of Washington. It is frequented by politicians, high-ranking officials and movie stars. I'm guessing they aren't used to a circus quite like mine and the curious gazes of the other diners follow us as we make our way to the table set by the window.

The fact we come with an entourage of men in black suits who position themselves by the exit and at nearby tables, tells them something unusual is happening and they stare at us with curiosity, causing Allegra's friend to grin with excitement.

"I feel like the First Lady." She whispers, "I don't believe it. You see that man over there with the woman in the white fur coat? That's my boss."

We follow her eye and I notice an older man dressed in a tuxedo with a slim, petite blonde on his arm, shrugging out of a fur coat and dripping in diamonds.

"I'm guessing that's his wife." Allegra says in awe, and

Cecilia laughs out loud. "That's his secretary. Marcia Billings. It's well known they are fucking their way through the working day and obviously after hours, too."

"Does his wife know?" Allegra whispers, her eyes wide with shock and Cecilia shrugs. "Probably, but she's too busy fucking the pool boy to care."

I watch with amusement as they burst out laughing and I love seeing Allegra so happy. It's a pleasure knowing she has forgotten the shit we are wallowing right now.

I decide I like her friend. She is right up Kyle's alley. Tall, beautiful brown skin, with intriguing dark eyes. Her hair is dyed blond and is dancing in waves across her shoulders and her slim figure is disguised by a slinky electric blue silk dress. She is wild, untamed and exactly how he likes his women, and I note the impatience in his eyes as he stares at her. I know that like me, he only wants to be fucking right now, but we need to eat, and Allegra needs some time with her friend.

So, I let them chat about shit and nod to Kyle in the direction I'm staring.

His amusement matches my own because striding into the restaurant is the man of the hour himself. Judge Lucas Stevenson and his long-suffering wife, Mary.

They ignore the waiter and head straight to our table and I watch Allegra's face tighten with anger when her uncle stops and says angrily, "A word please, Allegra. Outside."

To her credit, she gives nothing away and just smiles pleasantly.

"Uncle Lucas, Aunt Mary, what a coincidence." She turns to Cecilia and says happily, "Do you remember my aunt and uncle, Cessy?"

She nods and smiles in return. "It's so nice to see you again."

They remember their manners at least and greet her

politely and then Allegra turns to Kyle and says, "Kyle, this is my uncle. This is Kyle, and this…"

She turns to me and reaches for my hand, smiling lovingly into my eyes. "Is my boyfriend, Shade."

I nod to the enraged couple, loving the fact they are among their peers and can't create the scene I'm guessing they are desperate for.

"Um, well…" Mrs. Stevenson is trying so hard to deal with this disaster and she turns to her angry husband and says softly, "Lucas, please go and put the poor waiter out of his misery while I have a quick word with Allegra."

She addresses the table.

"You don't mind if I borrow her for a moment, do you?" She fixes me with a steadfast look, and I shrug, watching Allegra's reaction to that. She merely nods politely and pushes back from the table, making a show of kissing me defiantly provocatively, before saying, "I won't be long."

As she leaves with her aunt, I nod to the nearest guard, who stands and follows them out of the room. Her friend stares at Kyle and shakes her head, whispering, "That's a conversation I'd love to listen in on."

It makes him laugh and as I watch Allegra walk out of the room, I hate the fact she's no longer in my view, so I nod to another guard to secure the exits. This is a well-rehearsed drill that we have used many times before. When we secure a restaurant, we lock it down tight and there is no way in hell Allegra will make it out of this hotel without me by her side.

I glance across the room at Judge Stevenson who is typing furiously into his phone, his anger laid bare for the entire restaurant to register. I'm guessing this is no happy coincidence. He knows their secret is out and is in the process of dealing with it.

Well, so am I and as I lean back and lift the glass of

bourbon to my lips, I flash him a knowing wink as I drain the glass in one.

CHAPTER 43

ALLEGRA

I am so angry. Seething, in fact, because the minute I saw my uncle I wanted to be sick. I can't even look at him, and it took a superhuman effort on my part to keep things civil.

When Aunt Mary requested a word, it was an easy yes because it removed him from the situation.

We head into the bar and Aunt Mary directs me to a secluded booth and I notice Shade's men watching us at a respectful distance. It comforts me knowing he is protecting me even now and I will do everything to protect what we have.

"What's going on Allegra. Why the rebellion?"

Aunt Mary was always the calm voice of reason and I pity her almost as much as I do my father.

"It isn't a rebellion." I smile ruefully. "They say you can't help who you fall in love with. I'm a shining example of that."

"Along with every woman I know, darling." She smiles and appears a little sad. "Your mom called. She's worried about you."

"Did she tell you why I left?"

I am really interested to hear this, and she nods, a flicker of distaste passing across her face.

"Their secret is out."

"You know?" I'm stunned, and she nods, leaning back, appearing smaller, more fragile all of a sudden.

"I've always known. I just chose not to make a big deal of it."

"You chose?" My blood boils as I stare at the woman I always admired. Not so much anymore.

"It's not uncommon." She shrugs. "Unfortunately, Lucas fell for his brother's wife. It was most inconvenient and when they asked for his help regarding their parenting issue, he was ecstatic."

She stares at me with a sad expression in her eye.

"He would have married her. Left me and Jefferson and risked everything."

I still can't wrap my head around the fact she knew all the time and it must show because she shrugs. "Darling, you will discover this for yourself one day. When you marry a powerful man, it's unlikely you will hold his attention for long. They are a certain kind of animal. They must be strong to be successful. It's not uncommon for men like that to have affairs. They always come back though because their position is worth more than any scandal. If you take things further with your current beau, it's almost certain he will become bored and toss you aside for the next pretty face pouting in his direction."

I ignore her words about my own situation and say in disbelief, "I can't believe you accepted it."

I shake my head and she smiles as if we are discussing what to order.

"I understand it's a shock. Your father is most upset, and Lucas will have a hard time bringing him around."

"A hard time." I stare at her with so much pain in my heart I almost can't breathe.

"He has been having an affair with my mother for my entire life and whether you think it's acceptable or not, I don't."

I stand and she says softly, "Sit down, Allegra."

"No." I brush a tear from my eye and sob. "You are as responsible for this as they are. What sort of woman allows this to happen? For lives to be ruined just to keep up false pretenses. To play the upstanding members of our community and look down on the rest of us, knowing you are far worse. I despise your way of life, your reasons and you as it happens because even now, you are desperately trying to conceal your secret so you look good. Well fuck you, Aunt Mary, and fuck that man who calls himself my uncle. I will see you in hell before I ever speak to you again."

I turn to leave, and she stands, quickly grasping my arm with an icy, "You will…" Before she can even finish her sentence, two black-suited guards appear and push her arm away with a threatening, "I wouldn't do that if I were you. Never touch her again."

I don't stick around to watch her reaction and tear back into the restaurant and head straight to the table of the man I hate most in the world right now. Judge Stevenson.

He stares at me as I approach and makes to speak, and I shout for the entire restaurant to hear.

"Do not say a word, you traitorous bastard!"

"Allegra." He makes to stand, and I scream, "How could you? Your own brother's wife. You make me sick, both of you."

I stare around the restaurant at the shocked faces watching us and I yell, "Here is a man who pretends he's better than all of us."

"Allegra!" He yells, but Shade appears by my side and

moves between us with a menacing expression that would have any man cowering in his seat.

"Carry on, princess." Shade says quietly and I shout furiously, "This is the man who sits in judgment on us all and yet is guiltier than most. Well, for your information, he has been having an affair with his brother's wife for twenty-five years and guess who's the lucky result of that? Me!"

I turn and stare at him with anger and hiss, "I'm guessing you thought you could bring me in line too. Threaten me perhaps, paint me out as having some kind of episode. I know how it works, well not this time. You've made your bed now fucking die in it. You are *not* my father. I have one who is more of a man than you will ever be, and I hope you rot in hell, you bastard. I never want to see you again."

I turn and walk back to our table, everyone's eyes trained on the Judge, and I say to Cessy and Kyle. "I'm sorry guys, I really do need to leave. We'll catch up soon, Cessy."

She makes to speak, and Kyle says firmly, "Let her go. Give her time."

I smile my thanks and head for the exit, Shade walking beside me, watching my back as he always seems to do.

* * *

WE HEAD STRAIGHT to the penthouse and as soon as we step into the room, I burst into tears and place my face in my hands. Then I am pulled against Shade's chest and his arms wrap around me and he whispers, "Let it all out, baby girl. You did the right thing."

"Did I though, Shade? I have unboxed our dirtiest secret in public and there is no going back from this. Everyone will know, including my brother, and I should have told him first."

"I'm guessing he already knows."

"How?"

Shade holds me tightly and murmurs. "Your mom called him earlier."

"How do you know?"

He winks. "I tapped their phone."

"You did what?" I am so shocked he has that capability, and he shrugs as if it's normal. "I have a friend who specializes in that kind of thing, and when you're fighting a war, intelligence can be the difference between winning and losing."

"So, you've won."

"Not yet."

"I don't understand."

He pulls me down onto the couch and drapes his arm around my shoulder, kicking off his shoes while he loosens his tie.

"We've been listening in for weeks. When my grandfather told me about your uncle's secret, we needed to discover everything we could. I was to use you to ruin them. To open their pandora's box and let the demons out. Destroy you to destroy their perfect lives.

"Thanks for telling me." I sniff as he tells me something I don't already know and I sigh heavily, "I'm not stupid, Shade. I realized you were fighting a war with my uncle and using me as a weapon. I also know things changed, and you dragged me over the line to fight with you. I can take that, but Rafferty is innocent. He doesn't deserve this, and he didn't deserve to be framed for murder, either."

Shade nods and there is an expression in his eye I can't place and then he sighs and drops a light kiss on my head.

"My life is shit, Allegra. You see me as the guy who doesn't give a fuck and does what the hell he wants. I do to an extent, but it's all an act. A rebellion of sorts and a front to hide behind."

I stay silent because I can tell he needs to get this off his chest, so I just tangle my fingers in his and listen.

"I've never known any different. We were brought up by a bastard and thought that was normal. We became him but had a greater sense of loyalty than he did. He cheated on my mom and drove her into another man's arms and because of who we were, she left. She was given no other choice. Now, along with my brother and sister, we are to carry on the family empire. It's always come first in our family, and we accept that. However, somewhere along the way, I forgot the man inside the mafia bastard and it's only since I met you that I found him again."

I turn and stare at a face I could live seeing for a thousand years and never grow tired of it, and I nod.

"I feel the same, Shade. Despite what you may think, I don't really do this kind of stuff."

I laugh softly. "You are my bad. Everything I shouldn't want and yet you bring out the worst of me along with the best. The thing is..." I smile into his eyes. "It turns out the worst part of me is better than the rest. With you, I feel alive. You have given me a shot of living and I don't want to stop. We can move mountains, Shade. Fate brought us together for a reason, and whatever demons you carry along with you, they are mine now. Just like you have taken mine and made them your own. We fight together."

His lips crash against mine before the last word makes it out of my mouth and as his hands tangle in my hair and he deepens it further, I am drowning in darkness. He *is* darkness and, as it turns out, I prefer dark over light any day of the week.

CHAPTER 44

SHADE

TWO DAYS LATER

Kyle grins as he shows me the headlines on his phone, and I laugh softly. "It went well."

"Better than expected."

I type into my search engine and bring up the glorious downfall of Judge Lucas Stevenson in glorious pictorial form.

We stare at the screen of revenge. The result of our planning has never appeared so magnificent, and Kyle laughs out loud.

"This is the sweetest victory."

I nod and read some of the headlines.

Judge, jury, and downfall.

Judge Stevenson and his sister-in-law.

Judge Stevenson and the affair with his sister-in-law.

Two decades of infidelity.

Judge Stevenson steps down from his position amid scandal.

Judge Lucas Stevenson, the disgraced adulterer.

Jet Star's family betrayal.
When a family breaks.

"That's my favorite one." I say with a wicked grin and Kyle says with concern. "How did Allegra take the news?"

"Better than expected. She says they deserve it, and her only concern is her brother and father."

"Has she spoken to them?"

"Yes. She's meeting her brother now at his apartment."

"Of course." He nods. "I sent Sam and Vincenzo to guard her."

I think about how strong Allegra has been through this whole plot to bring her family down, and she has surprised me repeatedly. She is strong. Stronger than most and I love that her main concern is for the innocent ones in her family. There is nothing I don't love about her except her desire to carry on working. She is enjoying running my campaign and likes working with her assistant. Evangeline is happy because her agency was credited with the success of a campaign that lit up the socials like a firework. We have sold out our first masquerade night with a waiting list to fill several more.

It drags my thoughts back to this evening and I say sharply, "Is everything in place for tonight?"

Kyle nods. "All invited and their welcome arranged."

"Good. This has been a long time coming."

I stand and set my inner bastard firmly in charge and say with a wicked grin, "Then we should get to business."

* * *

WE GO in convoy to the warehouse near the city docks I use as an office of sorts. It's a legitimate import business that also doubles as an office for the visitors I prefer not to sign in on my guest book.

We head through the warehouse; a silent army of menace,

and I note the workers avert their eyes as they pretend there is nothing happening out of the ordinary.

There isn't. It's business as usual in the Vieri household and even my brother has decided to join us for the occasion. It's a rare sighting indeed, which is why security is at an all-time high.

Killian Vieri, mafia don in waiting, prefers to run the respectable side of our business, leaving me to have all the fun. Not this time. He is particularly pissed that it's taking so long and wants answers, and fast.

I reach the office and note his right-hand man, Saint, talking to one of their guards and he nods with respect as we join them.

"Shade, Kyle."

He points to the office. "Kill is inside checking a few things. He asked you to join him."

I nod and leave them to talk and head into the office we use for the less pleasant side of our business. Killian is checking his phone and stands when I enter.

"Shade." He brings me in for a hug, kissing me three times as is customary with family and then says with a grin. "I enjoyed the results of your weekend."

"Not as much as I did."

I laugh and drop into the seat opposite the desk and light a cigarette.

"Fuck, Shade, haven't you quit yet?"

Sighing, I stub it out and groan. "Habit."

"Then I had better keep you otherwise occupied."

"Shall we?" I stand and he nods, the light of revenge dancing in our eyes as we head out of the door, our men falling into step behind us, and we move as a hunting pack toward the door at the end of the barren hallway.

We enter and the bare concrete walls offer no luxuries

and the man sitting on a chair in the center of the room hasn't been granted any.

He is stripped naked with a bag over his head. Stark lightning glaring down harshly on his shivering frame. He is handcuffed to the chain that is suspended from the ceiling and is waiting for his fate to be decided.

Kill nods to the enforcer standing behind him and he rips off the bag over his head, causing our guest to blink against the harsh lighting.

His eyes widen with fear when he sees who's come to play and he whispers, "Don Vieri. I am honored."

Killian grabs a chair and sits astride it facing him and growls, "You pre-empt my title. Don Vieri couldn't be with us today and sent us instead."

I step beside him and smirk. "Two for the price of one. You are indeed honored, Freddie."

He starts to perspire, his tongue running along the ridge of his lips, and he says quickly, "Ask me anything."

Kill chuckles. "What, no attempt at a fight, no denials, just ask me anything and I'll tell you what I know?"

Freddie nods nervously. "If I thought I was going up against the Vieris, I would have come to you willingly. He didn't tell me you were involved. I didn't know. You must believe me."

Kill says nothing and makes him squirm for several seconds and then he growls, "Then you had better start at the beginning."

Freddie nods, shivering in the cold room.

"I was asked to blackmail that new star of the Jets. A woman was found murdered and the person asking saw an opportunity." He shakes his head.

"I used River. He does work for me like this occasionally and I knew I could rely on him."

His voice shakes as he whispers, "The dude's sister got involved and took over. She made the drop, and River sent Diego to mess with her head. We were going to split the money as payment, but our instructions were to intimidate her. Terrify her even and if the opportunity arose, we could have some fun."

I actually feel my blood boiling and Kill must sense it because he turns and fixes me with a hard expression, designed to get me to back the fuck down and yet how can I? I was there. I saw what Diego was going to do to her and I want to drive my fist through this fucker's head.

Kill says icily, "Who was the man behind it?"

Freddie starts to shake and says in terror, "I was never told his name. I swear to God, I would tell you if I did. He used one of those voice changers and his phone wasn't registered. He paid ten thousand up front and told us to keep the blackmail money. It seemed an easy job, and I never questioned it."

I share a look with my brother who rolls his eyes because there's a reason guys like Freddie Connor stay low-life villains. They don't have the brains to move on from the gutter.

I am so frustrated because this is getting us nowhere and Kill says suddenly, "What does the name Jefferson Stevenson mean to you?"

I stare at Freddie's reaction with interest and note the confusion in his eyes.

Killian sighs. "That's inconvenient."

"What is?" Freddie says nervously.

"The fact you can't tell us the identity of the man hiring you. How did he contact you?"

"He called. I told you."

Kill nods to one of the guards who tips out Freddie's belongings onto the stone floor and reaches for the cell phone nestling among his clothes.

Kill taps into it and says roughly, "Password?"

Freddie says quickly, "Whore."

I stare at him with growing distaste because this man is something else. He is both stupid and careless and I fucking detest men like him, even though I surround myself with them every fucking day.

Killian scrolls through the phone and occasionally shows me images of women tied up and fucked, badly beaten and used like trash. This merely adds fire to my fist because if Freddie thinks he's getting away with this, he is in for a shock.

Kill locates the incoming calls and shows me the evidence. Most calls come from unknown devises which isn't unusual for a man in Freddie's line of work. Whoever hired him knew we would get nothing from him, and I am so frustrated.

We are at a dead end, and I don't have a clue where to move next, and then Freddie says quickly, "I can't tell you who hired me, but I know who murdered that girl."

Killian looks up quickly and says with a low growl, "Tell me."

"Some creep from the city. One of my whores saw it happen. She was working in a nearby alley and as some guy fucked her against the wall, she saw the girl walk past. A car pulled up, and the door opened and a man in a pin-striped suit got out. They spoke and then he grabbed her hand and she struggled to get away. Greta was angry for her because she fucking hates that shit but before she could shake the guy off her, the girl was pulled into the car. She told me she will never forget that creep and said she has the license plate fresh in her mind."

"She never told the cops?" Killian says with interest. "Why not?"

Freddie shrugs. "Because she's an illegal. It's not worth

getting on their radar because they'll deport her back to Mexico."

"Did she tell you the license plate?"

Killian asks, and Freddie nods. "It was a Washington one with three letters and one number EV1L. She said it was easy to remember."

Killian leans back and turns to me, a satisfied smirk on his face. Then he stands and says to Freddie, "Our business is concluded. You are free to leave."

Freddie stares at him in astonishment.

"Are you serious?"

Killian growls, "Do you want me to change my mind?"

Freddie shakes his head wildly. "No, of course, thank you. Thank you, sir."

Kill nods in my direction.

"But not before my brother has a word. He's all yours, Shade."

He whispers as he passes, "Just don't kill the bastard. When you've finished with him, I'm guessing he will be covering his ass with the man who hired him and if it's who we think it is, revenge will be sweet."

He leaves with Saint and Freddie stares at me with terror as I shrug out of my jacket and hand it to Kyle, rolling up my sleeves with a murderous glint in my eye.

"Stand up." I hiss as the enforcer kicks the chair he is sitting on away from him and Freddie says in fear, "Please, I have told you everything."

"I know."

I shrug. "But that woman you were told to have fun with. The woman I found sobbing in the alley also happens to be my girlfriend and I can't let this go unpunished."

I watch the blood drain from his face as he realizes the shit he's in and I say in a voice edged in darkness, "Shall we begin?"

CHAPTER 45

ALLEGRA

Rafferty is broken. As soon as he entered his apartment and found me waiting for him, he broke down and I ran into his arms and sobbed, "I'm so sorry, Rafe. I should have told you when I found out."

He clings to me and says in a voice that kills me inside, "I fucking hate them both."

"Me too."

He pulls away and the anger in his eyes is hard to witness as he growls, "Tell me everything."

As I fill him in, his face is frozen into a blank expression. It's as if all emotion has deserted my brother and left him a machine. A broken machine with no life left in it and it breaks my heart.

I finish up and he runs his fingers through his hair and says with a slight hiss, "It was all over the fucking internet before I could deal with it. One of the guys showed me on his phone and I had no place to hide."

He shakes his head. "Mom called when you left and told me the happy news. She broke down on the phone and asked me to forgive her."

"What did you say?" I ask, not surprised when he growls, "I cut the call. That was the last time I spoke to her."

He grabs a beer from the fridge and leans against it, a sad expression in his eye as he whispers, "I called dad. I asked him to come and meet us here."

"Is he coming?"

He should be here soon. I want to check he's okay."

"Are *you* okay, Rafe?"

I'm concerned because my brother appears to have changed overnight and become harder, emotionless and no longer the sweet, friendly guy he's always been.

"I'm just fine, Ally. Don't you worry about me."

I am worried though. He has adopted a hard edge that I'm convinced is to protect himself. I don't like seeing it because Rafferty isn't this man before me.

There's a knock on the door and Rafferty sighs. "We may as well get this over with."

My heart lurches because what if it's not our father? It could be anyone and even though Shade has positioned his guards outside, I am still mindful there's someone out there with a grudge against us. What if it's something else entirely?

"Come in dad."

My heart sags with relief as my father walks into the apartment, a shadow of his former self.

He appears weary, tense and on edge and my heart breaks for him as he hugs his son hard.

"I'm so sorry, Rafe." He says with a break to his voice and as his eyes connect with mine, I sob as he opens his arms to let me into the hug.

We stand for what seems like ages as we hug it out and it strikes me that this is the new face of our family unit. Just the three of us.

We break apart and as I join my father on the couch,

Rafferty tosses him a beer and nods toward the coffee machine. "Want one?"

"No. I'm good, thanks."

I note my father's fingers tremble as he holds the beer and I rest my hand on his arm and say softly, "I'm so sorry dad."

"It's not your apology to make, Ally." He sighs. "I should be the one apologizing to you. To both of you."

He shakes his head. "We should have told you the story from the beginning. Your mom didn't want to, though. She didn't see the need because you were still tied to me by blood."

He sighs heavily. "I was so happy when Lucas offered to donate his sperm. It was the most precious gift a brother could give. I didn't realize he took it literally though and did it the old-fashioned way."

He sounds bitter and I'm really not surprised about that, and I put my arm around him and say with concern, "What are you going to do now?"

"Divorce Meredith. There is no going back from this."

"And uncle, I mean …"

"My brother." He interrupts, sparing me from having to name the man himself.

"We met the day after you exposed his lies in the restaurant. He was hiding away from the press camped out on his doorstep and I stormed around there to have it out with him."

"Did you?" Rafferty says angrily, and he nods.

"We fought. I'm sure you get the picture. The worst thing was, he never fought back. Just took the punches and told me constantly how sorry he was. It wasn't helping, so I left. That was the last I heard from him."

"And mom?"

I enquire gently, and he shakes his head. "I moved into a hotel. I'm never going back. She will be served with divorce papers and I'm walking away. But not from you. Never from you."

He says roughly, "I don't care what anyone says. You are my children. I love you and I always have, and I will fight for you. You may have your mother's family name, but you are my kids. I'm here for you and I always will be. You are not on your own."

He draws me in for a hug and I cling to him, the tears cascading down my cheeks as my heart crashes and burns. Rafferty joins us and we hug it out, knowing that nothing will ever stop us loving the man who will always be our dad.

* * *

Later, I fix us some lunch and, as expected, the conversation soon turns to my love life and they both stare at me with concern.

"This man." My father says with a sigh.

"Shade." I add with a smile.

"What's going on, Ally? Is he blackmailing you?" Rafferty says angrily, and it makes me smile.

"No, Rafe. I love him. He's, well, he's been amazing."

"Are you sure about that?" My father says with a worried frown.

"Of course. You know, it didn't start out that way. I'll be honest about that, but I believe he loves me. He's not your typical boyfriend, but at least he's genuine with me. I appreciate his honesty, even if I don't always like what I hear."

"Those photographs tell another story, Ally."

My father's expression is loaded with disapproval and Rafferty says in a worried voice. "He's a criminal, Ally. Some say he's mafia. He's not for you."

The fact we have two of his guards outside his apartment makes for no denial and I merely shrug and say lightly,

"Look. I'm aware of what Shade represents. He has never tried to disguise that from me and if you think I'm his prisoner or something, that he's playing with me, you're wrong. Who knows, we may end things when the shine rubs off. We may wake up one day and decide we're not right for one another, but not today and probably not for the foreseeable."

I shrug. "I can't help that I love him. I really do before you tell me I'm a fool, but I'm not going into this with my eyes shut, whatever you both think and those photographs…"

I take a deep breath. "They represent the best weekend of my life, followed by the worst, and Shade is responsible for the first weekend. So, give him a chance, give *us* a chance and if it all ends tomorrow, at least I had the best time ever."

I smile at them both. "Trust me and don't judge me. That's all I ask."

My father nods and shares a look with my brother, who sighs heavily.

"Okay, but if he does anything to hurt you, conker, I'll be looking for him. Mafia or not."

"Don't call me that!" I yell, laughing as they join me.

For a moment, I could believe everything was normal in my life. It feels so good I almost don't want to leave, but then I remember what tonight is and I'm needed back at the club.

Tonight is make or break for my career but I didn't realize it was also make or break for my life with Shade.

CHAPTER 46

SHADE

That felt so good.

As I wash the blood from my knuckles, Kyle watches me through the mirror.

"Fucking lightweight." He growls because Freddie really didn't put up any fight at all.

I always let my prisoners free and encourage them to fight back. I'm not interested in fighting a man who is defenseless. Where's the fun in that?

I gaze at my reflection and frown.

"Fuck, he didn't even land a punch. There's not a scratch on me."

"And you're upset about that?" Kyle shakes his head. "I can rough you up a bit if you like."

It makes me laugh. "You could try. It may even be fun, but we must head back to the club. We have a revenge to enjoy."

We make our way back and I think about what Freddie told us and say to Kyle, "That number plate. I kind of wish it was mine. Do you know who it belongs to?"

"Yes." Kyle pulls out his phone. "I was on it the minute he

told us, and it came back registered to a man called Alexei Komonov."

"Who is he?"

I'm curious because I have never heard the name before.

"Some guy who owns half of Russia. He's a big shot businessman there."

"Then why is he picking up women off the streets of New York who end up minus their heart the next day? Something isn't adding up here."

"I agree." Kyle shakes his head. "Komonov wasn't even in the country on that day, or even the weeks surrounding it. He was on vacation at his home in Hawaii and his car was having some work done on it at the time of the abduction."

"Maybe we should dig a little deeper."

Kyle nods in agreement and I add, "Check out anyone who fakes license plates. I'm guessing it was a decoy. Somebody wants us to believe it was this guy. Possibly somebody with a grudge against him. Discover everything you can about him. Who he is friends with, who he fucks, and who he entertains. The person doing this is running circles around us, and I want to know why."

Kyle makes notes into his phone and places it in his pocket as we pull up in the underground car park.

As we leave the car, I hate the feeling of losing control. Something is going on around us and nobody will be safe until we find out who killed the girl and who is framing Rafferty Powell for murder and why?

* * *

"I AM SO NERVOUS. What if it's a failure?"

I hardly hear what Allegra is saying because I want to rip that dress off and fuck her until she can't walk.

She is wearing the same gold dress she danced in the

night she came to my club and the fact she's wearing nothing underneath is like a red flag to a bull. Her hair is long and the mask sexy and the six-inch heels she is wearing make her legs go on forever.

"Come here." I say with a low growl and her eyes light up as she drags the zipper down, low enough to tease and says huskily, "Does sir want me to dance for him?"

"Sir wants you to do a lot more than fucking dance, sweetheart." I growl and she throws her head back and laughs before sucking her finger and saying suggestively, "Then you will have to pay the going rate and rent a room."

"I'll pay a lot more than the going rate if you come over here and get on all fours."

"Don't tempt me." She says with a sigh and then glances nervously at the nearby carriage clock.

"It's time."

I know she is right to dismiss my request because tonight is too important to us both for any distractions getting in the way, but she looks so good in that dress I just can't help myself and with a short stride, grab her wrist and push her face first against the wall, inching her dress up around her waist and hissing, "Spread your legs."

"Fuck, Shade." Her voice is dripping in lust and as I release my throbbing cock, I waste no time in plunging in deep from behind, slamming her against the wall as I do what the fuck I want as always.

It's a good job Allegra gets off on me treating her like a whore. It's become a favorite game of ours, which is right up my alley. I have definitely met my match with her. Princess by day and whore by night. She is my perfect woman and as I fuck her hard, I grip her hips and slam in relentlessly, loving her heated gasp as she clenches my cock and milks it until I explode inside her with a loud, "Fuck, yes!"

A knock on the door makes her giggle and I smirk as I

pull out and say huskily, "Go and clean up. You have five minutes."

I grab a wad of paper tissues and clean up, loving knowing my cock is wet from her pleasure. I will never get enough of my pretty princess, and she will soon realize that.

I open the door as Allegra scurries into the bathroom and Kyle and Cecilia head inside, dressed for business.

It makes me laugh at the pained expression in Kyle's eyes as he stares at his girl, who is dressed the same as Allegra.

We thought it would be fun to let them blend in and become our own personal dancers for the night. We are expected to join in the fun and will lead the way to depravity. It wouldn't look good if we had our girlfriends with us, so this was the perfect solution. Fantasy is the theme and this one ticks every box I own, and Kyle was more than happy with my suggestion.

"Where's Ally?" Cecilia says, her eyes wide as she stares around my penthouse.

"I'm here." Allegra waves from the doorway and heads toward us with a wicked gleam in her eye.

"Man, you're one hot bitch." Her friend yells and they dissolve into a fit of the giggles, causing Kyle to roll his eyes.

I shake my head as we study the two women whispering behind their hands and I say with a resigned sigh, "Come on. Let's not keep our guests waiting."

* * *

ANGELZ HAS BEEN TRANSFORMED. For one night only the place resembles a theater. There are cages suspended over the dance floor with dancers inside them, wearing revealing costumes that are designed to excite and titillate. The stage is filled with smoke and a lone pole in the center surrounded by a backdrop of flowers and lanterns. The tables are dressed in candles and champagne buckets with various adult toys littering the top.

All the guests are required to wear masks and the tables are filling up already with men hiding behind them. For one night only they can be anonymous and as we cut through the club, I'm aware of every set of eyes following us.

I leave my customers in no doubt who is in charge around here as we walk in a pack, the two women apparently our private dancers for the night.

We head to the roped off booth that surveys the entire club and as we settle down, I pull Allegra astride my lap and whisper, "I fucking love this event. You're a genius."

She whispers against my lips, "You look so hot. How long before we can slip away to that hotel room?"

It makes me grin and I tangle my fingers in her hair and pull down sharply. "Business first and then pleasure."

"Why am I so turned on right now when you're being an asshole again?" She hisses furiously into my ear, and I hide my laughter and shrug. "Because you're as fucked in the head as I am."

I smirk as Cecilia adopts the same pose on Kyle and I'm guessing that anybody watching won't think anything is going on that isn't repeated around this whole club. Everywhere I look, women stand astride men, giving them a show they will never want to forget.

The place fills up and soon every seat and table are taken. The promise of sex and depravity hangs heavy in the air and as Allegra sits by my side, I stare around the room, intent on only one thing.

Then my prayer is answered when I notice a man slap one of my dancers on the ass and tuck a wad of dollar bills into her G-string. She moves off his lap and they leave through the hotel exit.

I nod to Kyle, who whispers something in Cecilia's ear,

and I say to Allegra, "Enjoy time with your friend. I won't be long."

She smiles and is wise to keep her questions to herself as we leave the girls under the protection of the guards surrounding our booth.

We make our way to my office and as I switch on the monitor, I notice our guest has arrived in the room with the dancer. We take our seats for the show and Kyle groans when Jefferson tears off his suit and says roughly, "Strip you bitch and suck my hard cock."

"Nice." Kyle shakes his head as she crawls across the floor and Jefferson grasps her hair and thrusts in hard and deep, causing her gag as he fucks her mouth violently.

"Do we really need to watch this?" Kyle says with disgust, as he waves his hand at the screen, and I laugh softly. "I'll admit he's not my type, not many women's either, but we'll allow him some fun before we have ours."

As he shoots all over her face and hair, the disgust on her face obviously turns him on because he snarls, "This is my fantasy bitch and I have paid good money for this. Do your fucking job."

He slaps her hard around the face and she yells, "Fuck! What are you…"

She doesn't finish because he slaps her again and pushes her against the wall by her throat and hisses, "Don't move or you'll see just what I'm capable of."

The tears fall from her eyes as he sneers, "It's my needs that matter here. I'm the important one, not you. Never the greedy whore who fucks men with her eyes before emptying their wallets. I'm the big man. I'm the one who says what's happening here and you will do what the fuck I tell you to or face the consequences."

Kyle stands and I place my hand on his arm and say firmly, "Wait."

I stare at Jefferson Stevenson with disgust as he reveals exactly what kind of monster hides inside him. As he rips the dancer's dress off, he squeezes her throat, so she's struggling to breathe and whispers, "This is what turns me on, whore. The terror in your eyes, knowing there is nothing you can do about it. I will fuck you and I will hurt you. I will rape you and I will ruin you. The more unwilling you are, the more it turns me on and when I have finished, I will cut out your heart and keep it as a trophy, leaving you yet another worthless corpse that nobody will miss."

"Now!" I say darkly and one call from Kyle has the door to the room crashing open and several of my guards pouring inside, grabbing that fucker by the throat and punching his fucking head in.

I watch with growing excitement as they drag him out naked while he offers them money to stop and as another dancer heads inside the room to comfort Heather, who volunteered for the role, I breathe a sigh of relief that we got what we needed.

CHAPTER 47

ALLEGRA

Cecilia hands me another glass of champagne and whispers, "I'm in heaven. This world is wild. I can't keep up."

She grins. "Now I see what made you into a wild woman I don't blame you at all."

I nod and sip my champagne, loving how well the evening is panning out and Cessy says with concern, "Are you okay though, honey? I mean, the shit with your folks sucks. What are you going to do about that?"

"Nothing." I shrug. "I've spoken to my dad and Rafferty, and we are both of the same opinion. Nothing will change between us, and mom can go and fuck herself."

Cecilia says with concern. "It's all anyone can talk about at the office. Many love that the great Judge Stevenson was brought down, the smug bastard."

She shakes her head. "He was always so sanctimonious, and I overheard two of my bosses saying they wish he had taken his son with him when he left."

"I've always found him a little creepy." I shiver when I think of my cousin and Cessy nods. "One of the girls in my office knows his girlfriend, Gina Di Angelo. Apparently, she was seen wiping her mouth after he kissed her in public at a restaurant. My friend said she stared at him with hatred when he wasn't looking and smiled lovingly at him when he was. There's a story there."

It makes me laugh because Cecilia is such a gossip and loves the drama.

"Tell me about you and Kyle. What happened when I left?" I'm interested in their story, and she smirks and from the expression in her eyes rather a lot happened.

"Well, when you left, he poured on the charm. I mean, these guys are hot and when they look at you as if you are the sexiest creature alive, it kind of makes you drop your guard, along with everything else."

She giggles. "Anyway, he told me you wouldn't be back, and we were going to have our own party."

She rolls her eyes. "I'm not gonna lie. I gave him a hard time because I was worried about you. I told him to tell me where you were, but I got nowhere. I was angry, and he used that anger against me and dragged me into some room they have attached to that club and my anger turned into passion pretty damn fast."

She sighs, a dreamy look in her eyes at the memory.

"He ripped off his shirt and man, that body is a weapon all muscled and inked, I couldn't keep my hands off him. I figured I may as well enjoy my evening and so I let him fuck me all night in a room he called a sex room."

"I've been there. Well, in one similar." I say with a wicked grin.

"So, you know how hard it was to say no." She sips her champagne and grins. "I was a goner. I mean, he could have asked me to do anything in there and I would have done it, no questions asked. I was up for anything, and I think we did

—everything that is and when I woke up, we did it all over again."

It makes me laugh, and she says, suddenly serious, "Do you think he likes me? It's just, well, he is so cool one minute and hot the next. I waited for him to call me in the week, but all I got was a text telling me to meet him the following weekend. Then another one telling me to meet him at that hotel in Washington instead. What if he's just using me for sex?"

She looks so concerned it makes me smile and I say reassuringly, "He has a lot on his mind with work. Shade keeps him busy and to my knowledge, there isn't anyone else. Shade finds it amusing that Kyle is so taken with you. He didn't think he had it in him, so if you're asking if he likes you, then yes, I think he does."

"And there's nobody else, not that he owes me anything, of course."

I'm so surprised at how anxious she is because Cecilia is never anxious about men—ever. She must really like Kyle and so I nod, smiling my reassurance. "I'm guessing he's in unfamiliar territory with you, Cessy. Just don't make it too easy for him."

"Like you." She raises her eyes and I shrug. "I play Shade at his own game. He ruins me and I love every minute of it."

"I could tell from the photos. Man, that sex must have been something else. You looked fucked. I'm happy for you. You needed to get laid; you can thank me later."

She grins as I roll my eyes and glance around me.

"Where do you think they are?"

"Beats me. Do you think we can dance somewhere?"

"You could try, but I'm guessing we wouldn't make it out of this booth."

Cecilia sighs heavily. "This sucks. Not that I mind

spending time with my bestie, but we're all dressed up like whores, with no one to fuck. Fuck my life."

She takes a drag from the bottle and passes it to me and as we sit waiting, I'm just grateful for some time to catch up with my friend.

CHAPTER 48

SHADE

They bring Jefferson to my office and as he falls headfirst into the room, I stare at him with disgust as he cowers naked on the floor.

Kyle reaches down and grabs his arm and forces him into the chair before me and holds a gun to his head, causing Jefferson to say fearfully. "What's going on?"

"You assaulted a member of my staff." I reply coolly and replay the recording and his eyes widen as he says in disbelief, "You filmed me. Do you record every person that comes here? That's against the law."

"And what you did is within the law." I shake my head. "I wonder what daddy would think about that?"

Jefferson shakes as I sneer. "The trouble is, daddy has a lot more on his mind than dealing with your problems, doesn't he? Was that your plan all along? Remove the competition. Secure your inheritance and drive your half siblings into madness."

"I don't..." I hold up my hand and drop the photograph of Taylor Sutherland on the desk. The one Heather copied from the murder scene.

His eyes widen as I play the recording of him threatening her in the hotel room and I say angrily, "Bit of a coincidence wouldn't you say? Is that what happened to Taylor?"

He surprises me by laughing out loud and hissing, "Is that all you've got? A set up recording and a dead girl's photograph. Your evidence is as pathetic as you are."

The door crashes open, causing him to jump, and I love watching the blood drain from his face when he sees who has joined us.

I stand and head around the desk and offer my chair to my grandfather.

Killian and Saint accompany him and, as my grandfather sits down, he removes a cigar from his jacket and taps it on the desk.

I move to stand beside my brother and leave my grandfather to run the show, as he has done my entire life, and he says in his deep husky drawl.

"Jefferson Stevenson."

He shakes his head as if disappointed.

"I am here to inform you that your membership of the Dark Lords has been terminated."

Jefferson opens his mouth to speak, and Kyle presses his gun in further, effectively silencing him.

"This is a sad moment in our history." My grandfather shakes his head.

"A member using his position to act out vicious, sordid murders in the name of our great organization."

"It wasn't me." Jefferson stutters, and my grandfather sighs. "Even now, you are dishonorable. Blaming others when it was you all along."

He leans back and twirls the cigar between his fingers.

"Mario Bachini." He says with a dark expression and Jefferson begins to shake with nerves.

"You were his best friend. You idolized him, wanted to please him and be like him."

He shakes his head and sighs heavily. "You copied him. He let you into his sadistic world and involved you in ritual killings, all in the name of the organization your father was high up in. You thought you were better than him and pledged allegiance to a man who believed he would sit in my seat one day."

He hisses. "Mario Bachini was *never* going to be a Dark Lord. His own father was about to be stripped of the title because, contrary to what you were told, we do not murder anyone on an altar after we allow hooded figures to fuck them."

Kyle presses the gun in deeper as Don Vieri spits, "When Mario and Carlos were removed, you carried on. You saw a way to deal with a problem you had. You discovered your father had another family. Two siblings who were named alongside you in his will."

Jefferson says nothing and hangs his head, as if he can't process what's happening.

"You discovered this by bribing a corrupt lawyer who had access to the files. You were enraged and decided to use one of your indiscretions to frame the man who stood in the way of your inheritance, and you got two for the price of one. Your own half-sister became another one of your victims when you blackmailed her."

I am so close to dealing with this fucker myself, but I know my grandfather will have a well-deserved ending planned for him and I stare at him with an enigmatic expression that disguises the blood lust in my heart.

Don Vieri hisses, "You paid a low-life criminal to do your dirty work, telling him to keep the money and use the woman, hoping she would end up dead."

"I never–" He attempts to defend himself and Kyle strikes

him hard across the head with the gun and growls, "Shut the fuck up when Don Vieri is speaking."

Jefferson shivers uncontrollably as my grandfather fixes him with an angry glare and hisses, "I instructed my grandsons to deal with this. Shade was to deal with your father, and Killian had the delight of dealing with you."

Kill says darkly, "Gina was working for me."

Jefferson's head snaps up, and he shakes his head wildly. "She loves me, she told me."

We all laugh at the pathetic expression on his face as Killian says with a shake of his head. "She despises you. She begged me to speed things up so she could leave. You disgusted her."

"No!"

Jefferson is in denial and says almost to himself, "She loves me. I am everything to her. She told me."

Killian laughs darkly. "The night of Taylor Sutherland's death, you returned home, and Gina was sleeping. What you don't know is that while you were in the shower, she was gathering evidence and sending it to me. Your shirt had blood on it, and she hid it to preserve the evidence. You see, I instructed her to look for anything we could use against you. It turns out the shirt had the blood of Taylor Sutherland smeared across it and she can swear an oath that you were missing at the time of the murder."

Jefferson shakes his head in obvious distress. "It wasn't like that."

My grandfather leans forward. "Then tell us what it was like."

"I found her." He says pathetically. "I was driving home, and I saw a body by the side of the road. I stopped and, as I bent down, my shirt brushed against her. I swear I didn't kill her."

"Then explain why you had a fake license plate attached

to your car when you picked her up while she walked from the hotel after sleeping with Rafferty Powell. Explain how she was found with your hair under her fingernails and your semen in her body. Tell us how an eyewitness saw you pull her into your car against her will and explain why your car with the fake plates was seen leaving a lock up a few hours before her body was found."

Jefferson stares in horror at my grandfather as the odds stack against him and my grandfather taps his cigar on the desk and hisses, "Can you explain that Jefferson?"

He says nothing and my grandfather reaches into his pocket and pulls out a series of photographs that he drops on the desk before a disbelieving serial killer.

They are taken from inside his lockup. It resembles a church with an altar in the middle. It has stone walls and a stone floor, restraints anchoring the victim to the hard surface of the altar. There are candles set around it and various tools attached to the walls. It resembles a freaking sacrificial chamber and I feel sick knowing what he did there.

"Show them in." My grandfather leans back in his chair and Jefferson jumps as the room is filled with cops and one steps forward and says, "Jefferson Stevenson. I am arresting you for the murder of Taylor Sutherland. You have the right to remain silent. Anything you say can and will be used against you in a court of law. You have the right to an attorney. If you cannot afford an attorney, one will be provided for you."

He nods to another cop, who steps forward and cuffs him as Kyle lowers his gun and the cop says wearily, "We can take this from here."

He nods with respect to my grandfather and smiles. "It's good to see you again, sir. I hope you and your lovely wife are keeping well."

"Couldn't be better, detective."

My grandfather grins and the detective nods. "You can safely leave this with us, sir."

He turns and acknowledges the rest of us. "Enjoy your evening."

As they leave, I feel a sense of loss. What I wouldn't have given to finish the bastard off myself and Killian places his hand on my shoulder and says in a low voice, "It had to be done. Total humiliation and no comeback. We must be within the law to hold on to our power. It's the only way."

My grandfather stands and says wearily, "It's done. Another problem solved, as another takes its place."

I stare at my brother, who says to the men still in the room with us, "We need a minute."

As they leave, I hate the feeling that this isn't over and as the door closes, my grandfather shakes his head and points to the chairs before the desk.

"Now, for the real reason I'm here."

As we take our seats, I wonder what's on his mind and something about the expression in his eyes tells me I'm not going to like it.

"Serena." My blood runs cold and I say roughly, "What about her?"

"She will need your help."

"Why?" I say quickly because if our sister is in any danger, I'm liable to stage a fucking war.

He sighs heavily and I note the worry in his eyes.

"I had a visit from Dimitri Constantine. You are aware his sons were following your decoy."

"I was aware." I stare at him in anger, and he hisses, "They heard word there's a contract out on your sister."

"What the fuck!" I jump up and my grandfather roars, "Sit the fuck down and keep your head. Your anger won't help her now."

I do as he says but there is no way in hell we are putting

Serena in danger and he taps his cigar on the desk and says in his customary drawl, "They came to me with the information, knowing I will take steps to protect her. We have a good relationship with the Constantine's, and I asked them to help. Dimitri sent his sons, and they pulled in a few favors, which led to us discovering Jefferson's lock up. They were working on my behalf with Killian to wrap up this mystery and discover what they could about the person responsible for targeting your sister."

Killian nods. "They were close to discovering Jefferson's secrets and knew of his interest in Allegra. They were following that day to watch over her, knowing that Jefferson had no regard for her safety. They didn't realize we had placed a cop in as a decoy and just wanted to make sure she was safe."

"Will somebody please tell me why all of this was going on and you neglected to tell me?" I say irritably, and Killian answers as my grandfather looks on with interest.

"Because the woman at the center of it is too close to you. Anybody watching you both would have seen that, and we wanted to keep our investigations under the radar. When you are close to someone, it becomes personal, and mistakes are made. We were doing it to protect you both."

"I don't need protecting." I hiss, so angry I almost can't see straight.

My grandfather shakes his head. "You need protecting against your own ignorance with a statement like that."

He stares at me with a hard expression in his eye and, as always, I back down under the force of it.

His eyes flash as he snarls, "Your sister is the same. She will learn nothing of this threat."

"Why? She needs to protect herself, and knowledge is the best defense." I say foolishly because questioning the Don's instructions isn't the best idea in the world.

He merely shakes his head, followed by a deep sigh.

"Shade. You have a lot to learn. There are reasons why we do things in a certain way, and it all boils down to the same point. We use knowledge to protect, to defeat, and to secure. Serena is headstrong, like you, and if we tell her she is in danger, she will make certain she puts herself in the firing line to flush them out. She will be safer in ignorance with us watching her back and, with the help of our friends, the Constantines, we will discover the man responsible and remove him."

"The man?" I lean forward. "It could be a woman."

Killian adds. "Doubtful but Shade is right. We must consider all the options."

"Then consider them but make it fast."

My grandfather leans back and I hate the pain in his eyes as he says sadly, "I'm getting too old for this shit. Now the Stevenson problem has been resolved, we move onto Serena's. Use every resource you have and when she is back from visiting your mom, I want this city to be the safest one in the world for her."

"You are seriously letting her go ahead with her visit." I say incredulously, and my grandfather nods.

"As soon as she is on the plane, she is protected. I will send someone with her, and Australia is the perfect place for her to hide. Stoner's ranch is in the middle of nowhere and he is the perfect guardian to keep her safe."

"Does he know?" Kill says, and my grandfather shakes his head.

"No. Only us and the Dimitris. That is all, and I am relying on you all to work together to keep your sister safe."

He stares at us with an evil gleam in his eye and hisses, "Nobody messes with the Vieris and lives to boast about it. Do what you must but do it fast. Serena is now our number one priority, and we must move fast. I am relying on you. Don't let me down."

He stands and we follow his lead, and he moves before me and grips my face in both hands and stares at me with a dark expression mixed with love. I have always marveled at his ability to be the most commanding presence in the room, both fearful and demanding of respect, and yet I am always assured of his deep love for his family.

He kisses me three times and then whispers, "You have had your fun, Shade. Now it's time to grow up and take responsibility for who you are. This woman will be good for you. Make it work."

I nod because he's not wrong about Allegra. She *is* good for me and then he turns to Killian and says in a firm voice, "We're leaving. Work out a plan and work together. I will use my contacts and leave nothing to chance."

He smiles. "Now, I promised nonna I wouldn't be long, and you know your grandmother. My life won't be worth living if I cause her to worry."

As they leave, Killian throws me a look I recognize, causing the adrenalin to surge through my veins. This time we go in hard and where it concerns our sister, we will not leave anything to chance.

CHAPTER 49

ALLEGRA

It feels like forever before Shade enters the room, closely followed by Kyle and several of his guards. They don't seem happy, and I glance at Cecilia, who catches my eye and fans herself.

"Is it wrong that I find that so hot?"

She raises her eyes, and I can't help laughing because she's not wrong.

"Then there is something wrong with me too, because I feel the same."

As they reach us, my heart flutters because the first thing Shade does is throw me a wicked grin and pull me up hard against him, before leaning down and whispering, "Party's over."

"What…?" I don't get a chance to ask why before he grips my wrist and pulls me along with him, inside the circle of menace. I gaze helplessly at Cessy, who is watching us go with wide eyes and I notice Kyle reaching for her in much the same way.

Shade is moving at speed and as we leave the packed club,

I struggle to catch my breath as we head through a door marked exit and into a long, dark corridor.

"Shade, stop. Where are we going?"

He completely ignores me and moves toward a door at the end and one of his guards opens it, revealing an elevator, and as we step inside, the door closes, leaving us alone.

I open my mouth to speak, but he moves swiftly in and kisses me hard, with more passion than before. His fingers tangle in my hair and he deepens the kiss, causing my heart to flutter and my legs to buckle.

This is so intense, *he* is so intense and as the elevator stops, he pulls me out onto the rooftop, as he did the night we met in Gyration. I stare in wonder at the gleaming helicopter waiting for us and as we run toward it, he grips my hand tight.

The noise is tremendous as the engine starts and he snaps my belt around me, much like before and then secures himself. Once again, I open my mouth to speak and he lays his palm across it and his eyes gleam as he says, "No talking."

The helicopter takes off and my heart is pounding as we fly over the city and away from the masquerade. I'm still wearing the ridiculous costume and I jump when his hand rests on my thigh, causing the desire to flood through my body at the mere thought of what pleasure he can bring me.

We leave the city and once again head over the water and it's not long before we see the lit boat dancing on the waves below.

I stare at him with my eyes shining and he grins, taking my hand in his and lifting it to his lips.

His eyes gleam and his intentions are clear, and I am more than happy about that.

As we land, this time there are no nerves. No doubts and no fear. I am excited, hopeful, and so turned on I hope we make it before I come at just the thought of what happens next.

Still in silence, we exit the helicopter and Shade pulls me at speed toward the cabin area and as the steward nods with respect, Shade pulls me down the stairs below deck, into a huge cabin that could rival a top hotel room.

I stare around me in awe, and he locks the door with a wicked grin and leans against it, dragging his eyes the length of me, before saying, "Now you have my attention."

I roll my eyes. "You really are a cocky jackass. Who says I wanted it?"

He smirks and shrugs out of his jacket and lays his gun on the table, unbuttoning his shirt and ripping it off, revealing his toned abs and inked six pack. I can't look away as he drops his pants and steps out of them with the hugest erection I have ever seen and he says roughly, "I want your mouth on my cock and you on your knees."

"Fuck you." I can't help grinning at the mischievous twinkle in his eye and he shrugs, "Are you backing out of our deal already, princess?"

"But you said…"

He shakes his head. "You agreed to seven nights and seven days."

I nod, disguising the delight in my expression and holding his gaze, I unzip my foul dress and let it fall to the floor, standing before him in nothing but a gold G-string and my mask.

I run my hands over my body and moan as I sway from side to side, putting on a show that causes him to palm his cock and groan, "You look fucking amazing, princess."

I place two fingers in my G-string and ease it down gently, keeping my eyes trained on him the entire time as I suck in my lower lip and flutter my lashes.

His eyes are dark and filled with lust as I sway toward him and just as I press my lips to his, I drop down before him and cup his balls, rolling them around my fingers and squeezing them hard.

"Fuck." His low hiss makes me smile against his dripping cock and as I lick it slowly, his eyes roll back and he groans, "You're amazing."

I slide him into my mouth and grip his ass, pulling him in deeper, groaning with pleasure, and as he thrusts gently, I taste my man and a shiver of pleasure passes through my entire body.

This is what I love. Our dirty moments alone when nobody else exists. Two people who are crazy about one another, playing the most wicked games. Will it last forever? I fucking hope so and if it doesn't, at least I had the time of my life while it did.

As he grips my hair and face fucks my mouth, I find I get as much pleasure from pleasing him as myself. More, in fact, because right at this moment, I am the only thing on Shade's mind. I have his attention one hundred percent, and nobody can touch us.

As he comes hard down my throat, I swallow every drop, happy I brought him pleasure and knowing he will not be leaving it here. From the expression in his eye, I'm in for a long night and I'm more than happy about that.

* * *

I WAS RIGHT. We don't sleep at all and spend the entire night exploring our bodies, pushing our limits, and driving one another insane with lust. Shade is the perfect lover and my dream man and as we sit on the deck wrapped in a blanket, we watch the sunrise naked, holding hands and exhausted.

"It's so beautiful." I stare at the majestic rising of the most brilliant, magnificent star.

"It is." He turns to me and kisses my lips slowly and then whispers against them, "This is my happy place. You naked in my arms, on my boat, watching the sunrise, knowing we have the rest of our lives to enjoy moments like this."

"You're a little presumptuous, aren't you?" I laugh softly as his stubble grazes my cheek and he whispers, "Did I say you had a choice?"

He strokes his finger lightly down my face and his eyes gleam as he says huskily, "The sun may be magnificent, but it's dull in comparison to you. I never thought I'd say this in my entire life, but I love you, Allegra Powell, and you are going to become my wife."

I stare at him in surprise as he smiles gently and whispers, "Whether you agree or not."

It makes me laugh and despite how tempting it is to say no just to annoy him, I grip his face between my hands and hold it gently, staring into his eyes as I whisper, "As it happens, I can't think of anything I'd like more, so yes, I will become your wife, Shade Vieri, on one condition."

"There are conditions?" He raises his eyes with amusement, and I giggle against his lips. "On the condition you never stop surprising me. We live life to the extreme and don't settle for anything ordinary."

"That's two conditions. One has to go." He grins and I shrug. "You choose. I couldn't really give a fuck, anyway."

He laughs out loud and pushes me back onto the deck and strokes my face, while gazing into my eyes with a loving expression as he whispers, "I told you I loved you. It's customary to say it back."

"Then earn it, asshole." I giggle as his eyes glitter with lust, and he pushes inside me, slowly, in no hurry, while staring into my eyes the entire time. He rubs my clit with his thumb, building me to an orgasm that causes me to moan his name on the soft ocean breeze.

My entire body shakes as my orgasm crashes through it, ripping through my defenses and chaining my soul to his. Yes, I'm in no doubt at all that I love this man with my entire heart, but he really doesn't need to know that at all.

EPILOGUE

SERENA

My heart is heavy, and the tears burn as the car takes me away from the only people I love and trust with all my heart. As send offs go, this one is bittersweet because my brothers have introduced two other females into our tight circle, and I am interested in getting to know them.

I almost pity them and wonder if they understand what they have let themselves in for.

It's not easy being a Vieri and especially not a woman. I'm just surprised I was allowed to go and visit the one who got away.

Mom lives in Australia, and you couldn't get much further than that, but she obviously decided it was her best shot at happiness when she divorced my father.

I miss her and I'm desperate to reconnect with her. It's just a shame I must travel halfway across the world to do it.

As I watch the familiar scenery passing, I gaze out of the window and wonder if I will be as happy as my brothers obviously are because I never have much luck meeting guys.

When your brothers head up the local mafia, there really aren't that many takers.

Then there's me. I am made of the same stuff and I'm not the innocent young woman many guys like to have by their side. I'm a challenge. I realize that and I won't ever be anything else.

The three cars in our cavalcade must be an interesting sight as we speed on our way to the airport. My grandfather wanted me to take a private plane, but I insisted on traveling in a commercial one. I want to be among normal people for once. To live their life and merge into the shadows. I don't want to be Serena Vieri, the mafia princess. I want to be Serena Vieri, a daughter visiting her mom.

I'm dressed in black leggings and a black hoody, my hair hiding under a black baseball cap. I'm wearing sneakers and carrying a black leather holdall, my luggage in the car behind. I am invisible. At least I certainly hope so and the only stipulation my grandfather insisted on was that Connor came with me.

He sits in the car in front, on red alert and watching out for danger, and my heart sinks. When will I ever be free of this shit? Trust me to travel with a bodyguard. An assassin who doesn't require a weapon to protect me when his hands are more than adequate for the job.

I'm guessing he's not that happy about it either, and I almost feel sorry for him. Almost. The trouble is, I'm too busy feeling sorry for myself.

* * *

WE REACH the airport in no time at all and as the cars pull to a stop, the doors open, and the occupants spill out like an oil slick. Black suits, black shades, and black souls form a tight guard of honor as my cases are loaded onto a trolley. I must wait until the door is opened and as I step outside, the black shades covering my own eyes cause passers-by to stare. They will wonder if I'm a celebrity. That can be the only explanation because the mafia isn't something ordinary people think a lot about.

I follow Connor into the terminal, toward the first-class check in and as I wait, I note the curious glances thrown my way from a nearby line. As always, the guards crowd around me and I sigh inside. Not long now and I will be free. For the next three weeks, anyway.

We check in and the agent stares at me with interest as she hands me the boarding card with a polite smile.

"The first-class lounge is through security and to your right, up the escalator and toward the back, near Starbucks."

"Thanks." I smile and Connor takes the boarding passes and says to the nearest guard, "Keep eyes on us through security. Report any problems in the usual way."

They nod and as we walk toward the fast-track security point, it's as if I leave behind the burden that sits heavily on my shoulders.

Soon I will be free. Nothing can touch me when I reach my destination and with a happy heart I leave all my troubles behind and head into security and I don't look back.

ALEXEI

She enters the lounge as if she doesn't belong here. I observe from my table as I eat a fine lunch for one, unusually alone.

The man with her is obviously paid protection, judging from the way his eyes scan the room and he appears on edge.

A SHADE OF EVIL

I stare with interest at the girl. A slight figure dressed head to toe in black, with no designers present in her choice of clothing. If I saw her on the street, I wouldn't look twice, but there is something about this scene that interests me.

I carry on eating and the guard ushers her into a booth before sitting opposite and scanning the area.

A waitress stops and hands them a menu each and as she studies it, the man with her glares around him with an air of menace that warns anyone from approaching.

The fact I'm here at all is an irritant I'm still dealing with. Usually, I travel on my private jet, but a technical issue at the last minute had me boarding a commercial flight instead.

I have no time to wait for an engineer because business comes before my comfort.

As I eat, I stare at the scene, averting my eyes when the guard throws his glance in my direction.

I finish up and the waitress stops by with an invitation in her eyes as she whispers huskily, "Mr. Komonov. May I interest you in anything else?"

"Vodka. Make it a double." I say with disinterest and lift my phone, that is awash with incoming texts.

As I pretend to scroll through them, I am more interested in the scene at the table across from me as the two strangers carry on ignoring one another.

When my drink arrives, I nod toward a booth near the window that offers a better view of my fellow travelers, and the waitress places my drink on her silver tray and follows me over to it.

Once I settle in, I am happy with a different view because now I can see the woman herself, not her guard. She is wearing dark glasses and appears to be staring at the menu but I have an overwhelming sensation she is staring directly at me.

I raise my glass and her menu is quickly raised to cover

her face, causing me to smirk. My senses never fail me, and it has almost become a game pitching my skills against my fellow humans.

I register everything about them. What they are wearing, carrying, and their mannerisms. I am a studier of people and I'm good at what I do. It's a hobby with me, usually enabling me to bring my enemies down.

Yes, Alexei Komonov didn't get his billions from sitting back and letting people in front of the line. I take what I want and use my competition's weaknesses against them. It's no different in my private life and it's become more of a game to me of proving I can win than wanting to keep my prize.

I love the chase, the intrigue, and the steal. Women who don't belong to me are fair game. I want what everyone else has and when they are mine, I don't want them anymore and there is something about that girl that makes me hope she's on my flight. It will pass the time, all twenty-three hours of it and when we land, I will leave a ruined soul behind me.

Yes, I really hope she is on my flight.

I keep my eyes on my prize for the next hour and follow them when the flight is called to the gate.

I tuck myself in behind them, several paces back and delight in gazing at her sexy ass as she sways in front of me.

Her guard is doing a bad job of remaining unobtrusive as he walks beside her, holding their bags in both hands, which in my mind is a fatal error. I always have one arm free to reach for my gun, knife, or just a man's throat if he gets in my way.

I almost pity her for the protection she has because it's doubtful she would stand any chance of survival if she was in danger. It makes me smile to myself because she is in danger. From me and my interest in her.

As we near the gate, they head to the front, anxious to be

among the first to board and as I reach the woman checking our boarding passes, I drop a silent word in her ear that causes the alarm to heighten on her face.

She nods at me gratefully as she waves me through and as I head to the window, I lean against it and stare at the young woman through the glass. She is averting her face from the other passengers and staring at her phone, but there is something telling me she is studying me right back.

My phone buzzes and I'm interested to see the text from my assistant Gleb, and I wonder if I can really pull this one off.

The trouble is, I can't even refuse a challenge from myself and so I text back my reply and turn my attention to getting what I want — as always.

SERENA

That man. I can't tear my eyes away from him. He is something else. There is something so incredibly powerful about a man like him. His rugged good looks complement a body that appears to be made from sin. Jet black hair slicked back, revealing a handsome face that could grace any aftershave campaign. He is wearing a black polo shirt and jeans, a tan suede jacket making a casual statement. His expensive watch is one money can't buy purely because there were only ten made in the entire world. I happen to know because my grandfather has one and delights in telling us the story.

A man of means and an attitude of arrogance. My favorite blend of rugged temptation. I have his interest and he has mine and I wonder if he's sitting anywhere near me.

"Excuse me, sir." I am so invested in my study of the stranger, I didn't notice the cops approaching.

"Is there a problem, officer?" I say sharply and Connor moves to stand in front of me, a statement that obviously doesn't go down well with the cops.

"Sir, please come with us." He says to Connor, who says roughly, "Why?"

"We need to search you. Purely routine."

"Like fuck it is." I say angrily, and the cop merely nods respectfully. "It won't take long."

Connor is angry but realizes there is nothing he can do and turns to me and whispers, "Stay here. Talk to no one, look at no one and I'll be back before we board."

He thrusts the documents in my hands and whispers, "Just in case they board and I'm not back. Take your seat and wait for me."

I say angrily, "I'll call my grandfather. He will sort this out."

The cop shrugs. "Call who you like, madam. We won't take long."

I watch helplessly as they escort Connor from the gate and, as my hand hovers over my phone, I find myself delaying the call I promised. I'm not sure why, but my eyes flick to the window, and I notice the man has gone and I'm not sure why a huge wave of disappointment hits me.

Then a sexy husky voice whispers behind me, "It appears that your guard was carrying drugs. Shocking when you think of his blatant disregard for airport security."

My heart beats erratically and yet my voice is calm as I reply, "We both know he is carrying nothing but a bag, Mr…"

"Komonov. Alexei Komonov, Miss…"

I ignore him and a shiver of excitement passes through me as his lips brush against my neck and he whispers, "It's a long flight to Australia to take alone."

"I'm not alone." I say, his breath against my neck causing me to shiver.

"I have a proposition for you."

"I'm not interested." I am aching to turn and stare at the stranger who is doing something strange to me inside. His voice is husky and loaded with promise as he whispers, "I think you are extremely interested. I think you are searching for an adventure. Aching to do something reckless and against the rules."

"You don't know anything about me, Alexei."

I turn and stare into the darkest eyes that are loaded with power, and it takes my breath away.

I know those eyes.

I live surrounded by them, but none excites me in the same way that these ones do. Up close, he is even more handsome. A rugged beauty that tells of hard beginnings. A real man. The kind of man I'm used to. A man who takes no shit and doesn't care about the consequences and I smile as I stare into those eyes and whisper, "It was you."

He raises his eyes with amusement and shrugs, not even bothering to deny it.

"You called the cops on my companion." I shake my head. "You're a wicked man, Alexei. I kind of admire those qualities."

"I thought you might."

We hear the announcement to board and Alexei glances at the exit.

"It appears your friend may be some time."

"Apparently so."

He leans forward and whispers, "It turns out I won't be traveling on this flight after all."

I hate that my heart crashes with disappointment, but I give nothing away and he whispers, "You have a choice. Board this flight, or my private jet that is waiting nearby."

"You're crazy." I stare at him in disbelief, and his eyes flash as he nods in agreement. "Crazy for adventure. What do you say, my mysterious woman? Go on an adventure with me or endure twenty-three hours of boredom alone."

He stares at me with the hottest look I have ever had directed my way that sends delicious flutters through my entire body.

I picture my grandfather and my brothers, their furious faces urging me to walk away from him. I picture my mother's shocked expression when I arrive in Sydney on a different flight, and I picture my one shot at adventure disappearing in a jet stream as I take the easy, safe option.

I grin. I'm not that girl. I'm not a Vieri by blood for nothing and the safer option is nowhere near as appealing as the one in front of me now.

In the extremely short time this man has captured my attention, I have experienced so many emotions I'm struggling to keep up. So, I lean forward and tiptoe to whisper in his ear, "I kind of like the idea of an adventure. Make it a good one."

He nods and reaches for my hand and as we walk to the exit, I have a feeling this is going to be one adventure I may never recover from.

* * *

If you want to read what happens between Alexei and Serena, check out Pretty Evil.

Pure Evil
Killian & Purity's story

If you want to read about The Ortega's and Mario Bachini, check out Ortega Mafia.

Thank you for reading this story.
If you have enjoyed the fantasy world of this novel, please would you be so kind as to leave a review?

Join my closed Facebook Group

Stella's Sexy Readers

Follow me on Instagram

Carry on reading for more Reaper Romances, Mafia Romance & more.
Remember to grab your free book by visiting stellaandrews.com.

ALSO BY STELLA ANDREWS

Twisted Reapers

Rebel
Dirty Hero (Snake & Bonnie)
Daddy's Girls (Ryder & Ashton)
Twisted (Sam & Kitty)
The Billion Dollar baby (Tyler & Sydney)
Bodyguard (Jet & Lucy)
Flash (Flash & Jennifer)
Country Girl (Tyson & Sunny)
Brutal Sinner (Jonny & Faith)

The Romanos
The Throne of Pain (Lucian & Riley)
The Throne of Hate (Dante & Isabella)
The Throne of Fear (Romeo & Ivy)
Lorenzo's story is in Broken Beauty

Beauty Series
Breaking Beauty (Sebastian & Angel) *
Owning Beauty (Tobias & Anastasia)
Broken Beauty (Maverick & Sophia) *
Completing Beauty – The series

Five Kings
Catch a King (Sawyer & Millie) *

Slade

Steal a King

Break a King

Destroy a King

Marry a King

Baron

Club Mafia

Club Mafia – The Contract

Club Mafia – The Boss

Club Mafia – The Angel

Club Mafia – The Savage

Club Mafia - The Beast

Club Mafia – The Demon

Ortega Mafia

The Enforcer

The Consigliere

The Don

The Dark lords

Pure Evil

A Shade of Evil

Pretty Evil

Standalone

The Highest Bidder (Logan & Samantha)

Rocked (Jax & Emily)

Brutally British

Deck the Boss

Reasons to sign up to my mailing list.

- A reminder that you can read my books FREE with Kindle Unlimited.
- Receive a weekly newsletter so you don't miss out on any special offers or new releases.
- Links to follow me on media to be kept up to date with new releases.
- Free books and bonus content.
- Opportunities to read my books before they are even released by joining my team.
- Sneak peeks at new material before anyone else.

stellaandrews.com

Follow me on Amazon

Printed in Great Britain
by Amazon